D0729307

Strip
FOR ME

GEORGIA COFFMAN

Dream big,

Strip for Me
by Georgia Coffman

Copyright © 2019 GEORGIA COFFMAN

This is a work of fiction. Names, places, characters, and events are fictitious in every regard. Any similarities to actual events and persons, living or dead, are purely coincidental. Any trademarks, service marks, product names, or named features are assumed to be the property of their respective owners, and are used only for reference. There is no implied endorsement if any of these terms are used. Except for review purposes, the reproduction of this book in whole or part, electronically or mechanically, constitutes a copyright violation.

STRIP FOR ME

Cover Design by Kari March
Editing by Hot Tree Editing
Proofreading by Marla Selkow Esposito, Proofing With Style
Formatting by Jill Sava, Love Affair With Fiction

"SHOOT FOR THE MOON. EVEN IF YOU MISS,
YOU WILL LAND AMONG THE STARS."

-Les Brown

CHAPTER 1

Sebastian

Thunder claps through the speakers.

Sounds of rain mix with the thunder as the curtain slowly parts.

Show time.

My adrenaline spikes as I count down to the start of our routine.

I take a deep breath as the music builds, followed by screams from the crowd. Ty and the rest of the guys surround me as we take steps forward, moving slowly and purposefully.

"It's Raining Men" blares through the speakers, and the lights blind me. They're my least favorite part of each show. They keep me from seeing the crowd and the excitement on their faces.

I wave my arms up to the beat, then squat before ripping

1

off my pants, leaving me in just a bow tie and spandex shorts. Women yell variations of, "Come to Mama," and "Work it this way, baby!"

I smile wider and try not to squint. Leo, our coach, told me I squint a lot because of the lights, and it makes me look constipated.

"That's not sexy, and women want sexy," he said at the time.

I countered, "But it's my signature smolder look."

He just shook his head but smiled.

As the first song comes to an end, we get into two lines, one in front of the other. I hold out my hands to Jordan, a nineteen-year-old with wavy hair parted to one side and a smooth face. He's probably what I looked like when I started eight years ago—wrinkle-free. But he has dimples to boot.

Jordan braces himself on my shoulders with one foot in my hands. When it's our turn, I assist in his backflip and clap in encouragement at his perfect dismount. If this were a gymnastics meet, judges would raise 10s all around.

During the next number, "Feel the Thunder," sweat runs down my chest, intertwining with the rose tattoo on my pec. We disperse throughout the crowd, gyrating in every direction until we find girls to dance with.

I need a minute to adjust to the darkness of this half of the room, but I refrain from rubbing my eyes.

Once my vision clears, I see a few women wave at each of us to *come hither*, while others hide their faces in their hands. The latter group makes me smile because, even though they seem embarrassed to be here, it's usually a pretense. By the end of the show, they tend to let loose and join in on the fun.

I wink at a few, scanning the crowd for my lucky pick.

We all have our type. Leo goes for the young, petite women. Easier to flip them around like rag dolls. His acrobatic moves in such a small space are impressive, to say the least, and drive the crowd wild every time.

Ty usually goes for the loose, fun ones. We can always tell them apart from the uptight ones who were dragged out by majority rule. On cue, from the corner of my eye, Ty finds one whose nipple is an inch from exposure in her cutout top.

I chuckle to myself and spin, never missing a beat as I move my hips while girls fan themselves. I keep looking around, unable to settle on one woman in particular. My type is a little more complicated than the rest of the guys.

My chest heaves as I spin again and lean forward, coming face-to-face with a beautiful girl with blond hair and mouth agape.

Her wide eyes and plump lips.

Yoga pants and a simple cropped tank.

She's my type.

A girl-next-door type with eyes that hold a lot more than innocent thoughts, judging by the way she's eye-fucking me.

My step falters only slightly. As I regain my composure, I immediately know she's my pick for the night.

As I grind on her, the moves come naturally, having done this routine a million times. Which is a good thing because it's hard to completely focus in her presence with her looking at me like that.

I lick my lips, taking her in as she watches me curiously. Others usually paw at me or whisper crude comments in my ear, but she doesn't move or say anything.

Her hair hangs loosely over her bare shoulders, covering one side of her face. It's tousled like she just rolled out of bed.

It's fucking sexy as hell.

My heart beats a little faster, and it's not from my dancing.

I grin widely as I motion for her to get up. Her expression transforms, panic seizing her eyes instead of lust, before she screams, "No fucking way!" She's reluctant, but her group cheers her on. One even pulls her up by the arm like she's a child being forced to go to the doctor.

She gives that one a scowl and another one a middle finger, which makes me laugh and intrigues me further.

I climb onto the small table where she and her group sit, then help her up too. I spin her around so we're face-to-face. She's tense, refusing to move her hips, but I welcome the challenge.

I can tell she's got some spunk in her, and I want to see it.

After all, it takes balls to come out to the Strip in yoga pants, especially when the rest of her party is in sequins and so much dark eye makeup they look like raccoons.

I push her hair to one side, getting a large whiff of vanilla. Leaning in close, I'm careful not to burst her eardrum when I say, "I've got you." With that, I hold her even closer and rub myself on her warm, toned body, starting low and working my way up as the table continues to cheer us on.

When I meet her eyes again, only one is peeking out from behind her hand—fucking adorable. I pull her hand down from her face, then spin her around. Now that her back is pressed against me, I repeat my previous motion.

But this time I have to fight the urge to groan as I feel her up.

Her perfect ass is firm and round, and it makes me want to bend her over and slap it a little.

This is a racy show—Vegas's hottest male revue show, at that—but it's not *that* kind of show.

So I grind my teeth, tamping down my urges—I'm a professional, damn it.

Her friends whistle, reminding me further to keep myself grounded and my mind out of the gutter. I will myself to think instead of something non-sexy, like Ty's disgusting gym socks.

Or just Ty himself.

But it's difficult once this girl finally loosens up and moves her hips in sync with mine.

I bite my lip and look up to the ceiling, begging for mercy as my cock strains against my shorts.

This kind of immediate arousal is foreign to me. I'm usually better at keeping myself at bay when it comes to sexy women at our male revue show, Naked Heat—especially after what happened the last time.

After *her*.

The song is almost over, and although I know I should let this be the end, let her walk away and out of my life, I can't.

Perhaps it's the simple boredom from my repetitive routine lately, but I ignore all logic knowing what happened the last time, why I set my rules in place to begin with. My very clear rules that forbid me to ask out women I meet at our shows.

My rules are meant to protect me.

Despite it all, I lean in with my hands firmly on her hips, enjoying the vanilla scent radiating from her hair like pheromones, intoxicating me and clouding my judgment. "Meet me after the show," I say.

She turns around, uncertainty in her wide eyes.

But then, I catch a hint of mischief there too.

I gulp, my step faltering for the second time in her presence. This hasn't happened to me in a long time—the moves are as natural to me as spinning on its axis is for Earth. Like neurons firing involuntarily. But this girl is causing nerve damage in my brain.

And I don't even know her name—*yet.*

I continue my performance by some miracle, stealing glances in her direction the whole time. She's drinking and clapping, watching my every move, curiosity consuming her features.

It fuels me to move just a little more sensually, a little more provocatively, like I'm giving her a private show. And when we end the next number, turned around with our asses bare, I'm not supposed to look back at the audience, but I chance it.

Her mouth hangs open.

My heart stops.

And I know I'm in trouble.

CHAPTER 2

Kendall

I watch as the stripper who danced with me moves his sculpted body to the seductive music.

Veins pop out of his biceps as he holds his arms out. There are guys around my gym with veins bulging out of their biceps, their necks, even their fucking eyeballs. But this is different.

Natural.

Sexy.

Fucking turning me on.

When I first arrived, late and in my most casual outfit I own, I didn't think this night would amount to anything exciting. Not with my bitchy sister and her lame friends, who are still sneering at my attire for her bachelorette party.

Even though I tried to explain that traffic was horrific and I didn't have time to change, they still mocked. My sister Lauren was even more annoyed with me than when her kid dental patients won't open their mouths for her to clean their teeth.

As annoyed as she was to come to a stripper show to begin with. Before we came in, I asked her why we were even here, and she robotically said, "Because this is a bachelorette party. Going to this kind of show is what you do."

She covers her eyes now like she regrets her decision to be here. Like her Alabama church friends are lurking in the corner and judging her.

Thank God I moved to LA, away from them and my family's prying eyes.

Now I can freely ogle shirtless men with their junk on display as often as I please, like right now.

Each guy comes back out into the crowd and dances on the tables again. As they do so, the other women share in my awe, except most are drunker than I am and are actually salivating.

One woman at the table next to us hasn't stopped screaming profanities at one dancer in particular, one with a smooth face who makes me wonder if he's old enough to be in Naked Heat to begin with. It's probably his dimples that make him look so young, but his chocolate eyes and six-pack are definitely all man.

Another woman keeps standing up to pat the guys on their asses as they pass by. She sits down just as quickly so that if you blink, you might miss her.

But my eyes constantly roam to the one who danced with me. The one who licked his lips at the sight of me like it was an honor to be in my presence, lighting a spark in me

I hadn't felt in a long time. I even almost echoed the crude woman and yelled profanities at him too. I had an escape plan and everything—to point at Lauren.

God, the way he danced with me.

My heart races just thinking about it, imagining running my finger along the tattoo on his chest. It's a simple rose on his pec, but I can't read the writing that serves as the stem. I'd have to get closer—something I would not mind doing right about now.

He's so hot even my prudish roommate Emma would seriously consider screwing him in the bathroom, like I am now.

I'm still staring at him on stage, not bothering to look away when he catches me. Then he disappears as a tall stripper in a caveman outfit pulls an older woman on stage. She's wearing a birthday hat, and when he asks her what birthday she's celebrating, she answers that it's her sixty-fifth.

I double over in laughter at her horrified expression when the guy pulls off what little clothing he had on, leaving only a leopard print Speedo. As he grinds his dick in her face, Lauren glares in disapproval at my endless laughing. I shoot back, "You're going to gain eight wrinkles at the edge of each eye if you keep this up all weekend."

I watch my sexy stripper when he comes back out in his sailor costume, dancing like he was made to be on stage, like he owns the whole room. At the very end, he drops his pants once again and winks back in my direction.

I'm speechless. Frozen with my hands mid-clap. Fascinated by this guy I don't even know—but *want* to.

To know how he is in bed, anyway.

He looks like he knows what he's doing, which would be a nice change of pace for me. Haven't had a good roll in the hay since… ever. Not even my ex, Adam, could give me what I wanted, and we were together for almost a year.

Then again, he was always too concerned about himself, in bed and out of it, to worry about what I really wanted.

At the end of the show, the emcee comes back, the one from the beginning who kept touching himself. He refrains from doing so now and instead encourages everyone to stay for pictures with the dancers.

The room quiets down, and I search for the tall guy with dark hair and a short, kempt beard lining his square jaw. The one with a teasing smile and sparkling brown eyes.

The one who lights me up like a cigarette, and I don't even know his name.

The other guys are on stage, taking pictures with girls who are too eager to touch their biceps. The guys are good, never breaking character, never removing their smolders.

I inhale deeply as Lauren chatters away like a squawking parrot, tossing her long honey hair over her shoulder. At least her previous glare is now missing. All she needed was another martini and a shot to finally loosen up. I take a mental note for future reference, for when I need to wipe that resting bitch face off her, for not only my benefit but those around us too.

It's information I should let her fiancé Rhett in on because in one month, he's going to vow to spend the rest of his life with her.

As for me, I'm only buzzed, my tolerance much higher

than hers and her friends'. Which is probably why I can't stop thinking about the slow, sensual way that hunk of man ran his hands down my sides. The way he whispered in my ear and tickled me with his short beard. My face is hot thinking about feeling the length of him along my ass— and that was with clothes on.

I can't imagine what it'd be like to feel him skin to skin.

I gasp quietly at the thought, covering my mouth.

Lauren's old sorority sister Elaine bumps into me then. "You were hot dancing up there. And fun. You're so fun. Especially when there are two of you." She bursts out laughing, my eardrum taking a hit, but I'm relieved all is forgotten about my outfit.

They even stopped joking with me about waiting on people hand and foot for my job. "But oh wait, it's just the foot."

Because I work at a shoe store. *How clever.*

Because I'm not a trophy wife like most of them or a wife at all. *Not even close.*

Because I moved out of our suffocatingly small town and its even smaller minded culture that takes pity on me for not having a man—my parents included. Add it to the lengthy list of things they're disappointed in me for.

Vodka shoots from Elaine's nose and down the front of her purple blouse—this is the kind of crew I can get used to.

I laugh, wondering what's so funny, but when my stripper enters my peripheral vision, the sea of people parting in his godly presence, I forget my entire existence. It's his turn to take pictures now, and he's wearing his pants again… unfortunately.

But *fortunately*, he's not wearing a shirt.

His abs are on full display for my shameless perusal.

And his pants are riding so low, his strong V makes my insides tingly and heat creep down my spine.

He adjusts his bow tie around his neck, then tips his sailor hat in my direction as he gets into position on stage for pictures.

"Kendall." I jerk around at the sound of my name and find my sister's childhood friend Sam. "Let's get a picture with your man! He's right over there." She tugs on Lauren's arm. "You come too, bride-to-be."

Lauren lets out a howling laugh as though the idea of being a bride is hilarious. It's not, really, seeing as how she's been waiting for this ever since she first went out with Rhett a year ago.

It was love at first sight.

A true southern fairy tale.

The perfect couple that even Mom and Dad approve of.

Barf.

The only reason we're having her bachelorette party so early is because most of her bridesmaids only had this weekend free. Not that I'm complaining. I'm happy to have met this mysterious stripper sooner rather than later.

Sam sways to the right, dragging Lauren out of her seat, but she doesn't have to drag or ask me twice.

I tuck a small strand of hair behind my ear, suddenly very aware that I'm underdressed compared to everyone else. But instead of cowering, I straighten my back and pull my short tank down so that my cleavage shows.

Game on.

It's finally our turn, and I give the attendant twenty dollars for my pictures. When I turn, I'm met with a searing gaze from my stripper, and when his nostrils flare at me, I would've gladly given two hundred dollars just to watch him do that again.

As I approach him, he takes my hand and sits with one knee on the ground, setting me on the other.

"I'm happy you stayed," he whispers, tickling my earlobe and sending shivers down my neck.

"Couldn't pass up the opportunity to touch your abs."

He chuckles, his minty breath mixed with faint cigarette smoke.

My face flushes at the idea of having a smoke. I stopped smoking so much after my ex and I ended things—he was the reason I picked it up in the first place. Since moving on and picking up a new habit of working out so regularly, I stopped.

But I could really use one now to settle these nerves of being in this guy's presence.

We don't make eye contact, smiling at the camera instead and waiting for Lauren and Sam to sit still. The photographer snaps the picture, but their shoulders still move up and down from their inability to quit laughing. They turn out blurry in the picture, but I tuck mine under my arm for safekeeping, anyway.

I tell myself it's a keepsake for Emma to ogle shirtless men for once. Not for any personal reasons.

When we're done, his hand leaves my exposed waist, but there's a burning there that longs for more. I have an overwhelming need to sneak off with him to the bathroom *stat.*

But I keep walking in the opposite direction. Once I reach our table again, I take a big gulp of my drink as sexy thoughts of him and me getting it on in the bathroom take over. Watching ourselves in the mirror as he fucks me from behind.

Deep breaths.

As much as I want to ditch Lauren, I'd never hear the end of it. Especially if I left her for a stripper.

I shake my head. It'd be a bad idea from every angle, anyway. My vision is fogged by Captain Morgan and lust. I have no control and am way out of my league here. I'm normally more confident around guys. I'm usually the one giving *them* thoughts of doing me in the bathroom, not the other way around.

"Care for a lap dance?"

I pause, my knees buckling at the sound of *his* deep voice in my ear.

I down more of my drink, taking my time to swallow before I find my voice. "Um… actually, we… were just leaving. Weren't we, Lauren?" I pull her toward me and frown at him. "Yeah, we have plans, so… we should really be going."

I cringe at my weak voice, but I'm confident I'm making the right decision in trying to leave.

Lauren puts her arm around me and kisses my cheek. "You're so cute, you know? I forgot how cute and funny you are."

I stand back, shocked that she gave me a compliment

and actually kissed me, like she's forgotten all about her distaste for me. Alcohol really does change people. "Okay, I definitely think we should be going."

"Even in your ridiculous cropped tank at my bachelorette party, you're just *so* cute."

Ah, there she is—the *real* Lauren.

I nudge her with my elbow to get up, but she doesn't budge.

I don't know where she gets the shot from, but Lauren takes one and holds the empty glass in the air. "Now who has a stick up their ass, huh?" She points at me. "No, we're staying here all night and partying with McDreamy and McSteamy over there." She points to two other strippers who wink in our direction. Her eyes aren't even open.

Wide-eyed, I turn to my stripper, lifting my chin to meet his gaze as he towers over me. "I guess we're partying with the cast of *Grey's Anatomy*." When I look back at Lauren, who has another shot—*where are they coming from?*—I shake my head and decide I don't care. I need one too, so I just take hers. "Give me that."

I throw back the shot, watching as he swallows like he's the one drinking it, his Adam's apple moving up and down.

"I'm Sebastian," he says with a wide, knowing smile.

From up close, I can see his eyes are dark brown, almost as dark as his irises. A few freckles are sprinkled under his eyes and on his cheeks, giving him a boyish charm to his otherwise manly build.

A sexy combination.

I gulp—and it's not because of the shot.

CHAPTER 3

Sebastian

She quickly averts her gaze as she pulls at her short tank, like she's suddenly nervous that I can see her belly button. "Can you smoke in here? I need a cigarette."

I pat my bare chest, then lean forward and grip my own ass, which makes her lips part and my dick twitch. "Fresh out. Nowhere to put them." I wink, her blush growing in front of my eyes as she watches me carefully.

It's adorable. *She's* adorable.

And hot.

I wrap a small piece of her hair around my finger, loving its velvety texture. "Am I ever going to get your name?"

"I need a better pickup line than that, dude." She takes another gulp of her drink, staring at me through her long lashes. When she swallows, I'm mesmerized by her every movement, especially when she smiles in challenge.

I dwell on how she called me *dude*—I like it. I also like her faint southern accent, but she doesn't look like the average southern belle. No hoity-toity outfit or attitude to match. This girl has a down-to-earth quality, an energy I can't quite place, but she also has some city girl in her.

"Kendall," someone says behind me, "you can't hog him all for yourself. Share!"

It's another girl from the bachelorette party, and what strikes me isn't the way she drew out the word *share* to give it extra *r*'s and extra whine. Or that she's now touching my bicep. What strikes me is that I finally got her name.

Kendall.

Kendall yanks on my other arm, surprising me with the amount of force coming from such a small person. Although, I shouldn't have been that surprised. She clearly works out, judging from the definition in her arms as she tugs on me.

And from her legs. With those thin yoga pants, all I can see are legs. My dick throbs at the thought of them wrapped around me.

"He's mine. Get your own, slut," Kendall spits, which has me reeling. I can't contain my laughter at the way these two are playing tug-of-war with me.

I say to them both, "There's plenty to go around, ladies."

Another girl with a "Bride-To-Be" sash around her and a tiara on her head comes over. She looks a lot like Kendall, although a little more petite and taller in her heels. She's holding her hand up like we're in class and she has a question.

"I want in." Before I can move, the bride wraps her

arms around my neck. "I like your sailor costume." She wiggles her eyebrows, and the vodka on her breath reminds me of my bastard uncle. It was his drink of choice, always emptying water bottles and filling it with vodka.

But instead of going down memory lane straight to Hell, I smile as I always do. And just as I'm about to say something, Kendall stops me. Not with her words, but with her glare.

She's not laughing.

In fact, she's now giving her bride friend a scowl, and not the cute one she gave earlier, but a fatal one.

She looks legitimately *pissed*.

CHAPTER 4

Kendall

Now I'm *pissed*.

Lauren can't have Sebastian. He's *my* stripper.

But of course, she wants *him* to give her attention, just to take his attention off me. Why else would she leave the other one to waddle over here like a stupid penguin?

She can't even handle her liquor.

She's always wanted my stuff. Whether it was my shoes or lipstick, she'd take them without asking and not give them back for weeks, at which point she'd say they were hers all along.

The one time I inadvertently took something of hers, we ended up giving each other the cold shoulder. To this day.

And that was seven years ago.

I even tried apologizing back then, but she wouldn't

hear it. So I stopped trying. Stopped trying to apologize for that or any of my life choices since then.

I'm about to stalk off, but I can't. I physically can't move, dizzy just at the thought of making a dramatic exit. The alcohol fumes are clouding my vision, and the anger is fueling the fire.

Too bad I don't have a cigarette to light with that flame.

Lauren rubs her hands over Sebastian's chest, making matters worse, but then something smacks my right shoulder. It's Sam, but it might as well have been reality.

Suddenly my vision clears, and I notice the other strippers leaning closely to giggling women who are batting their eyelashes.

Sebastian is also just doing his job by flirting and humoring drunken women.

The anger is just tied in with the liquor.

Well, and the fact that I want Sebastian to get naked with me.

Heat radiates between my legs. The intense physical attraction to him is almost more than I can handle. My need to feel the ultimate level of ecstasy is so extreme that I contemplate yanking him from Lauren. Maybe in doing so, Lauren will fall and break her nose.

I'm drunker than I thought.

I normally wish Lauren ill, but not to the extent of physical harm. It's mostly for a large zit on her nose or added weight to cover her six-pack.

I'm about to go splash water on my face when Sebastian turns a sly eye to me. My eyebrows shoot up, meeting each other in confusion.

He gently pats Lauren's arm as he whispers something to her. She covers her smile with one hand as she walks away, and I wonder what he said, jealous that it made her giddy while I glare.

He moves over to me and murmurs, "Where'd you go, huh?"

"I'm right here." I shrug lazily.

He leans even closer and runs a hand through my hair, keeping it there like he can't help but touch me. He says something else, but I can't hear it. I'm too focused on how close he is to my face, mere inches, with a handful of my hair in his hand.

I part my lips, my fantasy coming true...

When he leans back, I curse that I was so close to feeling his lips on mine, the pool between my legs increasing the longer I'm in his presence.

Sebastian now has a twinkle in his eye that wasn't there before. "I have an idea." *Is that what he said before?* Letting go of my hair, he winks at me before getting his friend's attention—his *hot* friend. If Sebastian wasn't so damn sexy, I'd be making bedroom eyes at his dark friend with the tattoos covering his chest and arms.

Sebastian says something to him in hushed tones, where I can't hear, so I take this opportunity to admire his lean torso, my need for control lost for a good half hour now.

I jump when his friend pulls back abruptly.

"Are you serious?" he asks. "Yes! I'll text the other guys." He high-fives Sebastian before smiling at Amber, my sister's friend from high school. Bad choices are waiting for her to be made, and I couldn't be happier for her to take advantage.

This is Vegas, after all.

"Get you some, bitch," I call out to her.

Too drunk to scold me, she winks and pulls the guy closer.

"Let's go out." Sebastian wraps his arm around my waist, his hand resting on my lower back.

"We *are* out," I say weakly.

"Somewhere better." He's only a few inches away, his manly cologne drawing me in further. "What do you say?"

I lick my lips, Sebastian watching my every move like he's sketching me on his mind's canvas.

I slowly nod, against all logic.

I agree to step into the ring for this little game that started when he pulled me up to dance with him.

As a slow smile spreads across his face, I know I'm playing with fire. I'm going to get burned like I did the last time I lost control. But I take his hand, anyway, telling myself that I know better. I'm more prepared now to protect myself.

I can play the game long enough to get the pleasure I'm after.

I can play with fire and win for one night.

CHAPTER 5

Sebastian

I'm breaking every one of my rules just by talking with her after the show. I vowed never again. Not after the Hell I went through the last time.

And now I'm asking her to go to a club? To drink and dance with me?

The similarities between her and my ex are too similar. This can't end well.

But Kendall is looking at me like she wants to climb on top of me. I'm two seconds from asking her back to my place, or to get a hotel room here. The latter being much faster.

But she's here with a group, and I don't want to tear her away from them. At least with us all going out, it's a win-win.

Even Ty was surprised I suggested going out, since I

hardly do that anymore. It has to be a special occasion to make me come out to the Strip, and even then, I'm a drag.

As I gather my things in the locker room, there aren't many people left back here except for a couple of new guys gloating about the women they're going to meet afterward.

Ty tells them to bring the girls to MGM with us, and they nod enthusiastically.

I shake my head and remember my beginner days when I was eager for everything. Eager to hang with the veteran dancers. Eager for the next fuck. I didn't think I'd ever get enough pussy back then, but I sure as hell tried. With my job, I had an endless stream of it, so I indulged, picking off every dangling apple of temptation that I came across.

But I learned.

I learned it would've been the end of me had I continued the sleepless nights, threesomes, and drinking beyond consciousness night after night. I started missing workouts, coming late to practices, and getting wrapped up in more drama than *Jersey Shore*. Minding my own business and establishing boundaries have kept me not only in line with my job, but also sane.

I'm myself again.

At least partly, anyway.

"Dude, nice work with the bachelorette party." Ty whistles, rubbing his hands together like he's ready to put a plan into motion. "Found me a hot and desperate divorcée. Bet she's never had chocolate dick before, but we're about to change that."

I nod, laughing at the stars in his eyes.

"And she used to be a *cheerleader*. A cheerleader!"

He tilts his head to the ceiling. "Thank you, Jesus. Who would've thought I, former nerd extraordinaire, would get the cheerleader? If only I could pat my younger self on the shoulder now..."

I roll my eyes, unable to picture this massive human as a dorky teen. Especially one who never got laid. His younger self would indeed be proud now.

Once outside, I drink Kendall in and scratch the back of my head, kicking myself at what I've gotten myself into.

"Don't back out on me now." Ty steps in front of me and holds me by the shoulders. "Don't you fucking back out now. You need this. It's been far too long——"

"I'm fine."

He pins me with a hard stare. "I know that look. You're already regretting this. Just promise me you'll wait until tomorrow, until after you spend the night naked with that blond angel. If you still regret *that*, then damn. You're so far gone, not even angels can save you."

He smirks as I push him off me and walk toward said blond angel.

And that's exactly what Kendall is.

With every step, my dick throbs with thoughts of her light hair splayed on the pillow around her head like a halo.

I rub my hands together and inhale, preparing myself while I get back into my old charming routine.

Before I can say anything, Kendall points at me while the girls laugh behind her so hard they're holding their stomachs. "Wherever we're going, no lap dance. I'm... I'm good with just getting a drink, so... you're off the hook."

"I was kidding about that." I chuckle at the visible

release of tension from her shoulders. "This isn't that kind of place, nor am I that kind of stripper. Have you never been to a show before?" I feign disappointment, stepping back and clutching my chest.

Her cheeks turn a light shade of pink, making her look innocent and vulnerable, although she doesn't seem like either.

And that's when I see it.

Her smile.

A shy, sexy one that I'll dream about long after she's gone.

My chest warms and swells like the pump I get from working out.

I'm most definitely *fucked*.

CHAPTER 6

Kendall

Sebastian holds his arms out wide. "MGM then?"

He changed into faded black jeans and a white V-neck tee. His denim button-up is open with sleeves rolled up, exposing his dark forearms.

He's not oily like when he was on stage. No, here, he looks normal. As normal as possible, anyway. He's still too good-looking, it's almost painful.

I'm about to answer him when Amber pushes me aside to walk toward Sebastian. She points a manicured finger to his chest, bats her long, fake eyelashes, and says, "I'll go anywhere you want to take me." My eye twitches at her dazed expression, one she wouldn't have if we were within a seventy-five-mile radius of our hometown.

I want to rip Amber's extensions right out of her head.

Instead, I peel her off him. "I think that's enough. You

don't want to embarrass yourself, right?"

"Hey, what happens in Vegas stays in Vegas. Am I right?" She turns to the other girls, holding up her hand as though there's a drink in it, and toasts to the cliché. "Not like I have a husband to go home to anymore."

I wince, remembering Amber got divorced a few months ago. My mother makes sure I keep up with the gossip of our hometown, even though I moved across the country so I could stay out of it.

I almost feel bad for Amber, but she seems to be having fun now as she hangs off Sebastian's friend. Nothing like a dark, muscled stripper to make her forget about her balding-at-thirty ex-husband.

Sebastian introduces his friend, Ty, but it's barely out of his mouth before Lauren cuts him off.

She claps, then hooks her arm into Sam's. "Let's go!" She takes off down the sidewalk away from Excalibur like she knows where we're going. Like she's on a runway and not a cracked sidewalk lined with poor street performers and their big dreams.

Sebastian's lips tilt at the corners in a sexy smile. "I guess we're on, then."

I roll my eyes and follow Lauren with Sebastian by my side. He leans in to me to thwart a group of pedestrians and people handing out flyers, but instead of moving back once they've passed, he stays close to me, smiling down at me as he snakes his arm around my waist.

He really has no sense of personal space.

I smell his masculine cologne and imagine him being the guy in the Dolce & Gabbana commercials, half-naked and oiled up sitting in a boat on the open sea.

My mouth waters for him.

More than that, I welcome him and his warmth in the slight March breeze, so different from the hot sun before the show. He's also protecting me, keeping me company while the other girls walk ahead, their arms looped together like they're about to play Red Rover with the other tourists.

If it weren't for Sebastian, I'd be walking alone. Alone like I was when Lauren would have friends over, and I had to stay out of their way. Apparently, I was too young to hang out with them, even though I'm only a year and a half younger.

I tuck my hair behind my ear to keep it from sticking to my glossed lips. Elaine, of course, has a purse full of cosmetics, and she's drunk enough to have let me borrow them. Thankfully, I freshened up in the bathroom while one of the other girls was puking.

Being this close to Sebastian, I regret not having my usual makeup on and hair fixed. That I'm not wearing something a little more appropriate for the Strip—something low-cut with sequins comes to mind.

But he doesn't seem to mind. If anything, he enjoys what I'm wearing, based on the way he keeps eyeing me up and down.

Crossing the bridge, I watch the cars moving beneath us. Their headlights mix with the lit-up buildings like I'm inside a Christmas tree.

Mesmerized, I veer off the path, Sebastian's hand falling from my waist. Holding my phone up, I cross to the rail overlooking the street, bumping into a few people along the way, and take a picture of the Strip. Even though the picture doesn't do it justice—all you can see are blurs of lights—I save it as a memento.

"Cool picture," Sebastian says, wrapping his arms around me and nuzzling his face in the crook of my neck. I like it. I like the feel of him against me.

I turn the camera toward us, wanting to capture this moment, the night Sebastian and I met.

With the camera facing us, I see him watching me instead of the phone, and my heart swells at how handsome he is. At how comfortable he makes me, which never happens, especially when first meeting a guy.

I nudge him to get his attention. "Do it for the Gram," I say sarcastically, which makes us both grin widely. In the picture, we look more candid than posed.

From the outside, passersby probably think we're a couple instead of two strangers.

I'm glad I have this picture to remember this night—to remember Sebastian before he becomes a stranger indeed.

After all, I'm sticking to the promise I made myself moments ago.

One night—that's all this can be.

CHAPTER 7

Sebastian

My buddy Charlie at the door is surprised to see me. It's been a while since I was last here, and I only came then to peel Ty's drunk ass off the dance floor.

I place my hand on Kendall's lower back, leading her and the girls in. I can't seem to stop touching her, the instinct so natural like I've known her for a long time.

When she took our picture, I almost asked her to send it to me, the request on the tip of my tongue. But I bit it back. I didn't want to give her a reason to give me her number other than the fact that she wanted to, on her own.

But that would be a bad idea too. I might be breaking my rules, but only for tonight. This can only be a onetime thing.

Tomorrow, my rules are in full effect, and having her number will be too tempting to make more exceptions where she's concerned.

Once inside, I nod at the familiar server coming our way. She wears a seductive smile and practically purrs, "*Sebastian*. Nice to see you out and about again. The other guys coming too?"

I recognize her, Abby something. A woman from my past discrepancies. She was a fun one indeed, a former gymnast if I remember her backbend correctly. But fun was all it was, for both of us.

Ty and I give her a hug. "Hey, Abby. Good to see you. Some of the others are on the way." With my hand still on Kendall's lower back, I ask, "Got a table for us?" I'd called in advance to get us in. Hard to do on a night when Calvin Harris is here, but my friends here made it happen for old time's sake.

She scans the rest of the group, some of which have scattered to the dance floor, swaying to "We Found Love." "Right this way."

Red lights flash across the dance floor with fog surrounding the stage. The large dome-like ceiling reflects the enormous size of the place, but with so many people in here, the club feels small. Especially with the smell of alcohol and pheromones clouding the air above us.

Instead of following us, Kendall makes a beeline for the bar. I hold out my hand to the bride. "Follow Abby. She'll get you set up with a table and bottle service."

She waves me off like I'm her servant and she no longer needs me.

I find Kendall in the crowd around the bar. She's on her tiptoes, which makes her ass even perkier. It's all I can see.

It's out in the open for me to squeeze.

I rub a hand down my face and beg myself to be cool, but then she raises her arm, her tank sliding up to reveal a small tattoo on her side. When I get closer, I see it's a black cactus.

My skin heats at the sight of it, all my blood rushing to my cock.

So much for being cool.

I walk up behind her and lean over the bar so I'm pushed against her ass. Her eyes widen as she stiffens in front of me. I push her even harder against the bar, my cheek an inch from hers. "What're you drinking?" I ask her.

"Captain and Diet Coke."

I raise an eyebrow, impressed by her choice.

She relaxes against me and asks, "What?"

"I would've thought you were more of a cosmo, or appletini type of girl."

"Get me a cosmo and I'll shove the whole thing down your throat, glass included."

I hold my hands up in surrender and watch her eyes follow my every move. Glass shards are not in my strict diet plan, so I nod in response.

As I attempt to get the bartender's attention, I watch Kendall out of the corner of my eye, her perfect lips forming a small smile. The bartender nods at us, his gaze lingering on Kendall, whose breasts are on display over the counter. I whistle at the guy to get his attention and stop him from eye-fucking my girl.

Not that she's *my* girl, but if all goes as planned, she will be for the night.

Because I can't stop myself from wanting her. Others come here to live their fantasies, and I should be able to do the same and break my own rules just this once. I was never good at following the rules growing up, anyway, the one thing my teachers would always complain about at parent-teacher conferences. On the rare occasion my mom actually went. Otherwise, my uncle went and high-fived me afterward.

The asshole.

The bartender comes closer and reaches for my card. "Two Captain and Diet Cokes," I order. I'm about to tell him to start a tab, but the way Kendall's looking up at me, her bottom lip full and kissable, I don't plan on sticking around long enough for one.

The bartender grabs my card, the tattooed sleeve up his right arm visible and the sides of his head buzzed. I don't recognize him, so he must be new. Or it's been that long since I've been here.

Since I set my rules in place—since I had my heart ripped out—I don't tend to hang on the Strip anymore, going instead to small bars in Summerlin where the other locals are. At times, we go out to Fremont. No dancing, strangers, urge for adventures. Just calm nights with friends, beer, and the occasional one-night stand, but even those have been extremely rare lately.

"Oh my God." Kendall's body stills against me. "Is that Calvin Harris?" She squints toward the stage and screens surrounding the deejay table. Before I can answer, she jumps up and down in the enclosed space with so much enthusiasm I'm surprised she didn't just break my nose with the back of her head. "That's Calvin Harris! Calvin *fucking* Harris!" She claps excitedly and turns, her breasts pushed against me.

I swipe at my lip and chuckle at her childlike excitement, so unlike anything I've seen from her tonight. "Yeah. You know him?" I mean it sarcastically, because obviously she knows him, but she takes me literally.

She grabs me by the shoulders with her small hands. "Duh! Did you know he was going to be here and didn't tell me? Why were you withholding important information?" She slaps me playfully on the shoulder and pouts, but she can't stop smiling at the stage.

The Calvin Harris has one hand on his headphones and the other on the turntable while he bounces to the music. She watches him with wonder, like he's the inventor of all music.

"Guess I like teasing you." I wink as I lean in to her to retrieve our drinks, then hand her one. I stay flush against her, refusing to give her space, as a gentleman would. Not that the crowd surrounding us would allow it.

I'm about to clink my glass to hers, but she cuts me off with a narrow glare. "I could've gotten one for myself. Let me pay you for mine."

"Not a chance." I'm so close to her face that I could easily kiss her. Instead, I hold her gaze in a challenge, amused that she doesn't let up. "Let me show you a good time."

She runs her tongue over her bottom lip, and the earth beneath me feels like it's crumbling. I get an eyeful of her cleavage from this angle, being a foot taller than her. I'm definitely enjoying the view, but I'm positive the vein in my neck will burst from tamping down my urge to kiss her.

"You have no sense of personal space, do you." She says it as more of a statement, so I don't answer.

I just smile and clink my glass to hers. "Cheers."

She takes a sip. "Is this the part where you charm me into bed?"

I'm not sure I hear her correctly as "Titanium" blasts through the speakers. "What?"

She places a hand on my chest and leans closer so I can hear her loud and clear. "Is this the part where you say something cute and funny and ask me to reserve us a room upstairs for the night?"

I hold her hand against my chest and keep her close to me, her proximity soothing. "Is that what you want me to do?"

Her eyes briefly widen in confusion, perhaps surprise that I didn't simply ask her outright to do just that.

I narrow my eyes at her now, like we're having a staring contest to see who breaks first.

"We can talk... for now." I smirk without removing my gaze from hers.

She raises an eyebrow in doubt. "*Talk?* About what, lover boy?"

Her nickname makes me smile wider. "Have I mentioned I like your outfit?"

"That's a short conversation."

"Let me try again. What accent is that?" I tilt my head to the side, still close enough that I could kiss her if I wanted, but instead, I listen. And shield her from the tattooed bartender who keeps peering over here, even though there's a large crowd requiring his attention.

Her eyes flutter and then open with my question like she expected something else. She takes a sip of her drink and sets it on the bar, taking a step back and putting distance between us—distance I don't like.

"What accent?" Her jaw clenches.

"*Your* accent. The southern one?"

She shrugs, avoiding my gaze.

"Hey." I nudge her chin toward me, closing the minute distance between us. "Did I say something wrong?"

Her normally full lips form a tight line before they give way to a fake smile—one that's less endearing than her real one, to say the least. "No. I'm from Alabama originally, but I live in LA now." She puts her hands on her hips. "A move I should've made long before I did."

I pull her to me, but she doesn't come willingly. "I like a small-town girl with city attitude."

"Shitty attitude?" She cuts her eyes at me, her hands still on her hips. "You don't know anything about me, asshole. Don't—"

"*City* attitude. I was giving you a compliment." I chuckle when she visibly relaxes and even rests against me.

"Oh. Okay." She reaches for her drink, her throat exposed and begging for me to kiss my way across her jawline. Make my way down her smooth neck before I nip at her shoulder.

"Are you always this on edge?"

"I don't like my hometown" is all she says. Then she puts a wall up, closing the conversation off.

Interesting.

That's one of the things I like about her, that she's complex. She has a diverse background that goes beyond her high cheekbones and long legs. There's more to her attitude too—I know it.

She's a mystery I need to solve, and the more time I spend with her, the closer I can get to the answers.

Her hair tickles my lips as I say, "I like your accent. I like *you*."

She fights a smile as someone beside her bumps into us. If she wasn't already glued to my chest, she would've fallen on me, but she apologizes to me, anyway.

"No need to apologize."

"Southern charm, I guess." She winks, but her edge is still there.

Nodding, I search for her group and Ty. "Shouldn't you be out there dancing with your friends?"

Her face twists in disgust like I asked her to eat a pickle coated in dirt. "Have they seemed to notice me at all?"

I halfway nod, unsure of what to say.

"They're hardly my friends," she clarifies. "I thought that was obvious."

"So why are you here?"

"The bride is my *sister*." She emphasizes the last word as though that should explain everything. It partially does; although I don't have any siblings, I know plenty of people who aren't close with theirs. So I pry for more.

"But you're so…"

"Different?" she says, and her face lights up, clearly relieved. "Thank God for that. I'd hate to know what having a stick up my ass feels like."

I grin, brushing her hair from her face. "I was going to say *mean*. You're very mean to each other."

She smiles sarcastically while twirling the straw in her drink. "Loving sisters at their finest."

I wait for more, to unravel more of her story like a greedy bookworm eager for another chapter, but that's all she gives me. I don't push her further—for now, anyway—and I shrug instead. "I don't have any siblings, so don't know the difference."

She watches me again, studies me as though I gave her a complicated math problem instead of a simple fact about myself. She finishes her drink and sets her empty glass on the bar, not noticing the bartender who's still eye-fucking her.

"One Kiss" fills the room around us, and more people crowd us. In Vegas, the later into the night, the more people come out. This should really be called the city that never sleeps; always a club to go to, alcohol to drink, a sidewalk to pass out on.

"Let's stop this dance."

Unsure if I heard her correctly, I ask, "You want to dance?"

She shakes her head slowly at me, lowering her gaze to my lips.

And like an unsuspecting twig on a busy sidewalk, I snap. I never stood a chance with this woman to begin with. Not sure why I even tried to kid myself into thinking my rules ever applied to her.

She set my rulebook on fire the minute she danced with me, searing me with the slightest touch.

I close the small distance between us and crush my lips to hers. She meets my kiss just as fiercely and grips my shoulders with both hands, like she doesn't trust herself to stand up alone.

She may have some southern charm in her, but the way she claws at me, there's nothing polite or apologetic about it.

And while this kiss is everything I knew it would be with her, I need more.

Now.

CHAPTER 8

Kendall

Sebastian kisses me like I've never been kissed before, his lips warm and inviting, yet greedy and demanding. He takes over my whole body with one kiss, while Calvin Harris's "One Kiss" plays in the background.

I didn't even think to Instagram the fact that I was in the same room as Calvin Harris—that's how distracted by Sebastian I am. Being around famous people was never a thing back home in Alabama. Part of the reason I left to find life, excitement, and adventure.

That's why I love it out west.

And why I'm intrigued by Sebastian. He's exciting and interesting and fucking *sexy*.

The minute Sebastian pressed his hard-on against my ass, I didn't stand a chance.

And now that I know how he kisses, how it makes my

heart race and core clench, I can only imagine how alive he can make me feel in bed.

He breaks the kiss but only to talk in my ear, his stubble brushing my cheek, further lighting me on fire. "Let's go," he growls.

My breath hitches at his obvious need for me.

"Where are you staying?" he asks, running his hands through my hair.

"Upstairs." I shake my head slightly. "But we can't use that room. I'm staying there with four other girls." My voice is loud enough to hear over the music, but it takes all my energy. "Although, fucking on Lauren's bed seems like a grand idea."

Maybe I could get off even more easily--I live to piss her off that way.

He leans his forehead to mine and shakes with laughter against me. "We need to go," he says, grabbing my hand before we charge for the door.

I glance around for Lauren in case she's looking for me, but she's still on the dance floor with Elaine and Sam. And drinks—so many drinks everywhere.

We pass by the rest of the girls at the table where they're doing shots. I take one out of their hands and knock it back. "I'll see you in the morning, bitches!"

If they weren't drunk, they'd probably roll their eyes that I was leaving early, but when they see Sebastian and me, hands intertwined, they start whooping and hollering.

Either way, they wouldn't have been able to stop me.

Not even Calvin *fucking* Harris can keep me here with Sebastian fully clothed for another minute.

I pull Sebastian toward the door, away from the flashing red lights. Once we're out, there's still a small line of people waiting to get in. We rush by, through the casino where the beeping and cheering from the slots fill our ears. Mix that with the multi-colored pattern of the carpet, it's almost too much for my senses.

I rub my eyes when Sebastian stops and kisses me next to a slot machine with the *Big Bang Theory* cast on it, their eyes watching us.

When we reach the lobby, the carpet ends and clean, beige tiles replace it. *Thank fuck.* My senses were on overload.

Once at the front desk, my face is flushed. I swallow, trying to regain any semblance to composure.

Sebastian opens his mouth to speak while reaching for his wallet, but I pull him back. "What are you doing? We can't get another room. Or at least let me pay for half."

He kisses me hard again, holding my head in place with one hand. When he pulls away, he stays an inch from my face. "You are so stubborn."

"I like to call it independent."

The man behind the counter pushes up his thick-rimmed glasses. "May I help you?"

Sebastian whispers to me, "Let me buy the room."

"I feel like a cheap whore." I scowl. "Is that what you want?"

"I'm trying to be a gentleman. Is that not what you want?" There's a gleam in his eye. He obviously likes to get me worked up, especially by invading my personal space. "Or I can throw you over my shoulder and carry you upstairs—your call."

"You wouldn't."

The glimmer brightens, his eyes full-on dancing now. "Don't test me." He doesn't take his eyes off me as he hands the man behind the counter his credit card. "One room for tonight, please. Smoking."

"I'll leave."

"Then I'm definitely going to do it."

"I don't believe you."

"And I don't believe you'll leave."

We have a staring contest as the older man with balding white hair types away at his computer. I break it to look sideways, suddenly nervous at the way he peers at me.

Like he's fascinated.

As soon as he hands us our keys, Sebastian thanks him, scoops me up as effortlessly as picking up a five-pound dumbbell, and throws me over his shoulder.

I yelp and punch his back, but I can't stop laughing. I have tears in my eyes from laughing so hard. And from all the blood rushing to my head, pushing the tears out of me.

He smacks my ass and carries me the whole way to our room, earning us a few stares and even some smiles along the way.

Once inside our room, I don't have time to look around. All I know is there's a bed big enough for the cast of *Magic Mike*. The white sheets and comforter are crisp, clean—and about to get *oh so dirty*.

He tosses me on the bed and pulls his shirt off, wasting no time at all. And while I'm also in a hurry to have him consume me, I can't move, too busy basking in his shirtless chest and abs.

So many abs.

He pulls his jeans down, revealing the firm V that disappears into his red briefs.

There's nothing *normal* about this guy. His six-pack and bulging biceps could make bodybuilders jealous enough to cry. His veins pop out in several places in his arms, and his chest rises high as he pants for breath.

I'm light-headed from the sight of him, and he knows it. He smirks and moves toward me, ready to pounce. Devour me, actually.

That small movement alone makes me feel more alive than I have in a long time.

He lifts me with one arm around my waist while the other pulls my tank over my head, making me gasp. *That's a neat trick.* One smooth, quick motion.

He growls against my neck, his words vibrating against me. "I need everything off. *Now.*"

And I don't argue as he nips at my neck and shoulder before pulling back enough for me to take my pants off, never taking his eyes from me. My legs are shaking from anticipation.

This is it.

This is what I've been hoping for tonight.

The world stops as the realization hits me that I'm about to feel something I've never felt before.

When I'm completely bare, lying on the bed alone, Sebastian stands close and studies me, one hand moving up and down my thigh. I'm exposed and needy. It's a rare side of me, one I'm not completely familiar with myself, and now I'm sharing it with Sebastian.

A stranger.

Someone I'll never see again.

So just for the night, I don't cover myself up. I don't try to control the situation. I let him watch me like this, my most vulnerable state.

And I prepare myself as best as possible to feel everything.

His nostrils flare, but he doesn't come toward me. "You're sexy as hell, you know." He runs a hand through his dark hair in hesitation, and for a moment, I think he's changed his mind. Indecision and something else—*fear*—cross his features.

So uncharacteristic of the fun and carefree Sebastian I've seen all night.

I sit up on my elbows, lifting my knees so my feet rest on the bed in front of him. I'm about to ask what's wrong when his nostrils flare even wider, along with his eyes as he watches me spread my legs farther.

Any hesitation that was there before is replaced with something else.

Hunger.

Need.

Desire.

All for me.

And it makes me wet with power that I have this effect on this sexy man.

"I want to taste you," he says, his jaw ticking like he can't stand it that he's not already doing it.

I exhale while he leans down and waits for me to say something, but I don't know how to say what I need to tell him. And to tell him what I need.

That I want him to give it to me and make me *feel* everything.

"I want to make you come. I want to see you come for me."

"I... look... I need to tell you something." I close my legs and lean forward to reach for him, then fall back on my elbows and watch his wild eyes fill with confusion.

"Right now?"

"It's important." I nod furiously, making myself dizzy. Then I spit it out, "I've never had an orgasm during sex. Well... or ever, actually... I've never had one, so if you—oh!"

I fall back on the mattress with a whoosh as his mouth assaults my most sensitive part. His determination and skill at finding my exact spot so quickly are impressive, turning me on even more to where I feel I might combust.

He pulls back an inch and meets my gaze over my mound. "Challenge accepted."

I reach down and grab his hair. Within minutes, Sebastian has me writhing, crying his name, getting me so close to what I've been looking for. What I haven't been able to get from anyone else before.

Before I know it, I'm on the brink, ready to fall over the edge. The sensation is new, exhilarating...

But I can't let go.

Can't let go of the control like I thought I could. Can't let go of my control with this guy I've only just met.

I stop myself, clenching and holding onto his hair like it's my rope keeping me from falling off a cliff.

And I can't jump.

CHAPTER 9

Sebastian

Her taste is better than the finest wine, whiskey, or unicorn water that exists in the fucking ether.

At the front desk, even at the club, she seemed nervous, and for a second, I thought she'd say no.

But I'm so glad she didn't. Having her moans fill the quiet room under my touch—it's better than the sound of waves of the ocean.

She trembles beneath me, and I squeeze that perfect ass of hers that I've been staring at all night, losing my mind. I suck on her clit until her core tightens, ready to burst beneath me.

But she doesn't.

She fights it.

I squeeze her ass tighter in encouragement as I continue licking every inch of her pussy.

When she clenches tighter, refusing to orgasm for me, I look up at her. Her eyes are squeezed shut like she's about to go skydiving but is afraid of heights.

I stop licking and instead, push two fingers inside her while my thumb rubs circles on her mound. Her eyes shoot open as she leans up, grasping the sheets. My voice cracks slightly when I say, "Let go for me, baby. Let go."

She meets my gaze and relaxes her expression with each passing second, her lips parting as her pussy clenches around my fingers. I watch her closely, her trembling body on display only for me.

And when she finally lets go, that's when I see it.

Her freedom.

Her eyes are no longer pained. She's not nervous or on edge—she's free.

And that freedom spills onto my hand while her body jolts in ecstasy.

She doesn't take her gaze from mine, the whole thing so erotic that it makes me want to come before I've even had a chance to feel her, to fit myself inside of her.

My dick is so hard, it's painful.

I step away from her as her eyes flutter closed, and I reach for a condom out of my jeans pocket.

She watches me again with wide eyes as I slide it on. "That was…"

I hover over her, her hair splayed across the white bedspread, just like I'd imagined it earlier tonight.

When she reaches for me, I waste no time sliding into her, as deep as I can go, holding on to her for dear life.

Her nails dig into my shoulders as I stay inside her,

pulling her farther up the bed so her legs no longer dangle off the side.

I hold her hands above her head and leave them to push against the headboard—I need her to brace herself.

She whimpers when I pull out and pump into her again. I hold her close by the waist, her hard nipples poking me in the chest. My cheek rests against hers, and her panting and whispering of my name fill my senses as I pick up speed, thrusting in and out of her wet heat.

She starts moving her hips in rhythm with mine, and I grunt, ready to burst if she continues.

"Sebastian!" she screams over and over, like she's cheering me on.

She digs her nails into me harder, and I know she'll leave marks, the thought so hot that I can't contain myself any longer. I bury myself deep inside her with a few more thrusts and exhale my release before collapsing on the other side of the bed.

We stay silent, staring at the white ceiling. The far wall is lined with floor-to-ceiling windows overlooking the Strip. Mandalay Bay fills the other side of the street, and the sky full of unseen stars stretches out over us all.

I can't see Excalibur from this angle, but I'm very aware that it's close by. Aware of the significance of that place now. It's where my life began and ended. Where I was heartbroken and my brothers helped me get back up again.

I may have left Naked Heat for a short while, but since I've been back, it's like I never left. I'm closer than ever with the guys.

Now I'll also remember sweet and fiery Kendall.

Her laugh.

Her scowl.

Her taste.

As I sit here, I'm aware that this is for one night only. I'll never see her again, let alone make her smile again or come on my fingers.

She rests her head on my shoulder, and I play with a strand of her hair before I kiss the top of her head. I pull her close, afraid to let her go, even though I know it's for the best.

I've had a taste of her. I've tried the forbidden apple and want the whole fucking tree full. I want to make my way through the deadly sins with this girl.

Greed, lust—and pride.

Pride, that I'm the first to ever make her come undone.

That I want to be the one to do it over and over again.

As the night continues, I'm disappointed that I won't get to.

CHAPTER 10

Kendall

My first ever orgasm.

It was… pure bliss.

Once Sebastian finally coaxed it out of me, my spine felt like the San Andreas fault, the orgasm an earthquake shaking me to my very core as I rode the aftershocks.

I lick my lips thinking about his tongue, his fingers, his body. He was *insatiable*.

He stirs to go to the restroom, and when he crawls back into bed, he gives me a small smile. I lie with my back against his front. He squeezes my hip and squirms, adjusting himself while he exhales in my hair. "Your hair is tickling me."

"Don't blame the hair for your uncomfortable hard-on."

He groans, then rests his forehead on the back of my head.

I trace his forearm with the tip of my finger, teasing him, thinking there's no way in hell he's actually ready for round two already. But then I feel him pressed against me, between my bare ass cheeks.

I stand corrected.

"Talk to me." The last thing I expect him to say.

I turn toward him with a sly smile. "Or we could…"

His grip on my hip tightens, and he squeezes his eyes shut. "I want to…"

"But?"

"I want to watch a movie."

"A movie? Now?"

"Yeah, I love movies. Grew up watching *Rocky* and every Quentin Tarantino movie ever made."

I smile, thinking of a young Sebastian watching *Rocky* and pretending he himself was a boxer, running up a set of stairs and punching the air in victory.

He flashes his round ass to get the remote from the nightstand, then settles close to me with his dick barely covered. I pull the sheet up over my chest, very aware that I'm exposed, but he doesn't seem uncomfortable with his nakedness.

The sight makes me blush, and I blush harder when he kisses me without a word.

When he flips the TV on, Freddie Kreuger's sunken face and evil grin fill the screen. I jump from the sudden screaming as Johnny Depp's character gets sucked into the bed, into his nightmare, but Sebastian changes the channel to something less gruesome—a mop commercial.

"Hey, put it back." I reach for the remote.

"I thought it scared you."

I scoff. "Yeah right. Freddie was my best friend growing up."

"Really?" He sounds surprised, maybe a little in awe. "What was that like? I'm asking because you're the only one who'd know."

"It was interesting, but I didn't sleep for weeks at a time. He's just so misunderstood."

He smiles as *Nightmare on Elm Street* comes back on, Nancy screaming from her window, trapped inside her house.

When it goes to commercial, Sofia Vergara stands in front of a Ninja blender with a wide smile. "I should get a Ninja for all my yummy protein smoothies." I say this with a bit of sarcasm, but the truth is I enjoy protein shakes. It's Emma's juices I don't care for.

Sebastian reaches for the phone, flashing me again with his ass. Hours earlier, I saw it on stage, but the private show is much better.

I lick my lips. "What're you doing?"

"Call out the number," he says without looking back at me.

I look between him and the TV with the toll-free number on the screen, then slap his back and jump over him. "You can't call the Ninjas!"

Chuckling, he wrestles me onto my back. With all his weight on me, I sink farther into the bed, ready to suffocate in bliss. Then he jumps back to his side, pulling me with him. "I enjoy protein smoothies too. Juices? Not so much."

"Juices are the worst. My roommate puts lemon juice,

spinach, and other green shit in them. Swallows it down like it's Gatorade." I shiver, remembering the last time Emma made me try one of her creations, convinced I could be a juice person. But that was the seventh time she'd failed.

I'm on board with healthy living, but I draw the line at juices.

"I haven't had a roommate since college. My first was Erwin, and he was also my very first stalker."

"You did *not* have a stalker."

Even in the dim room, his dark eyes seem lighter now that he's so animated. He's so different from the Sebastian I saw on stage, the one with a set routine and movements to sync with the other dancers. Here, in this hotel room alone, he seems relaxed and carefree.

And sexy—he definitely oozes sex.

"I'd finish class, and Erwin would be waiting outside to walk back to our room together like I was just getting out of preschool. One day he even tried to hold my hand while we crossed the street." He laughs and shakes his head. "But then I met Ty on campus. The big guy who came out with us tonight? The one with all the tattoos, who's half Samoan, half African American?"

"How could I have missed him? I thought Amber would have a stroke just by the sight of him."

"*Anyway,*" he gives me the side-eye like he's jealous, and it makes him look innocent again, like the subtle freckles sprinkled on his cheeks, "he didn't have a roommate, so I moved in with him within the week. We joined Naked Heat about a year later while we finished school right outside Vegas."

"You went to college?" I blurt, immediately worried he'll take offense.

"That's what got your attention?" He shakes his head again and flashes a smile full of teeth, his beard short enough that it looks drawn on. "Yeah, I went to college. Graduated summa cum laude, thank you very much." If I offended him, he doesn't show it. Which relieves me.

That's what's different about him—his smile and laugh. They're both fun and charming. Why I can't stop myself from snuggling closer to him rather than rolling away like I should.

I watch the TV as Nancy enters Freddie's world, cautiously crawling and waiting for him to attack. With screaming victims on low volume in the background, we turn to each other. He tells me more about his college experience, about how he majored in business and finance and that his old roommate continued to follow him the rest of that first semester, then stopped when Sebastian got a new schedule.

The more he talks, the more I want to roll away. We're treading into dangerous water for me when it comes to college.

With a heavy heart, I keep the conversation going because I like listening to his deep voice. But I'm largely aware that he could turn the question around to me and ask what college was like for me—a sore subject. And I don't mean sore like two days after leg day—more like the soreness after bashing my head through a wall.

And that's the first time that I'm slightly jealous of him. Of having a cool college experience when the little time I did go is marred by unhappy memories of screaming at my ex and binge-drinking right after to forget it all.

Instead of dwelling on it, I smile at Sebastian, etching this night into my mind so I never forget the hot guy with an equally attractive personality who makes me feel alive.

I've never been able to find a guy as hot as him who also makes me laugh and feel special.

As we continue lying there, slowly drifting off to sleep as a new movie begins, I'm very aware of the minutes passing us by. The new day is right around the corner, and my heart sinks at the thought that I won't ever find a guy like him again.

What's more terrifying, is that up until now, I didn't even want to.

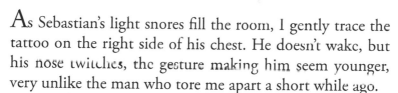

As Sebastian's light snores fill the room, I gently trace the tattoo on the right side of his chest. He doesn't wake, but his nose twitches, the gesture making him seem younger, very unlike the man who tore me apart a short while ago.

I study the tattoo, a rose with a stem made out of words. They're in small cursive letters, and I have to squint to read them. In the dark, it's hard to do so with the whole thing black, not a splash of color anywhere. I put my weight on my elbow and practically rest my chin on his chest. From this angle and with the help of the moonlight, I can read the words *I am laid low in the dust.*

His nose twitches again, and I pull my hair back so the

ends don't tickle him, although I want to wake him up, to ask him what his tattoo means, then to ask him to do that thing with his tongue and fingers to make me jump off the cliff again.

The pull toward him is strong and something I've never felt toward anyone, let alone a guy I just met.

I can't think clearly with him laid out like this, his mouth slightly parted, his dark muscles a sharp contrast from the white pillows and blankets around us.

My mouth waters, and my fingers itch to keep touching him, to wake him up.

But I let him sleep.

I'm too scared to do otherwise.

Too scared that I want to ask him for his number, address, and social security number so I know where to find him at all times.

At first, it was a raw, physical attraction. But now that I know a little about him, it's becoming more—too quickly.

He makes me feel warm, with his bear-like build and gentle smile.

I need to regain my control. I can't let a one-night stand have this much power over me. I'm not so much an amateur when it comes to dirty liaisons that I get attached—it's why I haven't had a relationship that's lasted longer than a Chick-Fil-A drive-thru line since college.

Since Adam.

I swing my legs carefully over the edge of the bed, watching his chest rise and fall in peaceful sleep. The sheet only covers his lower body, his V still visible—and delicious. To add, the slight bulge a few inches lower makes my body shiver.

Control.

I need control.

With trembling hands, I crouch to the floor and search the pockets of Sebastian's discarded jeans. From this position, if he woke up, it'd look like I was robbing him. I snort at the thought. I'm poor as fuck; I only came here because my parents paid my share of the hotel room and Lauren's spa day tomorrow. Sure, I'm broke, but I'm not that desperate for cash to steal.

I'm only desperate for one thing, which Sebastian already gave me.

I silently thank him for that, and the box of cigarettes I find in his back pocket.

When I stand back up, I'm facing the door on the opposite wall. The smart thing to do would be to sneak out, run away from him, and never look back.

The smart thing would be to quit while I'm ahead before I do anything really stupid and ask to see him again. To know more about him. To let him know me.

With deep breaths and eyelids heavy, I back away toward the large windows instead, unable to bring myself to leave. Something special exists in this room, and I want to hold on to it for as long as possible.

I set the cigarettes on the table, then raid the mini-fridge. I fully intend to pay him back somehow, as I know how expensive these are, but right now I need a ten-dollar mini tequila bottle.

Or five.

I scoop them up in my hand and settle into the

loveseat—also white, like everything else in this room—by the window. I unscrew the top of one and take a long swig before lighting a cigarette, the flame burning bright with the Vegas backdrop.

I take a puff to calm my nerves, thankful Sebastian reserved a smoking room with a view. The city laid out in front of me calms me, like I'm in charge here with the world beneath me. That, along with the cigarette and the sound of Sebastian's raspy snores, comforts me.

The hum of the fridge and light footsteps outside our door add to the mix of the makeshift music. All I need is to add the erratic beating of my heart and a turntable to finish the remix of tonight's one-night stand.

One full of feelings and natural sounds that sounded unnatural coming from me for the first time in my life.

I take another sip of tequila and take a pull from the cigarette, letting the smoke surround me like a lust-filled fog. Then I tear my gaze from the mesmerizing lights to watch him sleep.

I long to join him. To have him make me feel alive again. To feel *anything*.

But I don't move. I watch the city breathe below me while I inhale the smoke from his cigarette.

I breathe it all in and beg myself to retreat into my shell, to protect myself from feeling too much during a meaningless onetime thing.

My heart beats faster as I listen to Sebastian's snores, knowing deep down it was not meaningless. Not at all.

But I have to convince myself it was because the last time I felt close to anything this strong, when I lost control

of myself so quickly, my heart ended up broken and bruised.
And I never really recovered.

CHAPTER 11

Sebastian

With my eyes closed, I turn to my right and reach out to Kendall, but her side of the bed is empty and cold like she's been up for a while.

Or *gone* for a while.

I gulp in silence. Thinking she left, I settle onto my back and stare at the ceiling while disappointment crushes me like a four-hundred-pound sumo wrestler.

I touch my bottom lip, the one she'd bitten earlier tonight, and smile.

Movement to my right has me looking toward the window, and relief washes over me when I see Kendall's silhouette, her perfect shape, against the Strip outstretched for us to admire.

A perfect picture.

She swipes a loose strand of hair from her forehead and

tucks it behind her ear as a small puff of smoke surrounds her. Her gaze never leaves the window, even as she sips from a small bottle. Like she's mesmerized with the world beyond the window.

She doesn't seem to be watching anything, yet she sees everything.

Just behind the cage of her own existence.

Even in private, she puts up walls, curling into herself like she is now on the loveseat, like she's protecting herself from the world below. Her feet are tucked underneath her, one hand holding her toes while the other rests on top of her knee.

She's only wearing her tank and panties, the side of her thigh exposed.

My breath hitches at her innocent, insanely feminine look.

I want to know more about her, but this is a one-night stand, a casual hookup with a random, sexy-as-fuck girl I met in Vegas. One I'll never see again.

That's how the story goes. That's how all the stories go when they start with "Once upon a time in Vegas..." They aren't supposed to end with "happily ever after."

I know that better than anyone.

But I can't stop myself from kicking my legs over the bed and slowly walking toward her, tugging my boxers on before I reach her.

I don't move her or say anything as I contemplate what I want because even if this was our third or thirty-third night together, I know a happy ending isn't in the cards for me. But for now, I want to hold her while she tells me what has her so wound up, what keeps her from laughing.

From not smiling freely.

I could help. I also have those demons inside me, ones that cut deep from the lies, betrayals, and disgust from the ones I loved most.

I want her to let me take care of her, to coax her to let go like I did with my mouth on her, when she moaned my name and went completely limp before I revived her, bringing her back to life like she was drowning.

I want to do all these things, but I can't bring myself to ask for her number or even her last name.

If last year—the worst year of my life—taught me anything, it's that happy endings don't exist for someone like me.

She isn't startled when I gently touch her shoulder, just moves over for me to sit, but instead of scooting in beside her, I pull her onto my lap and hold her.

"Where'd you go?" I whisper in her hair as we watch the cars racing below us, always on the run even at four in the morning.

My heart races just the same as I continue holding her.

"I'm right here," she whispers against my bare chest, placing a kiss above my tattoo.

It makes me smile, and I look down at her, waiting for her to continue.

She leans back and hesitantly meets my stare. "You think you know me so well from a few hours together, huh?"

My gaze is unwavering while hers darts back and forth between the view and me, like she can't decide if talking to me, giving me her truth, is better than jumping out the window from the forty-fourth floor. "I know more than you think. I'm perceptive like that." I wink.

She smirks and rolls her eyes.

"Talk to me," I say, and because I can't help myself, I dip my head and brush a kiss across her lips, encouraging her to let me in. "What's your deepest, darkest secret?" When her eyes widen, I continue, "What's the harm in telling a complete stranger who you'll never see again?" I almost stumble over my words, not wanting to believe them, but I remain focused on her wide eyes and full lips.

"If I told you, I'd have to..."

"Kill me?"

"See, you don't know me at all. I was going to say 'leave right now.'"

She gives me a devilish smile and narrows her eyes. There's a faint tequila smell surrounding us from the empty mini bottles, but her eyes seem clear, focused, if not a little hazed from lust as she watches my chest rise and fall.

I reach around for a full bottle and take a sip, waiting for her to go on.

"When I was seventeen, I stole a pair of panties from the dollar store."

"A dollar *is* too much to pay for panties."

She giggles and shrugs, taking the bottle from me for a drink. She doesn't even flinch as she swallows, and the bold move gets me hard—something that was already inevitable since I'm very aware she's sitting on me in almost nothing.

I shift, and she looks down between us with a shy smile. I stop her, tilting her chin back up. "Don't go getting shy on me now. I still want more."

Her hooded gaze meets mine again. "I can give you more."

I growl, wanting her again and again, but I also want to know the story behind the shoplifting. The story behind everything, including her cactus tattoo, her sister. Fuck, I even want to talk about her childhood and high school. Anything and everything.

I want more than the physical.

There are so many questions I want the answers to, and I'm scared I won't get them. That she doesn't want to share them—even when I shared my own past experiences from college, she didn't share any of her own or if she went to college to begin with. I gave her an opening, and she didn't take it.

But instead of pushing her now, I try to soak up whatever she *will* give me.

She lifts her hands above her head, and I pull her tank up, kissing between her round breasts, her hard nipples ready for me.

I suck on each as she holds on, digging her nails into my shoulders and arching her back in pleasure.

I run my hands along her back and fist her hair while she whimpers, hungry for my touch.

I'm fighting with my self-control. With my urge to take it slow and savor every second, every inch of her skin, while my need for her wants to push her against the glass windows and fuck her from behind with Vegas as our audience.

Her squirming grows more and more impatient, but I hold her in place as I pull her face to mine, stealing as many kisses as I can.

Her plump lips are even more swollen when I move back, searing her with an intense gaze as I hold her up in order to remove my boxers.

She slides her own panties down at the same time, and when we settle back down, she wastes no time sliding onto me. She does, however, take her time moving up and down, watching me with lust-filled eyes and her lips parted. I hold her close while I switch angles in order to find that spot that drives her wild.

After a few moments and a little encouragement, she finds her release, slow yet earth-shattering as she goes limp in my arms. I follow closely behind but don't let go of her.

Her eyes flutter as I pull out, but I hold her in my lap while she whispers against my lips, "My deepest, darkest secret is my fear. My fear of caving in to my parents and their desire for me to settle down in our small hometown with a respectable man and have lots of babies." She looks down as though she's ashamed. "My fear is living an average life because I don't have the balls to do what I really want."

I squeeze her tightly, at a loss for words.

We both still, her secret hanging between us, bringing us closer.

Her courage gives me the strength to speak my own truth. "I want to own a hotel. Build it from the ground up and run it myself."

Her eyes open in wonder, mirroring my own.

I smile and say, "I found a lot right outside LA, close to where I used to hang around as a kid. With all the wrong crowds, of course. It would be a small boutique hotel, no more than thirty rooms. Just a getaway spot for both locals and tourists."

"Why don't you?" she asks out of innocent curiosity, but it's a question that plagues me every day.

Instead of answering, I kiss her into a stupor, then wrap my arms around her waist, holding her close to me.

With the Vegas lights against the dark sky to our side, we stay like this, savoring the warmth of each other's heart beating, and I wonder if she feels sad.

Sad that we'll never be this close again, that we won't share anymore secrets.

Because I do.

CHAPTER 12

Sebastian

I squint at the blinding sun, the curtains wide open from when we admired the city last night.

When she straddled my lap and nipped at my lips before we fell over the edge.

I reach for her, but she's missing from her side again. I roll onto my back and catch her at the end of the bed with one pant leg on. I groan. "Come back to bed."

She stops but doesn't turn around. Fighting with the second pant leg, she says, "I'm going to be late. And one of us needs to be sneaking out of here. It's in the one-night stand handbook." She takes one look at me with her hair tossed to the side. There are darker strands underneath the blond that are more visible at this angle and in the light. She smirks. "Clearly it's not going to be your lazy ass."

"Ouch." I pull myself up against the headboard and

clutch my chest. Halfway joking in reaction to her jab, but also because she said it out loud. That this was a one-night stand. We both knew it—I implied it last night when I asked for her deepest secret—but it's the first time I'm hearing it from her lips.

Like I didn't believe the words until I heard her say them.

And I don't like the way they sounded. They were too casual coming out of her mouth, and nothing about her mouth or our situation is casual.

I wonder if there's protocol in this handbook of hers for the turmoil happening inside me.

"I feel used."

"Right, because you don't look like you're enjoying the view." She tilts her head at me in sarcasm.

She's only in yoga pants and a sports bra—damn right, I'm enjoying the view.

But her eyebrows are drawn as close together as they can possibly get as she searches the room for her tank, for her escape route.

I eye her teal shirt crumpled in the corner by the nightstand and reach down for it, dangling it from my hand like I'm trying to hypnotize her. If I can get her to stare at its side-to-side motion long enough, maybe she'll stay. "Looking for this?"

"Yes, actually," she says, challenging me to another stare down. We're getting good at them. When she sashays to the edge of the bed by my feet, my nostrils flare. And when she leans over for the tank, her breasts are pushed together. It looks like she's ready to crawl toward me, on hands and knees, and I'm ready to let her.

But she snatches the tank from my hands at the last second and smiles. "Thanks."

She walks away then, pulling the tank on before sitting back on the edge of the bed. She puts her shoes on, one at a time, torturing me.

Her hair falls over one side, shielding her face from me. I want to know what she's thinking. How she really feels about this.

I may have only just met her last night, but I can sense last night was a big deal for her as it was for me. She came for me.

Under my touch.

From my tongue.

And from her moans and tinged cheeks before we fell back into bed, she clearly liked it.

My dick twitches, wanting desperately for one more go-around. Morning sex has always been my cup of coffee, giving me the energy to start the day off right.

But the sun's up. The twinkling lights from last night are gone. It's a clear day, and the fantasy is gone.

She spins around, scanning the room to probably make sure she didn't miss anything. Tucking strands of hair behind her ears with both hands, I can finally see her whole face, including her flushed cheeks.

"You are so beautiful."

She faces me, giving me her full attention with a dazed smile. "You're a real charmer, you know."

"It's the truth."

She averts her gaze, a sadness washing over her features.

"You wouldn't say that if you knew me in my real life."

My chest squeezes, wondering what she means. Wondering what she's like in her real life. Because although she told me her biggest fear, I don't know the most basic things about her: what she does for a living, what her hobbies are, what her favorite food is.

The thought of never finding out, of never knowing why she said that, sends panic to every cell in my body, nerves firing off like they do in a fight-or-flight situation.

And my panic overwhelms me—an unfamiliar sensation for me.

I don't want this to be a one-night stand at all. The realization is too much for me to handle.

But as Kendall finishes getting ready and makes her way to the door, I don't have a choice.

CHAPTER 13

Kendall

"Can I do my walk of shame now in peace?" I wink at Sebastian, who's outstretched and taking up most of the bed with his large frame. He's avoiding my gaze, so I figured I'd try lightening the mood, but it's not working. He looks worried, scared even, and it about breaks me. "If I can even walk," I joke, and this time I at least get a smirk.

I watch him, study him like he's a rare species. He is in my book, anyway. The only guy to make me smile more than I have in three years. The one to give me my first orgasmic experience.

Literally.

That's all I really wanted last night. To experience one for the first time. To feel something, anything, for once.

And I did.

But as I move around the room, the familiar emptiness

settles in the pit of my stomach.

And right on cue, my stomach growls.

Sebastian's head snaps toward me. "We need to get you some food."

"I am. We're having brunch," I say, with my hand around a fake cup of tea and my pinky in the air. I expect him to smile, but he just continues staring intensely at me, like he wants me as his meal. His look and mussed dark hair have me ready to jump back in bed and stay there. Order room service. Mimosas and strawberries too.

I use all my leftover energy to gather the empty tequila bottles and pillows that are strewn around the room like a scatter plot diagram, the dots leading me away from him.

When he climbs off the bed and starts dressing, his eyes follow me around the room.

This isn't my usual routine. I'm not sure how I'm supposed to act with him. Normally after sex, I make excuses to force them to leave, or if we're at their place, I sneak out quietly and unseen. If they do happen to wake, they're in the shower before I have time to put on my second shoe.

That's the reason I kick them out, before they have a chance to make me feel unwanted.

I never make it to sunrise with them.

Sebastian, on the other hand, seems like he can't get enough of me. Like I'm the rare carb he allows his lean body to eat.

When my wristlet is firmly in my hand, I exhale deeply, preparing myself for our imminent goodbye. I dig deep to gather more energy to meet Lauren and her friends. Enough energy to leave Sebastian, who looks like a buttermilk pancake—hot and delicious.

His nostrils flare when we stand face-to-face by the door, the windows stretching to our side. The Strip is so different during the day, almost like a normal city instead of a magical one that comes alive at night. The sky is a regular shade of blue, nearly as light as the clouds. Cars and people don't seem to be in a hurry. Sunday morning is a hungover person's worst nightmare, so they're probably seeking solace in a pile of biscuits and pots of coffee already or sleeping it off until noon.

"I'll walk you down," he offers with a firm kiss on my lips, his tongue parting my lips with ease.

I shake my head and move toward the door, swallowing my nervousness. Smoothing my hair down and wiping under my eyes for any runaway mascara, I say, "You don't need to. My sister is staying in this hotel, so I'll find her and her minions easily." I give him a small smile, nervous under his scrutiny.

"What kind of gentleman would I be if I let my lady walk all alone in the Vegas jungle?" His face transforms into his signature grin that's come to fill me with warmth.

"Right. You're a gentleman. And I'm a lady, a real debutante." I roll my eyes and tuck a strand of unruly hair behind my ear as the door clicks shut behind us, the sound echoing down the empty hallway and over our heads like we've shut the door on what's happening between us.

He takes my hand once inside the elevator and doesn't let go while we walk downstairs. I let him hold it, let my fingers curl around his and enjoy the moment.

I don't want to say goodbye, but I know I have to. It's

the only logical thing to do. He lives here, and I live in LA. We're from different worlds, in so many ways. It's a recipe for disaster.

Like Rachel cooking a trifle for Thanksgiving dinner on *Friends* and making it wrong, adding beef and sautéed peas and onions to a cold dessert—*disaster.*

We'd take a good thing, a fun and wild night, and I'd ruin it with my insecurities and drama. And let's not forget my family, who already thinks me a disappointment.

Even if I was ready for it, any kind of relationship with a stripper would send them over the edge.

When we reach the lobby, I spot Lauren immediately, sporting her "Bride" shirt while the others wear matching "Bridesmaid" shirts. The slim-fit ones with the V-neck tucked into their matching high-waisted jeans with a thick tan belt.

Trendy enough to be a Pinterest post.

I'm late just like yesterday, my time management skills extremely poor, another thing they gripe at me for. I let go of Sebastian's hand and walk to my sister. Hopefully, one of them will give me a key so I can freshen up and finally put some clean clothes on.

Before I open my mouth, Lauren swivels her head around like the doll Annabelle herself. Her eyes skim over my face and lock onto something—or *someone*—behind me.

Sebastian.

"Oh my God, aren't you the stripper from last night?"

Sebastian swoops in beside me. "As a matter of fact, I am. Good to see you again. Lilly, is it?"

"Lauren," she sneers and turns to me. "Don't tell me he's why you didn't come up to the room last night." She looks me up and down. "And why you're wearing the same disgusting outfit."

"Brace yourself, because he is." I roll my eyes and turn toward Sam, the only one who's usually reasonable. "Now, can I get a key to—"

"Seriously? This is why you bailed? I called you like a hundred times. I was close to calling the police."

Elaine leans in with arms crossed. "I told you she was fine, and with a guy."

Sebastian chimes in, proudly sticking his chest out. "Yes, she was." He then turns to Lauren. "And next time we'll be sure to change her voice mail to include 'Too busy fucking random hot guy to come to the phone right now. Please leave a message.'"

I cough a laugh, hiding it behind my hand. I should've been mad, but I can't be when Lauren's face is twisted up like it is when she needs to fart in public but doesn't because "it's not ladylike."

"Really, Kendall? This is so typical." She points a slender finger at me like I'm her child, not her twenty-three-year-old sister. "You show up late, screw the stripper, and then flaunt it around in front of me and my friends. You never fail to embarrass me." She throws her hands up. "For once, just *once*, you couldn't just be here for me. Show up on time, fake a few laughs, and go home. Can't do even the simplest of things for me." Her voice drops to a whisper as she checks around to make sure we haven't attracted an audience, I'm sure, and through her rude comments, I actually sense she's hurt deep down.

Deep, deep down.

Sebastian tenses beside me, so I place a hand on his chest to let him know I can handle Lauren and her hostility. I've been doing it for the last seven years. "How about you and your friends stop acting like you're better than everyone else, and then maybe I'll consider *your* idea." I take a step forward, curling my fists in a challenge that she better step down from. We're not teenagers anymore, but she never fails to make me feel like one.

One who'll tackle her to the ground.

Standing next to each other, we look like twins. Same wide eyes and lips so plump you'd think we get Botox. Only difference is the hair—blond to honey brown. She doesn't dye hers and claims to be naturally beautiful. Not in so many words, but with her attitude.

We're the same height at five four. Same body type of full hips with a small waist that Instagram models would be jealous of. Lauren's slightly thinner, her arms not as toned as mine. She doesn't work out with Emma like I do.

But the biggest difference is our personality.

She takes notice of my fists. "Calm down before someone's nose gets broken again."

"Good one." I roll my eyes and pull Sebastian to the side, embarrassed that he was a witness to our spat, but also nervous that Lauren would elaborate on the unfortunate incident from long ago when I lost my shit—not my finest moment in the slightest.

He steps in so close to me that I think he'll kiss me, but instead, he says, "Will you marry me?"

My eyes narrow, skeptical of his question. "After that? That childish argument?"

"Exactly." His eyes are animated, different from his previously intense gaze. "You are fierce, sexy as fuck, and I have half a mind to drag you upstairs like I did last night and settle in between your legs for the rest of the day."

I look into his eyes. He's serious, and hungry again. "As appealing as that sounds... I should go." My voice is strained and needy, even though I'm saying no. "At the very least, I need a clean shirt. A shower. A fucking comb." I stutter on the last word, thinking about the reason I need a comb. His hands mussed up my hair so much all night, I'll spend all day getting the knots out.

He looks down. "We have a show tonight, in San Francisco. Leaving in a couple hours."

"Oh..."

"Guess this is goodbye, then." He looks at me hesitantly, shy even. Almost boyish, like he doesn't want to say what he's really thinking.

I take a deep breath. If this were my game I usually play to keep me in control, I'd get his number, then give him a sweet peck on the cheek and walk away, swaying my hips more heavily for his benefit.

The perfect ending to a fun game.

But I can't bring myself to do it. This feels like more than just a game. "I guess it is." I offer a smile, but his face falls. Clearly not what he wanted me to say.

But his smile is back, in true Sebastian fashion. I may have only met him yesterday, but I've noticed his smile is second nature for him. It's always plastered on his face even if he's hurting deep down. And last night I got a glimpse of his true sadness when he talked about his hotel dream. The way he held on to it like a secret, not sharing the whole story.

As curious as I am to continue getting to know him, to uncover all his secrets like they lead to his heart of gold underneath, I'll save us both from the pain in the future if I walk away now. He doesn't realize it now, but he doesn't want to know me.

I'm doing him a favor.

He kisses me one more time, and heat envelops me, settling at my core. Nothing sweet or innocent about this kiss as his tongue explores mine. I lean my body against his and stifle a moan.

"We have reservations at Nobu," Lauren says behind me, and her disapproval might as well have slapped me in the face.

Elaine pokes her head around Lauren and adds, "I heard that's where the Kardashians eat." She practically squeals, like I care where they eat. Unless that magically makes the food delicious enough to pay the obscene price for it, it doesn't matter to me who eats there.

Sebastian interjects. "You know, I heard that place is also where that old jackass baseball player eats. Stack is much classier."

I stifle a laugh, once again happy he butted in. Although I can stick up for myself, it's nice to have someone there for me for once. Someone to fight for me. Aside from Emma, no one does that for me.

"Uh, thanks for your input." Lauren scoffs with obvious

sarcasm. She turns to me with her arms crossed, but her eyes are pleading, almost begging me to read her mind like we used to pretend we could. When we shared a bedroom and thought we were psychologically connected because we had the same dream *once*, at the same time. We never did again. "Are you coming?"

I glance briefly at Sebastian before turning to her, stepping out of the way for a big group of students in matching "Senior" T-shirts. "I'll be right behind you."

Before she turns, she gives me a small smile, only a hint, before she scowls and mutters to the other girls, "It smells like fucking smoke and feet. Let's get out of here."

Typical Lauren.

"You know the sad thing?" I fidget with my hands, turning my attention to Sebastian. "We actually used to be friends. You know, during prehistoric times, when we had a pet raptor named Blue and trained her to be our protector."

His throaty laugh blocks out all the dinging from the slot machines and the chatter from couples, groups of friends, and families excited to see the city. To get their day started, when it feels like mine's ending before it even began.

"I think I remember that," he says. "Was it you or your sister who created the monstrous Indominus Rex?"

I smile at how well he knows *Jurassic World*, but it doesn't reach my eyes. It mirrors his sad smile as he stuffs his hands in his pockets. I step closer and place my hand on his cheek, the stubble a stark contrast to my smooth palm. Before I kiss him, I hold his gaze and don't stop until his tongue swipes along my bottom lip, seductive and hot.

When he pulls back, he tucks a stray hair from my

forehead behind my ear and then kisses the back of my hand. "My lady."

I nod, too hot and overwhelmed to speak. I walk ten feet before glancing back to see he's still watching me. He raises one hand in a weak wave, and I continue walking.

I take the elevator up to our floor, feeling like I'm missing something the whole way.

And hoping he remembers this small-town girl he met in a city full of lights.

CHAPTER 14

Sebastian

I place my hand on my chest, over my heart, willing it to stop beating so loudly.

This is how it was always supposed to be.

I stand there a minute longer, but Kendall disappears in a sea of gamblers and sightseers with visors and fanny packs.

The tall ceiling and open room make me feel small.

I was on top of the world when I was on top of Kendall last night. Like the first time I reached the top of the Space Needle and rode the roller coaster—terrifyingly awesome. It was my first week after I moved to Vegas from LA, eight years ago. Before I met the woman who betrayed my trust and ruined relationships of any kind for me.

Of getting close to anyone else.

Of keeping me from chasing after Kendall and begging her for more time, or at the very least, her last name.

Last night made me want to dredge up my past, but I fight with myself to keep it in the dark. To bottle it up and bury it deep inside so I can protect myself. That's why I set my rules in place to begin with, and last night, I broke all of them. Now I'm standing here alone, being pushed by eager tourists and getting checked out by the cocktail waitresses.

I smile at one who's walking toward me, but before she gets too close, I pull my phone out and fake a call.

Feeling guilty, I mouth, "Sorry," to the young girl with skin almost as pale as her curly blond hair. Her lips pout while her eyes smile. My younger self would be backing her into a corner and asking her out before sticking my tongue down her throat. I was relentless and carefree back then.

The new me would've just asked her out with promises of only one night and nothing more.

But the even newer me, the latest version as of the last twenty-four hours, turns my back to her and pretends to be on a call.

Once outside, the sun blinds me, and I shield my eyes in an attempt to adjust to the brightness that matches many of the smiles on the tourists' faces. No clouds in sight. An otherwise beautiful day, if I didn't feel so empty. So restless.

I walk toward the bridge, heading to my car at Excalibur. My legs pick up speed the farther I get from MGM while past memories beg to be released, sweat running down my back when I reach my car. Once inside, once the silence consumes me, memories burst through my walls as I grip the steering wheel.

"Don't you want to know what I'm wearing underneath?" *She cocked an eyebrow suggestively. "Or what I'm* not

wearing..."

I groaned and raked my hands through my hair as she ran her pointer finger down my bare chest. Her deep red nails against my dark body made me groan even harder—*fucking sexy,* that's what this woman was.

Sexy and confident—a winning combination.

She flipped her long black hair over her shoulder and smiled, her teeth perfectly straight and white. She looked like a beauty queen, like she was on the stage at a Miss USA pageant with her flashy smile and full makeup. Especially when she waved to her friends, a small wave with her delicate wrist casually moving from side to side.

But she wasn't delicate in bed.

She wasn't delicate the morning after, when she put her number in my phone and told me to call her.

She wasn't delicate when she broke my heart a year later.

I claw at my shirt collar, thinking about Kendall's shadow in the moonlight when she sat by the window. When she told me her fear. When she moved above me with ease.

Kendall wasn't delicate, either, but she had a different kind of confidence, one that allowed her to still be vulnerable with me.

I shake my head, forcing myself to accept that it was a one-night thing. Better to think of it as a dream.

A sweet, wet dream.

Pulling out my phone, I see new texts from Ty.

Ty: *On my way to the gym. You coming or what?*

Ty: *Dude, I chugged pre-workout like a frat boy on New Year's Eve.*

Ty: *Already have two sets of bench presses down.*
Where are you?!

I run a hand through my hair and decide a workout is just what I need to rid my mind of all thoughts Kendall. Her smooth skin, the way she moaned my name, the way she tasted.

It's going to take a lot of heavy lifting to get her out of my fucking head.

When I walk into the gym, the banging of barbells and weights consumes my senses. I can feel the adrenaline rush already, and I didn't even need pre-workout.

The gym is the only thing that ever turns my mood to a more positive one. Dancing in front of a room full of appreciative women doesn't even compare to the natural high I get from lifting. The best part of my day is walking into this rusty-ass gym with fifty-year-old machines that squeak with each minor movement.

Ty and some of the other guys we work with are already taking up one corner of the gym, alternating between the bench press and tricep pull-downs. As a veteran dancer and gym buff, Ty is leading the new guys, coaching them through their sets. I'm just about to settle in with my headphones and continue pumping myself up, but I should've known I wouldn't get off that easily.

"There he is," Ty starts in. "Look, guys, the product of

a good fucking! This dude hooked up last night! With an atomic blond, no less." He grins from ear to ear, resembling Terry Crews with that crazed look in his eyes—probably from all that pre-workout he tends to inhale.

I take a deep breath, trying not to cough at the stench of sweaty gym socks and armpits. There's no air conditioner in this gym, just large fans in every corner and garage-style doors that are open. The Las Vegas heat is inescapable, trapping us with the stench.

I drop my bag by the rack. "Are you ready to do some work, or are we just going to gossip like a bunch of pussies?"

"Dude, you *hooked up*. We have to talk about it!"

I glare at him in warning. He knows the hell I went through with the last girl I hooked up with after a show. A one-night stand that lasted for a year until it blew up in my face, leaving me with nothing but a frail heart.

Ty and I have been friends for almost ten years and started at Naked Heat around the same time, so he knows me all too well, taking my hint to back off.

Too bad the newbies don't know shit.

Rafael picks up where Ty left off, gyrating his hips. "You give her a private show?" He rolls his *r*'s with his Spanish accent, making his question sound even dirtier.

Jordan chimes in. "I'm sure I could've given her a better one. Five stars. Do you even remember how to use your dick?"

He and Rafael high-five each other while I grind my teeth, blood boiling.

They don't know my exact history, but they know I don't go out much or take girls home. That's what my younger self used to do. The self that got me mixed up with a minx who ripped me to pieces.

I've been working for over a year to put them back together. Last night, I was stupid to get a room with Kendall. To revisit my past head-on. To let myself get attached in any capacity.

But it was a onetime thing. I can get back to my life now. To my rules and routine. Work out, dance, sleep. The occasional bus or flight for an out-of-town show. A few laughs with the guys in between.

Simple.

Instead of beating their asses, I chuckle sadistically while I put my wrist straps on. I widen my eyes to match Ty's and grind my teeth together in a forced smile. "Not only do I remember how to fuck, but I also remember how to bench way more than you. Let's go."

Rafael is the first to whine. "But we've already done two sets before you got your lazy dick out of blondie."

"You think you're a real badass, don't you?" I narrow my eyes at him. "Let's fucking *go.*"

"You heard the man." Ty claps and gets the bar ready, loading up the plates like we're training for the Mr. Olympia bodybuilding contest. I put my headphones on and turn it to my Tech N9ne playlist, ready to make these assholes throw up.

They don't know what's coming.

After three sets of heavy bench presses, doing as many reps as we possibly can and then some, we're all panting, our faces red. Rafael's curly hair sticks to his forehead. He pours water down his throat like we're in the desert. Which we technically are.

The thought reminds me of Kendall's cactus tattoo. Her smooth skin against mine. Her nails digging into my back. I made sure to wear a short-sleeve T-shirt here instead of going sleeveless even though it's hot as balls out. I wanted to cover the marks she left on my back and shoulders, not because I'm embarrassed that the guys would give me shit, but because I want to keep them for myself.

I shake the thoughts away and grin at Rafael's obvious defeat. "You done already?" I taunt him and Jordan, who's pacing with his hands on his head. I carefully take a small sip of water so I don't choke before I continue, "What's next? Some burpees? You like to jump around? Up and down, your stomach flipping upside down?" I watch their faces turn from pale to green and back to pale, then smirk.

Don't mess with me again, fuckers.

Ty waves them off. "Get out of here, pussies. I can't have you throwing up on my new Jordans." Ty flashes his new red sneakers like they're his most prized possession.

Once they're gone, Ty and I finish our chest workout in peace, aside from each of us yelling obscenities at the other for motivation.

"Don't you fucking quit, you sorry ass. Give me three more!" Ty yells at me.

My muscles burn by the end, worrying me that I won't be able to lift my arms later. The workout is more intense than it's been in a while, but it accomplished the main thing I was hoping for. I didn't think about Kendall but for two fleeting moments, the illusion of her vanilla scent more welcoming than the BO that surrounds me.

As we walk out of the gym, Ty nudges me. "I know you didn't want to talk about it before, but I just want to say I'm happy for you, for getting back out there. It's been over a year since Joelle."

I laugh it off. "Last night was a onetime deal, man. I won't ever see her again. No reason to have this conversation."

"Never say never and all that shit." He raises an eyebrow like he knows something I don't. Like he's communicating with the universe to send Kendall back to me.

The confident look in Ty's eyes unsettles me as I drive home.

But not in a bad way. In a way that gives me hope that I will see her again. That the universe is not out to get me after all. Joelle was a strange twist of fate sent to torture me for past sins. Maybe for sleeping around in college, and for years after that, without ever calling girls back.

Lesson learned—that's for damn sure.

Walking into my apartment, I shake my head at the living room, at the hole in the wall that I have yet to cover up. It welcomes me home every day, which is why I spend as little time here as possible. Too many reminders of what I lost... and *why*.

I shake my head at myself for letting Kendall get to me like this. To give me hope. I've never been one for wishful thinking.

Never had a reason to be.

CHAPTER 15

Kendall

My heart beats loudly in my chest, echoing in my head above the music blaring from my headphones.

Sweat runs down my face, my muscles screaming, but I don't stop.

One more rep.

When I do one more, I push myself to do another three before I drop the dumbbells by my feet.

Rubbing my shoulders while I take a break, I notice the room is empty, other than a guy doing rows in the corner with his back to me. This is rare, but when it happens, I take advantage. I grab my phone and stand up, twisting to the side and holding my arm out so it's not flexed but not completely relaxed, then snap a picture.

I sit back down on the worn bench and study my selfie as a small group of guys walks in laughing.

It's a good picture, Instagrammable even, if it weren't for the shadow over half my face and the love handle hanging over my high-waisted leggings.

Emma says I should post these pictures, especially if I want to become a fitness influencer on Instagram like many of the women we follow—the main one being Samantha Ray, my idol. I've been toying around with the idea for several months, but I just can't make the leap.

Drop out of college? Move to LA on a whim? Those leaps I had no problem making, but posting about my fitness journey is where I draw the line, apparently.

Shaking my head, I add the picture to the growing collection on my phone of others just like it, a graveyard of my progress pictures. But at least they're safe on my phone where no one can see or judge me.

As I push the dumbbells up for my last set of shoulder presses, one of the guys who walked in earlier watches me. He's laughing with another guy, but his eyes wander to me. I catch his gaze long enough to intrigue him, then turn back to my set.

With a deep breath, I push one knee up to get the dumbbell into position out to my side, then the other. Watching myself in the mirror, I count down the reps. I'm at eight when I see someone standing beside me, but I still don't stop.

Four more reps.

Calvin Harris continues blaring in my headphones as I finish. Since Vegas last weekend, I've been listening to his music on repeat. I've also reinstated my flirting game full force, and now is no different. I turn my attention to the guy next to me, ready to turn on the charm.

Sebastian is the only guy to ever throw me for a loop, but now I'm back.

Well, my game is, but *I'm* not.

Just as it has in the past, my game has worked every time I've used it in the last week, but I haven't gotten any dates. They've all asked, but I can't bring myself to follow through. I did actually say yes to one, then ended up canceling at the last minute because thoughts of Sebastian wouldn't allow me to function properly enough to even comb my own hair.

I pull one headphone to the side and meet this guy's gaze. "Oh, hey. You need this bench?" I ask innocently, like I can't read his smoldering look. Like I don't know what he needs is *me*.

My assumptions are confirmed when his gaze lingers on my lips.

He looks back up at my eyes then, giving me his full attention. He's tan with dark brown eyes, almost as dark as what I imagine his hair would be if he had any. There's a light shadow across his bare head instead. His tank top is unable to contain his muscles, his traps coming up high and tickling his ears. "I've seen you in here a lot. Never did get your name."

I raise my eyebrows, not impressed by his opener. If I'm going to get Sebastian out of my head, I need something better than this lame pickup line.

My eyes never leave his as I take a sip of my BCAAs—a godsend formula that Samantha Ray swears by for faster muscle recovery post-workout. "I'll do you one better and give you my number." I tear out a sheet of paper from the notebook in my bag that I keep for personal records and workout ideas. After I scribble my name and number for him, I hesitate, while he stands with his mouth open. His social skills are subpar, but his large eyes and sexy grin tell me he's got potential.

Sebastian's smile again clouds my memory. Shaking my head, knowing I'll never see Sebastian again, I hand over the piece of paper. The thin sheet leaves my hand like it's a contract, agreeing to a boring dating life until the end of time.

The guy closes his mouth as he accepts my paper, folding it and stuffing it into his pocket like it's no big deal. Pulling my bag over my shoulder, I take off with a small wave, all the while I can see him watching me in the mirror. This gym is full of mirrors, plenty of selfie opportunities for the newbies. And the Instagram athletes trying to get noticed, to make it to enough followers for a sponsorship or apparel modeling opportunities.

When I first started training after I moved to LA, I considered doing this myself. I posted a few pictures and videos of me working out in the beginning. It went well, but then the nasty comments started rolling in about my double chin and back fat. Some even called me fluffy. I mean, who the fuck openly calls a person *fluffy*? That's what I said to Emma. I acted tough, reassuring her that it didn't bother me, but then I shed a tear over it while in the shower.

I became convinced afterward that all kinds of cameras add ten pounds.

I got messages from my high school "friends" judging me too, saying I'm fake and mean, all the things people from my hometown used to whisper behind my back like I couldn't hear.

A couple more similar comments in the following weeks made the decision for me, that it's just not for me.

Although I still follow many Instagram athletes and wonder what it'd be like to do the same, I always shut down the urge. I take a few selfies but never end up posting them. I can never get the angle right, the proper lighting to show my abs, or my hair to fall to the side.

I can never make the whole picture effortless yet sexy, like the pros can.

On the drive home, I almost forget about the guy I gave my number to, my thoughts plagued by my insecurities.

I sip on a protein shake and turn the radio up as I continue driving through back roads to get to our apartment. The song ends, and the hosts start a game for people to call in with their funny, hopefully even painful, dating stories. I snort as I sort through all the possible ones I could tell, not that I'd ever call in.

I laugh in silence now, from the clichés I've experienced to the truly unique, ranging from a guy wanting to take me "home" to his parents' basement to going down on a guy whose dick tasted like Cheetos. After deciding it wasn't worth it, I made an excuse and ran out of there like Chester Cheetah himself was chasing me.

To this day, I can't eat Cheetos.

And now I can add "slept with a stripper" to my little black book. I could call in and tell them it was my best experience yet, but I'll never see him again. And my chest has been aching ever since. How's that for a story?

I roll my eyes at what my mother would call "my dramatics." It's what Adam used to call me too, saying I was too dramatic and why didn't I just "chill"—which usually meant get naked for him.

Which then meant me doing all the work. I cringe thinking about how selfish he was in bed.

The first few times we had sex, I faked my orgasms. I felt like I had to, not that he paid attention. He didn't know the difference, anyway—he never knew.

And I kept it that way for fear he'd think me dead inside. That he'd have one more flaw to harp on to emphasize my inadequacy. My urge to prove him wrong yet please him in any way overshadowed everything that I once was.

But all that did was kill the light inside me further.

Until Sebastian.

Until Sebastian said and did all the right things to breathe life back into me. To make me feel more alive than ever. One night with him is all it took.

He even made me believe there's nothing wrong with me at all—that I'm beautiful and funny. Fiery, even, but in a good way. He actually liked my spunk.

I blush as I turn onto our street, thinking about the way he touched me, gripped me, *owned* me.

The radio host's voice booms through the speakers with laughter at a caller's story. I was too lost in thought to have heard it.

It wouldn't matter, anyway. Cheeto dick is worse than any of them.

I rub my eye with one hand while the other blends my protein pancake mix, courtesy of the fabulous Samantha Ray. I'm slightly dreading the cardboard taste of the ground oats, but after having eaten them for the better part of the last year and surviving, I think I can make it through one more.

Which is what I say every morning.

"What're you still doing here?" Emma says behind me.

"Well, I do still live here, unless you kicked me out and didn't tell me?" I say, flipping the tasteless mixture in the skillet.

She bumps into me as she shuffles around the small kitchen we share for what I assume to be a quick and healthy snack. She's fully dressed with enough makeup for a lunch date, even though it's only eight thirty on a Saturday morning. Once she finds her granola bar, she turns to me and rolls her eyes. "Aren't you supposed to be at work in an hour? You're not dressed." She looks me up and down. "Unless you're planning on going in your sweaty spandex." She cringes like that is, in fact, what I was planning, then walks over to the table.

I join her with my plastic pancakes and sit with one foot on the seat so my knee reaches my chest. "What's up your ass? Thought you would've gotten plenty of sex while I was gone last weekend to put a smile on your face."

"Wouldn't that be a nice change of pace." She doesn't look at me, just continues scrolling through her phone, nibbling on her granola bar like a chipmunk.

"But the neighbors already think we're lesbians, so why set things straight now."

That gets her attention, turning her glare toward me with fire in her eyes like I took her coffee. No matter how much she likes telling people she's a morning person, I know the truth—that she despises mornings like I despise Cheetos. To make matters worse, she doesn't even allow herself more than one cup of coffee a day due to it being a diuretic, so her one cup is sacred.

In other words, off-limits.

"That's exactly why we need a change of pace."

"But you're my type. Am I not yours?" I ask as I smear more than a serving's worth of peanut butter on my pancakes while they're still warm. This way the peanut butter can melt and ooze down the sides like syrup. It reassures me that I don't need actual syrup.

She starts putting her shoes on, unfazed by my joking. Probably because it's normal for us, having known each other since elementary school. I'd be surprised if she wasn't used to these kinds of conversations by now. Which is why she plays along. "I can't have eligible people with male genitalia thinking I'm into... well, female genitalia."

I cringe at her choice of words. "But why? People with *penises* sometimes like that about a girl."

"I can't talk to you." Emma throws her hands up, unable to continue our banter. As always, I win.

"All right, sorry. *Male genitalia* it is from now on." I stick my tongue out.

"Speaking of *crude*"—another glare—"how'd your date go last night?"

I pause, pretending I'm chewing and don't want to talk with my mouth full. Which is unlike me, but she's rummaging through the refrigerator now so she doesn't notice. I consider lying and telling her I went, but I can never lie too well with her. Instead, I coolly say, "Didn't end up going out."

She pulls fat-free yogurt out of the fridge and watches me, waiting for an explanation.

I don't want to tell her it's because of Sebastian. That I can't get him out of my head. Seems too dramatic for someone I'll never see again, and I'd hate to actually give a reason for people to keep calling me that. "He's the one I went out with a couple weeks ago, remember? The funny one? Or at least I think he was. He kept laughing before his stories were over, and I could never understand the ending through the snorts. It was cute for about five minutes, but after that, I wanted to jam a fork through my eye. Or his."

"Wow, now I know never to withhold jokes from you."

I shrug and continue shoveling the pancakes in my mouth. Big bites help me eat it faster in order to forget that I dislike the taste, even though Samantha Ray swears it's delicious. Probably the only time I disagree with the queen of godly abs and legs awarded to her by angels themselves. "He also tried to cuddle me after sex." I wince thinking back to the mediocre sex. Not the mind-blowing sex with Sebastian—fuck-master extraordinaire.

"How dare he." She grabs her keys from the entryway table and turns back to me. "Why did you even sleep with him?"

"He was a good kisser. And pretty hot, actually. And I was horny as fuck, so why not?"

"Such a slut." She smiles at me. "At least with your

healthy appetite, people won't continue questioning our sexualities."

"You're welcome." I grin sarcastically, holding my arms out and taking a bow from where I sit. "Hey, guess who has a new boy toy."

"I swear, if you say Samantha Ray…"

I nod and swallow the last of my food. "Samantha Ray, and he's a mystery. She won't give any details."

"You act like you two are best friends. That's creepy, you know that, right?"

I continue as though I hadn't heard her. "She's calling him Gym Bae. She's going to start selling hats and tanks with *hashtag gym bae* logos. That Samantha, she's hilarious. I should get me a shirt when they release."

She just stares at me, like she does every time I go on ranting about Samantha. Or Britney Spears. I have fascinations with certain celebrity women that I can't explain.

Maybe I should revisit the lesbian thing.

When Emma doesn't respond, I mutter, "Maybe you'd laugh more if you had your own gym bae."

"No time for that."

I roll my eyes at her usual response. She says she wants a change of pace, but I know she doesn't mean it. She intentionally stays away from all *male genitalia*, having decided that all men are assholes like the one she used to date. Brant hid behind his sweet dimples and wavy hair, but underneath, he was really burning with Satan's fire for a heart.

Emma's gorgeous, with long black hair that reaches

just above her ass. A perfectly round, toned ass from all the hours of teaching yoga and Pilates. Her cream-colored skin is a blessing. Her whole family is naturally tan, but somehow down the line, Emma didn't inherit that gene. Instead, her skin is as silky as it is creamy. Not the sickly pale kind, but silky like almond milk.

It matches her icy tendencies, which she mainly acquired since said Devil betrayed her trust almost two years ago. It worked out for me, since it allowed me to move out here and in with her, but I'd never be thankful for it because of what it did to my best friend.

Ever since her ex dumped her with a figurative slap to the face, she's been extra wound up, working and volunteering every chance she gets in order to stay busy.

But I miss her spunk. I catch a glimpse of it every now and then, but she's still brokenhearted.

I reach across the table for a spare sheet of paper and write down the number from the guy at the gym this morning. He'd already texted me by the time I got home, but I decided not to respond. Now I have a better idea of what to do with it. He may not be worth the risk, but he could be what Emma needs to get back out there. A casual fling could do her some good.

"Here, you should call him. Easy smile and nice, toned shoulders. He'll help you out." I wink as I hold the paper out to her.

"Who's this?"

"Some guy I met at the gym earlier. Seems like you need him more than I do. You're into bald dudes, right?"

She ignores me and checks her Apple watch, her birthday

present she bought for herself last fall. "You're going to be late for work."

"Nuh-uh, I have plenty of time," I say without checking the time.

"No, you have thirty minutes before you need to leave."

"Plenty of time."

"You take an hour to get ready. At the very least." She shakes her head, her tight ponytail following suit. "I've taught you nothing about time management, no matter how hard I try. Text me when you're fifteen minutes late. I'm off to my class, and then I have that charity dinner tonight. Are you still coming as my date?"

"You have a class this morning? On a Saturday?"

"Yes, remember I told you last week that I added classes on the weekends to bring in more people, and therefore *money*? LA isn't cheap, as you may have noticed."

I shake my head, trying to jog my memory.

"We had a whole conversation? While eating takeout from that new Chinese place downtown for our cheat meal?"

"With the good egg rolls?" I nod, remembering the crunchy heaven. "Let's get some of those tonight."

"We have the charity dinner tonight. Please tell me you remember *that* conversation, at least? The one to raise money for the animal shelter?" She loops her purse onto her forearm. It's the Michael Kors one her dad sent her a couple months back, the one she told him she'd send back but then decided to keep once she saw how hurt he was on FaceTime.

"Yes," I say slowly. "Now will *they* have egg rolls?"

"I'm leaving. Get ready." With that, she shuts the door and locks it behind her.

By the time I get to work at the shoe store, Margo and George are already there. I check the time once I'm inside. Nine forty-five.

And of course, right then, I receive a text from Emma.

> Emma: *You just got to work didn't you? You owe me $5.*

Son of a bitch. For a woman who teaches yoga several times a week and volunteers—like on purpose—she can be a real minx.

I roll my eyes as I type out a response.

> Me: *I already gave you a boy toy to call. That's worth more than $5.*

I slip my phone into my back pocket as I make my way to the front where Margo and George are discussing what pair of shoes Margo should buy. She has yet to decide if she wants the strappy sandals or the heels for her date tonight.

I join their debate, the whole time wondering when my next date will be. Contemplating when Sebastian's smile and hands will leave my memory. When he'll stop being in my dreams.

I go through the motions of my shift, wondering when I'll stop missing the way he made me feel. I actually felt like my old self again. No games or front. Just me.

Even though we only spent one night together, it felt like I'd met him long before that. And now my chest hurts knowing it was a onetime deal.

That's what I've been telling myself, anyway. It's what I told Emma too. But the truth is, I'm holding out hope that maybe, just maybe, it wasn't a one-night stand.

There's a hope in the back of my mind that we'll meet again.

CHAPTER 16

Sebastian

LA.

That's what it says.

Fucking LA.

I don't know whether to grin or frown, to pump my fist in the air with excitement or pound it through the wall.

I'm left standing in the middle of our practice studio while the rest of the guys make their way out. But I can't stop staring at our schedule of upcoming travel dates and locations in my hands, gripping the sides so fiercely that I can only see half the paper.

LA shows are nothing new, but the location has a whole new vibe now, knowing she's there.

For the last two weeks, I've been doing everything in my power not to think about Kendall. Twice I thought about looking her up on Facebook, my fingers hovering over the keys of my laptop, ready to type her name in, but I talked myself out of it.

It's not like I would find her. I don't even know her last name. Every inch of her body? I got to know *that* very well. Like no one ever has, according to her.

Ty high-fives me, our schedule in his other hand. "Damn, I love LA. This is going to be dope."

I merely nod and reach down for my things, my stomach growling after that gruesome dance practice. Dancing is the reason I'm able to stay so lean. Otherwise, my weightlifting habits would have me barely fitting through the door. That and the fact that I eat like I have a bottomless stomach, never getting full.

Ty walks out with me into the desert heat, continuing around the corner of the studio to the parking lot. We pass a liquor store with windows caked in dust, but it does nothing to curb the urge to down a bottle of whiskey. Maybe Jack Daniels can help me figure out what to do, and how to find Kendall, because the universe knows I want to find her and bury myself inside her for just a little while longer.

Ty shoves his phone in his pocket. "Isn't that girl from LA? You going to look her up?" he asks hesitantly. I spent the whole day after Kendall and I hooked up talking about her with Ty, going back and forth about it being a mistake but also the best night of my life.

"Can't. Don't know her last name or even have the slightest idea of where she lives."

He tsks at me like I'm a kid who disappointed him, and it pisses me off. I don't need him to tell me how hopeless I am for this girl I just met. And how fucking miserable I am that I don't know how to find her.

"You give up too easily," he says.

I stop by my car, crumpling the piece of paper in my hand. He smirks at me, holding up his phone, though I can't make out what's on the screen from the glare.

Ty exhales and comes over to me. "I have your girl right here. Kendall, right?"

I take the phone from his hand and see Kendall's smiling Facebook profile picture, her blond hair slung over to one side while a monkey pecks her cheek. I don't know whether to laugh or cry that I found her. To hug or punch Ty for finding her. "How the fuck did you find her?"

"Well, there was a divorcée at the party, so…" He shrugs.

"So, of course, you had to get all her information for 'safekeeping,'" I finish for him.

"My *charming* talents came in handy, though, huh?" I roll my eyes at his use of "charming" when he knows we're both thinking "whoring" is more appropriate. "Found her mutual friend, who just so happens to have magical powers."

I give him his phone back, along with a confused expression.

"To have broken your dry spell? She definitely cast a spell of her own." He jumps back as I leap for him, missing him by an inch. He continues backing up and around my car to get to his own before he winks. "I got your back, bro."

I smile at Ty because he does, in fact, always have my back. Even when I don't ask him to, he's always there for me.

The minute he starts his car, I pull my phone out, not wanting to waste any more time. I pull up Kendall's profile,

and as the sun starts setting, I click "Add Friend."
Fucking LA.

CHAPTER 17

Kendall

"You have to come out tonight." I rest my phone on my shoulder as I finish eating my rice cake. I can still hear Emma's groaning on the other end over the crunchy chewing, but she already told me she doesn't have another charity dinner tonight like she did last weekend. She has no out.

And that was so boring I just can't have her going to another one on another Saturday night. I told her it'd make me feel like a bad friend if I allowed that, unless she finally hooks up with the young surfer guy who also volunteers. He's the only reason I went—to ogle his tan skin and wavy hair.

But even he didn't make me feel better about Sebastian.

"I'm teaching an early class tomorrow. No way am I going out tonight. If I did, I wouldn't drink or stay late, so it'd be pointless." She ends her argument like the whole conversation is over. Like I'm not also persistent.

"You never go out with us," I start, just as Margo comes in to warn me that I have one minute left for my break. "Just think it over. We'll meet some nice touristy guys and get free drinks. Maybe one of them will grind his dick on you while dancing. It'll be magical."

"Seriously, Kendall—"

"Oh sorry, *male genitalia*." I hide my smile behind my half-eaten rice cake like Emma is here in the break room with me.

"Not exactly the romance I'm looking for."

"Who said anything about romance? This is about getting laid." I raise my hand up like I've seen half my hometown do in church every Sunday. Right now I'm praising—well, *praying*—for the unsuspecting soul who's going to show my friend a good time tonight.

It's been two whole weeks since Sebastian made me come like he was bringing me back from the dead. Two weeks since I've had anyone else. Since I've even had a date. Haven't even sexted any guys I have on hold.

Emma even asked me if I've been ill.

I run a hand through my hair as I prepare to get off the phone and back to work. "Please come with us. And wear your sexy red pumps. They make your ass pop."

She pauses. "I might do that…"

"Yes!" I spin in place. "And you'll drink too. You know I love it when you get drunk, and I could use a good laugh tonight."

What I don't tell her is exactly how much I need a good

laugh since I haven't had one in two weeks. Since that night with Sebastian when I laughed so hard, a real laugh, like a holding my stomach and panting kind of laugh.

But drunk Emma might be able to do the trick and change all that.

The last time she got drunk, probably a month ago, she thought a guy was Zac Efron and talked to him for an hour about his transformation from *High School Musical* baby Zac to *Baywatch* sexy godly Zac. Poor guy went along with it, probably thinking he'd get some action, but Emma dumped him for a Chris Pratt look-alike.

Yeah, I need her to get drunk tonight.

"Gotta run. The new shipment of athletic footwear isn't going to unpack itself." I roll my eyes, preparing myself for the next hour of shelving new sneakers. Sneakers with sequins that are for looks, not function.

The only thing that gets me through my shift is George. He's in charge of the music and plays Lady Gaga every fifth song because that's his lucky number. He sings along but usually makes up his own version. The longer he's been at work, the more ridiculous his lyrics become.

Now there's no one in the store, and "Perfect Illusion" comes on. He stands across from me humming, ready to debut his own version any minute. And sure enough, when the chorus comes on, he abruptly stops unpacking the shoes from their boxes and uses a pink sneaker as a microphone. He whisper-screams along as he changes the lyrics to describe how bored he is and ready to go out later.

I roll my eyes but can't help the small grin tugging at my lips. But while I try to hold it in, a snort escapes.

This is what I need. Positive and happy energy.

As I focus back on the work in front of me, I will myself to think more positive thoughts. Like George's singing. Like Emma's aversion to the words *penis* and *dick*.

Like going out tonight with friends. We'll have a few laughs, and maybe I'll even find a guy who can make me forget a certain chiseled male dancer with magic lips that know the right things to say and do to make a girl moan, scream, and whisper her heart's secrets after.

"George!" Margo says, making him stop singing and pulling me out of my thoughts. "Customer."

George shrugs as we hear Margo put her professional customer service voice on. The one where she enunciates all her words and smiles too widely than is natural for her.

My phone vibrates in my back pocket. Thinking it's Emma backing out of our plans, I drop the shoebox and round the corner behind the cash register to check it.

But it's not Emma.

No, it's a Facebook notification.

The smiling face in the profile picture not one I thought I'd ever see again.

George sneaks up behind me and grabs the label gun from the counter. "Who's that hunk of man? Sweet Jesus, look at those smoldering eyes."

I hide my phone, speechless. *How did he even find me?*

"Don't you hold out on me, Kendall, you southern slut, you."

I scoff. "You're just jealous."

"Of course, I'm jealous! The ass you get on a weekly basis? What's not to be jealous of?"

I giggle halfheartedly, thinking about being off my game lately. But I don't tell George that. I haven't told him or Margo about ever meeting Sebastian to begin with. I can imagine George's howls now if he heard I slept with a stripper. Not because he'd make fun of me, but because his suspicions would be confirmed—that my southern accent is all a front.

I don't look like a southern belle, nor do I act like one.

I don't say anything as I finish my shift, or when Margo and George confirm our plans to go out. With Sebastian's face on my phone, I can't properly think about going out. Meeting new guys seems moot now that I have the one I really want waiting for my response.

When I get home, I hold the phone up in front of Emma's face without a word.

She squints at the notification. "Am I supposed to know him or how to respond right now?"

Exasperated, I click on his profile and shove the screen back in her face.

"He's hot...?" She draws it out and then pushes my hand out of the way. "Are you trying to set me up again? I've told you over and over again, I don't want to date. I definitely don't need you to find me—"

I hold my hand up to stop her and finally find my voice. "It's Sebastian. The guy on my phone is Sebastian, the guy from Vegas I told you about."

Understanding replaces her outrage from before as she reaches for my phone. "Gimme, gimme."

I hold the phone away from her and click on his profile picture. It's a closeup of him smiling in a dark room, perhaps a club. It's casual, natural. The easy smile that's kept me up at night now in front of me.

"How the hell did he even find me? I mean, that's some stalker shit right there. Right? The kind *Catfish* warns you about?"

"Stop watching that shit. Try the Discovery channel every now and then. You might learn something."

I glare at her, as this is not the time to discuss my television habits.

"Didn't you say his friend was talking to Amber at the bachelorette party? Maybe that's how he found you?"

"That's right. They did look like they were exchanging information at one point. That makes sense."

She rolls her eyes at my conspiracy theories. "Are you going to accept?"

"Should I?"

"Why wouldn't you? You accepted Cheeto dick, yet you're not going to accept the best sex you've ever had?"

"I told you that in confidence."

She looks around at our empty apartment.

"Okay, but you can't throw that in my face ever again."

She holds her hands up and plops down on the blush pink couch, holding a floral throw pillow to her chest. "So?"

My thumb hovers over my phone screen as I chew on my bottom lip, considering my options like this is a college algebra problem.

It's Sebastian.

The guy I had a great time with.

But he's also the guy who knows a lot about me, which, from experience, doesn't tend to end well.

"Stop that head of yours from spinning. You're going to have a stroke. This isn't Mrs. Chase's chemistry class. You're not going to blow up the classroom just by clicking a button."

I loosen my grip on my phone and sit next to her on the couch, letting my toes sink into the cream plush rug. It's so small our knees touch. "You're right. I'm getting worked up over nothing. It's just a friend request."

"Exactly, so what's the big deal?"

I don't answer her, not wanting to get into the details. I normally tell Emma everything, but I left important details of that night out.

Instead of answering her now, I respond to the friend request and shrug. "There. No big deal at all."

But my heart clamors in my chest, my whole body aware of Sebastian. That he found me. That we've been brought back together again, even if it is only virtually.

And that brings a smile to my face.

CHAPTER 18

Sebastian

She accepted my friend request.

She accepted.

I'm so happy—it feels like she accepted *me*.

I roll my eyes at my pathetic yearning for this woman. Ty would have a field day with the way I'm acting like a teenage girl waiting to be asked to prom.

I type as I head to the kitchen for something light to snack on.

> Me: *Missed me?*

I sit back down on the couch with my protein bar in hand, my eyebrows shooting up when Kendall's name appears on my phone. I could get used to that.

Before I answer, I lean my head back toward the ceiling.

I am definitely pathetic for this girl.

With my head tilted back, I can see the hole in the wall right above me, bringing me back to reality. I flex my hand, open and close it, remembering the way I punched right through the wall with no hesitation. Or regret.

I can hear Joelle's screams filling the quiet apartment as I recall the way she covered her face, like she was afraid of me. Like I was the monster when the real one was *her*. She was the one with the cold heart.

I rub my chest, my jaw ticking at the memory, but then I look back down at my phone, at Kendall's face right next to her new message.

She's different. This is different. I'll be more careful this time around now that I know better.

> Kendall: *Looks like you're the one who missed me, lover boy.*
>
> Me: *The girl whose first orgasm was my doing? Damn right.*
>
> Kendall: *Oh yes. Thanks for opening the floodgates, literally. Had many since then.*

My head falls back against the couch again, and a groan escapes me. *Fuck.* Why does the thought of her gaining pleasure from other guys make my skin itch with jealousy? Like a bunch of fire ants crawling up my arms.

> Me: *Hope you didn't scream my name out of instinct.*
> ☺

I nod at my casual response, while my insides are in turmoil. Just then, my phone starts ringing, and my heart stops altogether thinking it could be Kendall.

Instead, I'm disappointed that it's just my mom.

I scratch the slight stubble on my chin and reluctantly answer the call. "Mom."

"Hello? Can you hear me?"

"Barely." Her voice sounds muffled like she's talking with her hand covering her mouth. There are also loud noises, beeping, and a voice over the intercom in the background. "You at the airport?"

She whispers something to someone that I can't make out. I roll my eyes, not surprised that she calls and then ignores me. After a minute, she turns her attention back to me. "Uh, yes, I got called to do a last-minute trip, so I've been flustered all morning."

She's been a flight attendant since I was two years old. For twenty-five years, she's been running across the country and overseas, especially since she started working for a new airline a few years back. Growing up, she was always on a last-minute flight, or a flight in general, leaving me with my uncle next door. My own father was never around, and my uncle didn't have kids, so it was no issue. Except he worked just as much as my mom did, which meant I was on my own a lot.

"Huh," I say, "So… guess you're not going to make it to dinner, then?"

She whispers to someone again before answering, "What, honey?"

"Dinner, Mom. We were supposed to have dinner

tonight, remember? I thought you were staying in town for a couple days."

"Right. Shit, that was tonight, wasn't it?"

"That's what I said." I exhale, uninterested in this conversation. I'd be more bothered if it didn't happen all the time. We often make plans, but she usually cancels. Usually last minute or without warning at all, leaving me waiting at the restaurant like I've been stood up by a blind date.

"Sorry, Sebastian, I'm running late. Just called to see how you're doing." She pauses. "How's... your, uh... job?" I imagine her flinching at the question, one side of her perfectly red lips lifting in disapproval of what I do for a living. Which is her usual reaction, so the way she asks the question so hesitantly makes me wonder if that was really what she wanted to say.

"You mean stripping?" I say with more confidence than she had. "It's going great. What's not to love about it? I get to grind my junk on strange women every night, which is quite fulfilling." I put a fist to my chest dramatically and look up at the ceiling with fake tears in my eyes, as though she can see me.

She scoffs. "Don't be crude, Sebastian. Remember, you're speaking with your mother. Have some decency."

I roll my eyes again at the same conversation we always have. She demands respect yet doesn't spend any time trying to earn it. It's been three weeks since I last spoke to her, and six months since I've seen her. "Was there something else you needed?"

I imagine her snapping her fingers like she just remembered an item to add to her grocery list. "Yes, actually.

It's about your uncle. I think you really should speak with him. He's got a great business proposition for you. It's— hang on, I'm boarding."

My jaw tightens at the mention of my uncle and the idea of speaking to him. It's been a year since I've talked to him, since he took everything from me. Why would my mom bother bringing him up?

"Listen, honey, I know you've had your differences—"

Now it's my turn to scoff. "That's putting it lightly, don't you think?"

"But I think it'd be in your best interest to talk to him," she continues as though I didn't interrupt. "Having one conversation with him could get you away from your current situation."

"You say that like I'm in an unfortunate predicament that I can't get out of. You realize I *want* to strip, right? That I like it? It's not something I'm doing because I have to. I like it, and it's good money."

"But come on," she pleads. "You have a business degree. Why not put it to good use instead of letting it waste away on a greasy stage?"

I hate her choice of words, but I can't deny that something inside me comes to life at the idea of using my business degree. Of trying the business route again. "I don't care what he has to offer. I'm not interested."

"You always were so stubborn. Just think about it, okay? He really wants to talk to you and…" There's some shuffling that sounds like static through the receiver. "Shit, I have to go. A kid just spilled a juice box."

Click.

"Okay, talk to you in another month," I say out loud to no one.

When I look back at my phone, my Facebook messages are still pulled up.

> Kendall: *I had to bite my lip so hard that it swelled, but I managed to not scream your name.*

Fuck.

Images of her writhing beneath me play in my head like a movie, and I know I'll be getting off tonight with Kendall in mind.

CHAPTER 19

Kendall

I gape at Sebastian's message.

He's coming to LA.

In less than two weeks. And he wants to see me.

Well, his exact words were that he wants to make me scream his name without restraint. I had to squeeze my legs together tighter than a Catholic's mouth during Lent.

I went on a few dates with a Catholic once, right as he had to fast for forty days before Easter. I made it three days into Lent before I had to end it—not that we had even made it as far as *it*. I just couldn't date someone I couldn't go out to eat with. My friends thought I was nuts, but what else is new?

I put my phone in my bag when Emma rounds the corner into her studio, the one she bought a little over a year ago. We were here for a class when the owner put the

For Sale sign up. She hadn't finished taping it before Emma perked up and expressed interest. I was surprised, as I can't imagine owning my own studio at twenty-two like Emma, but that's just another way we're different.

She's bold in a different way than I am. She's ambitious.

"Hey," Emma says to everyone as she heads to the front of the room to set up. A couple goes to the front to talk with her, calling her *Ms.* Emma. And it's moments like these that I'm proud of her. She's so official and doing something with herself instead of continuing to live off her dad's money, which he insisted she take when she first moved out here.

Especially after Brant left her.

I'm jealous of her ambition. She got knocked down by Brant, but she got herself back up again. And declined her dad's help along the way, although he still sends expensive gifts that his new wife picks out.

I wish I had more of her determination and confidence. When I got knocked down, I ran. Not just to the other side of town, either. I ran to the other side of the country, to get away from Lauren, my parents, my old life. I wanted to be someone new, yet I'm just repeating old patterns. New town, but same me. The same me who goes out with guys, then dismisses them after a couple of dates, keeping only the ones who were good in bed on retainer like they're lawyers, and I keep needing them to get me out of trouble.

Sexual trouble, but still.

But even they didn't have what it took to do that. Only Sebastian.

The one guy who's made me feel anything beyond surface feelings is Sebastian. And now he's coming to town in less than two weeks.

The horror of seeing him again fills me as I settle onto my yoga mat with the rest of the class. Talking to him through brief messages is one thing, but seeing him again? Whole other monster.

I told him way too much about myself the last time we were together. I just have to watch how much I say to him next time.

The surfer guy who volunteers with Emma jogs in just as she starts the class. He winks in her direction, while I roll my eyes at her indifference. Settling next to me, he nods. "Hey, Kendall."

I smile in greeting, kneeling on my yoga mat and getting into child's pose.

We don't say anything more as the class starts, and I'm deep in thought about Sebastian.

I need to see him again. I need to kiss him again. I need to feel his hands on me.

I wiggle on my yoga mat, my body suddenly heated, but I have eleven days until I find that release.

So instead of dwelling, I let the soft music replace the thoughts in my head as Emma starts the class. Her soothing voice calms me further, and I'm at ease.

I've been doing yoga for months, and it's helped calm me down as a person. Well, yoga combined with not living at home with my overbearing and psychotic family did the trick.

Sometimes I think it's too good to be true that I haven't wanted to rip anyone's face off lately. Even annoying customers at work who try to return stained and obviously worn shoes don't bother me as much as they would have had my old self been working there.

I lie in child's pose and take deep breaths in, letting out all my nervous energy, and succeed in getting out of my own head, embracing the peaceful silence.

But when class is over, all I can think about is *eleven days*.

Eleven days of waiting.

Eleven days of torture.

CHAPTER 20

Sebastian

Ty high-fives me after he gets off the stage like we're playing tag.

My turn.

I run on stage with a few other guys for our smaller act, one with no props. Just our six-packs and dicks covered by small pieces of fabric. Those are what the ladies like most about us. Which doesn't bother me anymore. It did once, at the end of my first term of stripping, if you will. Before I quit and came back a year later.

Stripping is an art form, just like dancing. Dancers entertain, which is what we do. We just use our male parts to attract more audience members.

I clap my hands above my head along with the rest of the guys. The crowd gets out of their seats and claps along with us. But when the music starts, the guys and I get into position and go through our routine flawlessly.

I feed off the adrenaline and get lost in the moves. When I'm on stage, everything comes naturally.

I move to the end of one side of the stage while the others scatter for the final part of the song. Sticking my tongue out and catching the women's eyes there in front, I grab my junk and hump the air, earning every last penny I get from being here.

I keep going until I feel like my hips might jump out of place, which is timed perfectly for the ending of the song. Before I turn around to get into place for the last number, I wink at the ladies falling over each other to get to the stage. It sends them into another frenzy, and I feel alive, like a rock star.

That's what people like my mom and Joelle don't understand. This job is not a demeaning one, nor is it one I feel forced into. I like this job because I like the audience's enthusiasm, their zest for a good time. And it's a good time I can give them by dancing on stage.

It's a good time for me and the other guys as well. It's how we bond. We're more like brothers than coworkers.

There's so much positive energy swirling around, I feel drunk.

I use this feeling to enhance every last move of the final number. We wear top hats in this one, and I flip it around so quickly that it almost flies out of my hand. Laughing it off, I continue with my moves and rip my pants off so forcefully that they do fly out of my hands, but it's just as well. The women fighting over them is a humorous scene.

When the lights go out and the show is over, I run

backstage and dress as quickly as possible, a new sense of elation coming over me.

Kendall.

After almost two torturous weeks of flirting through text, we're finally in LA. And I finally get to see her again.

She would've come to the show, but she had to work the night shift.

"Hey, man, you ready?" Ty leans against the door, already dressed for our night out. Kendall said she'll be bringing her roommate, so I asked him to come along, hopefully to keep the roommate busy while I feel Kendall up in a quiet corner.

"Yeah, let me just…" I spray some cologne while Ty shields his face. "Okay, ready."

"Let's do it."

Arms wide, we go out into the warm night.

A warm night covered in stars and possibilities.

I search the crowd for her but can't make out any faces in the dark. Too many people around, and the disco ball flickers small but blinding light our way.

Ty slaps me on the back with a large grin on his face, but he doesn't look at me. Instead, he's watching two girls dance with each other, searching around them for another partner. Before he says it, I know what he's thinking.

I'm already rolling my eyes when he says, "I think they need some Nutella between that white toast." He wiggles his eyebrows at me and rubs his hands together before he makes his way over. Sure enough, he gets right in between the girls and grinds on one while the other turns and rubs her ass on him.

I rub my eyes, trying to unsee the threesome unfolding right on the dance floor. Used to be my thing too, on a particularly wild night, but I had to have enough to drink.

And two blondes.

Mixed all together, I had the perfect Long Island Iced Tea.

I scan the crowd again, ready to see my current blond obsession, the only one I need.

I spot Kendall by the bar with a dark drink, probably Captain and Diet. She leans back on the bar and gives me and the rest of the club an eyeful of cleavage in her low-cut, shimmery beige halter. My mouth waters as my mind races, wanting to cover her up and keep her for myself.

I draw closer, trying to catch her gaze, but another girl says something to her.

Kendall doesn't budge, her eyebrows drawn together at whatever the girl with the high ponytail says. She also has an ass to make your mouth water, perky but petite, unlike Kendall's full, round ass that I can't wait to dig my fingers into.

Another girl steps in on her other side and smacks her lightly on the shoulder.

Kendall's eyes light up when they finally meet mine, and her lips part in that subtle way that's been on repeat in my head for weeks. I bet if I were standing closer, I would've heard her gasp, a small feminine gasp like you hear from a

Disney princess.

A naughty one.

The other girls stand back, but I don't take my gaze off Kendall's. Her hands fall to her sides as she stands tall, her straight hair parted down the middle, covering her bare shoulders. Her skintight jeans are high-rise and hug her slight curves, and the top she's wearing is actually a bodysuit with cutouts on the side.

This is a different look for her than when we first met. Although I enjoyed the tank and yoga pants, I'm tipsy already over this look without even having a drink yet.

I feel like a dog with a piece of bacon dangling in front of me. As I approach her, I run my hand across my bottom lip to make sure drool isn't falling. She watches me, indecision marring her features, before she straightens her shoulders and smiles.

But it's not my smile.

It's not the one I've been so desperate to see again.

My step falters, but I catch myself. Now a foot away from her, I say, "Hey, gorgeous." I kiss her on the cheek and wrap my arms around her waist, but her body tenses.

Stiff, she lightly puts a hand on my chest and pushes me back. "Hey" is all she says before she sets her drink on the bar. "Meet my friends." She doesn't meet my gaze, her plump lips stained red form a tight line as she gestures toward the two girls on either side of her. "This is Margo. We work together. And this is my roommate, Emma."

Reluctant to tear my eyes off her, I turn to Margo. Her nose piercing glimmers in the dark, and her dark blue lips match the subtle blue streaks in her hair. She winks at me with narrow eyes but doesn't make a move, so I just nod and smile.

A tall guy bumps into Margo. "There you are, you bitch. I've been looking everywhere!"

"George, you made it!" She gives him a hug, while the rest of the group greets him as well. I shove my hands in the pockets of my jeans, waiting for another introduction, but George grabs Margo by the hand and practically runs to the dance floor. Even though there are people smashed together, he still manages to run gracefully.

Then I turn to Emma. She's naturally pretty with a ponytail high on her head, so tight it looks painful. She watches the dance floor with dismay, her frown reaching her eyes. Looks more like she's at a funeral instead of a nightclub.

I give her a one-armed hug, but she's even stiffer than Kendall and doesn't hug me back. I laugh, trying to ease the tension. "It's nice to meet you, Emma. I like your name."

Her thick eyebrows draw together, and her eyes widen at something—or someone—behind me, but she quickly recovers, turning her gaze to the floor.

I'm slapped on the shoulder and immediately know it's Ty. That's who Emma was gawking at. "Dude, this place is insane!" he shouts in my ear, still grasping my shoulder. "I texted Rafe and Jordan to come check it out too. They're going to—" He stops and slowly grins at Emma, who's sipping on her drink with her gaze focused on the dance floor. "And who do we have here?"

While Ty stares at Emma, I watch Kendall wrap her lips around the straw to her drink, driving me crazy.

Knowing the ecstasy she can infuse into my veins with just her kiss, I can't take my eyes off her.

Ty nudges me out of the way and takes Emma's hand to kiss the back. "My lady."

Emma recoils but doesn't immediately pull her hand away.

"Ty, this is Emma, and you remember Kendall."

He gives Kendall a once-over, and I shove him to stop checking out my girl. He merely laughs and pulls her in for a bear hug, her small frame swallowed by his large body. I'm a big guy myself, but Ty has a good two inches and fifteen pounds on me. His wide back strains against his plaid button-up, which rides up as he hugs Kendall. His purple briefs peek out from his sagging black jeans.

"Bro, pull up your fucking pants," I say, shielding my eyes. Mostly it was to get him to quit holding my girl. Especially because she actually hugs him back. It's obvious that she's enjoying it.

More than she enjoyed my hug.

What twists the knife in my heart further is that she's laughing by the time he pulls back.

Looking back at me, Ty shrugs. "Sorry you're not as smooth as me." Pulling his pants up, he stands close to Emma and asks to buy her a drink. She visibly sneers but cuts her eyes at him curiously.

She seems torn between disgust and fascination, but I want to reach out and tell her to stick with disgust. From what little Kendall has said about her, she does not want to get mixed up with Ty.

He's a tough nut to crack. Took me over a year to learn

anything more about him than his affinity for peanut butter and raisin sandwiches and fine wine—sometimes together—and that he loves basketball.

After many late nights of drinking and traveling, I finally got it out of him that his sister died when he was a teenager, when she was in her early twenties. Doesn't talk about it much unless the anniversary of her death rolls around, or when his parents call, which is rare.

Kendall hasn't said much, shifting from one foot to the other, her hip jutting out farther. She sets her empty glass on the bar, and I reach around her for the bartender to order us more drinks. "Two Captain and Diet Cokes, please." Then I peer down at Kendall. "No cosmos, if I remember correctly." I wink, hoping she remembers her threat to shove it down my throat.

She steps back and smiles, but it doesn't reach her eyes. Instead, she rolls her eyes and says, "You have a good memory." She briefly looks at me before turning back around, her breasts on display again as she rests her elbows on the bar behind her.

She seems uncomfortable, though I'm hoping it's because of her heels. They're strappy with a narrow heel sharp enough to cut into a porterhouse steak and tall enough that we're almost eye-level.

The next hour goes similarly, with awkward glances exchanged and even more awkward conversation about the weather. We talk a bit about the show tonight, but she doesn't seem interested, her gaze wandering from the floor to Emma and back, which starts to make me panic. Joelle was never interested in talking about my shows, no matter how many times I tried, until I quit for a short period.

When I ask Kendall to dance, she merely shakes her head and complains about her shoes. Emma doesn't leave our side but for a brief minute to use the restroom. I can tell she's not paying attention to us, her gaze never leaving the dance floor.

Even when we're alone, it's difficult to get anything out of Kendall, to ignite that spark I know exists underneath.

By the end of the night, I'm frustrated. I tell myself again it's because of the heels that she's not the same girl I met in Vegas, the carefree and daring one with snarky comments around every corner. The forward and direct one who took control in the bedroom, but also showed me her vulnerable side.

I tell myself that's the reason because admitting that maybe she was only that girl while in Vegas is not an option.

I can't accept that she's not my Kendall with a free spirit.

I meet her gaze and look for something, *anything*, that's familiar to the vulnerable part of her. Anything to suggest our connection was real.

But all I recognize is hesitation.

Indecision.

Indifference.

CHAPTER 21

Kendall

It's going smoothly, everything according to my plan to regain control, but it's not having the effect on Sebastian that it does on others.

Other guys fall face-first for me the harder to get I play.

But Sebastian's smile falters, and confusion fills the space between us.

When he looks at me, his expression indicates familiarity, but when I smile or say something flirty, he tilts his head to the side like he's seeing me for the first time.

And he is. He's seeing the real me, not the pathetic me he met in Vegas. The one who had a moment of weakness with a hot guy and opened up to him. This is me. The smooth and cool girl whom all the guys love. The one they all want.

It's the one my ex wanted, but he broke up with me

after a year when I couldn't be that for him on a daily basis.

Sebastian puts a tentative hand on my waist and talks in my ear. The closeness and smell of his cologne blanket me, causing my heart rate to spike like I'm on the treadmill, walking fast and panting.

"You're fucking beautiful," he says, his light stubble gently brushing against my cheek.

I can't help but lean into it, then pull back when I comprehend his words. He thinks I'm beautiful. The plan is working. The last time he saw me, I was a slob in my tank and yoga pants. This look was carefully picked out to show off skin but not be too slutty.

Gets them every time.

One side of my mouth tilts in amused victory. I lean in to him and rest my hand on his arm, perking my breasts up higher. My bare breasts that are loose tonight, not trapped in a bra. "You should see what's underneath." I idly but purposefully run a finger down my chest toward my cleavage.

His nostrils flare, gaze heated, but he's not following my finger. He's searching my eyes again, looking for something he's not going to find this time around.

My vulnerability.

I can't tell him any more about me. It'll make him run away. Then I'll be the girl who ran even a stripper off. Because although to me he's just Sebastian, he's a stripper I met at a show where he flashed everyone his ass.

That's how much of a fuckup I am.

From the corner of my eye, I catch a guy watching me. His chest is broad and peeking out from under a black button-up that's unbuttoned at the top. He's only a few feet away, but several people separate us.

Now *he* has the reaction I was looking for from Sebastian. This random guy is playing the game as expected, while Sebastian seems to be on the sidelines. An idea hits me to get a reaction out of Sebastian, something to get him riled up and eating out of the palm of my hand instead of the other way around.

I smirk at the other guy who's coming closer, watching me the whole way, even when a couple girls bump into him. The way they giggle up at him tells me it wasn't an accident, but he still stalks toward me. He's cute in a Hollywood kind of way with his black hair slicked back, tan, and fit. His nose is crooked like he got in a fight and lost, but as he gets closer, his smile is kind. He's the kind of guy I'd be dancing with on a regular night.

On a night before Sebastian.

My insecure subconscious toys with Sebastian as this other guy approaches. I twirl my hair with exaggeration and smile at him. Out of the corner of my eye, Sebastian's jaw tightens. *My plan is working.*

"Let me buy you a drink. What're you having?" the guy asks, glancing at Sebastian and nodding.

"Actually, I don't need another." I hold up my full drink. "Besides, my boyfriend here is taking care of it." I slide my arm through Sebastian's and rest my head on his shoulder while watching this guy through my eyelashes.

He holds up his hands and backs away with a scowl. I laugh when he walks away. "That was fun."

Sebastian pulls away from me and starts stalking off. I

turn to Emma, but she's not watching Sebastian—her eyes are on Ty. "Who the hell needs to have two dance partners?" she clips. Ty grinds himself on two girls at once, running his hands up and down one's side and watching them with a hooded gaze. It's almost as inappropriate as watching live porn.

"Did you see where Sebastian went?" I ask her. When she doesn't reply, I snap my fingers and wave in front of her face. "Hello? You there?"

"What?" she sneers like I interrupted her favorite TV show, which—just like the coffee—is a big no-no.

I step back with my hands up. "I'm just looking for Sebastian."

She slurps the rest of her drink, so unlike the proper etiquette she usually practices, before setting it down on the bar harder than is necessary—I hear it land even above the music. Good thing the glass is thick. "He probably left after your little show. Doesn't seem to be falling for your game, huh? So you pulled out the big guns and flirted with someone else?"

I take another step back now, not to give her space but because of her accusation, no matter how right she is. I didn't think she was watching, but even so, it doesn't give her the right to judge me. "I know what I'm doing. My flirting game works every time. It's my own scientific method."

She rolls her eyes, and I'm insulted even more. "I'm going to find Margo. I can't watch this."

I open my mouth with a witty comeback on the tip of my tongue, but then I realize she's watching Ty with the two girls again. As she walks away, I notice her shoulders slump with jealousy coloring her whole demeanor.

Jealous? Emma? That can't be right.

I shake my head, convinced I misread her. I make my way through the drunken bodies swaying to the music, a song I don't recognize but has a major techno quality to match the disco ball that sparkles like glitter over the dance floor.

I fight my way past the tables and booths, where a few girls dance barefoot on the tabletops with sloppy smiles on their faces. One tries to pull me up as well, but I hiss at them like a snake and continue to the large double doors. I nod at the security guards giving me the once over and push through the doors to the breezy night.

I rub my ears, trying to regain a semblance of normal hearing after being inside with the loud music. My hearing is still muffled when a deep voice behind me says, "Looking for something?"

Sebastian leans against the brick building behind me with one foot propped behind him. The faded red bricks of the wall are in direct contrast with his pale blue shirt and deep blue jeans. He looks Instagram worthy, like one of those trendy pictures where he looks out to the side with wonder in his expression. Especially with a lit cigarette between his fingers by his side.

The model-like stance gets me hot, my body growing hungry for his touch. My fingers itch to run through his hair while he fills me, reaching all the parts that ache for him.

No one else has been good enough.

No one's made me feel like he does, even when he looks

at me with a confused expression.

I deserve it, but I also can't help it. It's a game I've played for a long time that's protected me from heartbreak and disappointment. It's kept me safe.

I waltz toward him, bouncing ever so slightly, suddenly nervous at how hot he gets me with just one sultry gaze. "I don't suppose you have another one of those for me?"

He smiles down at the cracked sidewalk before pulling out his crushed pack of cigarettes. Then he watches me as I bring the cigarette to my mouth for him to light, holding my gaze against my will as I inhale, the first cigarette I've had in over a week. Since the first time he texted me.

Seems I only need a smoke when he's involved.

We fall into silence, with him watching me like I'm a puzzle and he's trying to piece me together.

Good luck.

I lean against the wall beside him, watching the cars drive by, the music from inside faint. I wiggle my ankle around to get blood flow to my toes in these restrictive shoes.

Still, Sebastian watches me, but I refuse to meet his gaze. It's too intense, and I'm trying to regain control, put up my necessary walls to keep him wanting more, because he's not going to want more if he knows more about me.

He shoves a hand down his pocket and takes a puff, then lightly laughs with his eyes cast downward, like the crack in the sidewalk is in the shape of a funny cartoon. "I've been dreaming about you nonstop since Vegas."

I'm offended by the way he laughs, as though he's disappointed that it's not what he expected. That *I'm* not what he expected.

Like he ordered a delicious supreme pizza, but only a cheese pizza was delivered, so he had to settle for the less exciting, less colorful one.

For the first time, I'm uncomfortable around a guy. One I've already slept with. *Maybe this is what it's like beyond the one-night stand?*

Determined to win this game, to stay in control, I smirk. "Why don't we head back to my apartment and give you some more material to dream about?"

He draws his eyebrows together, indecision crossing his features, and for a moment, I think he's going to decline.

For a moment, I feel it's over between us before it even began.

And the feeling leaves a large lump in my throat and uneasiness in the pit of my stomach.

CHAPTER 22

Sebastian

I don't know why I follow her into the Uber.

Back to her place.

Up to her room.

She's not the girl I met in Vegas.

She barely said anything all night, and she's even more silent now, if that's possible. Didn't say a word the whole way to her apartment, even when the Uber driver swerved and she landed on me. She only giggled and pushed back to her side.

The Kendall I knew would've at least flipped him off, cursed, scowled—anything other than giggle like a teenage girl getting her tit grazed for the first time.

And the way she flirted with that other guy right in front of me, on purpose, with the intention to hurt me? Make me jealous? I wanted to punch his perfectly white teeth out of his mouth, hoping he'd choke on them.

Especially when she called me her boyfriend like it was a joke to her. I haven't dated anyone seriously or been called "boyfriend" since Joelle, and then Kendall made a joke of it so easily.

To avoid causing a scene, I went out for air, not expecting her to follow me. Instead, I expected that to be it. To move on from the short-lived fantasy that my luck in the dating department had turned around.

But when she came outside, she tucked her hair behind her ear tentatively, almost shyly, and I remembered when I first laid eyes on her during my show. The way she watched me curiously and danced shyly with me on that table.

That's why I followed her here. I need to know that the girl I met in Vegas, the one I've thought about nonstop for weeks, is real.

I need her to be real.

And I know she is. Underneath all the mascara and hairspray, there's a girl wearing a wrinkled tank with a filthy mouth.

"Make yourself comfortable." She points to her queen bed covered in a pale blue comforter with gray throws. When she leans on the open door and winks with too much effort, I know this is still just a game to her. "I'll be right back."

"Wait." I hold her arm, not wanting her to walk away, even if it is just to the bathroom. "Come here."

"You naughty boy." She smirks. "Can't wait any longer, huh?"

I ignore her comment that sounds whiny and fake, very

unlike my Kendall, who is strong and speaks her mind. Even if she does so with her middle finger.

My small-town girl with city spunk.

I lower my head and kiss her softly, pulling her into my embrace. She stiffens at first, but I continue with my seduction. My hand grazes her cheek, savoring this moment with her.

Begging her to let go of the barrier she's put between us.

She slowly relaxes, and I dive in deeper. My tongue explores hers as I pull her tighter, flush against my hardening length.

She moans in my mouth, and I almost lose my resolve, but I talk myself down. Right now, I need to take it slow with her. Let her know it's just me. That she can be herself with me.

That I want her to be comfortable with me.

"Come here." I take both her hands and walk backward toward the bed. The room is rather small for both of us, so it doesn't take long before we reach the bed. "I want to see you."

Her hooded gaze studies our hands intertwined between us. She moves her thumb over mine, sending tingles up and down my whole body, but again, I refrain.

She nods and pushes me gently back, pulling her leg to one side of me.

I shake my head without breaking eye contact and rub her thigh before I place it back on the floor. "Strip for me. Let me see you."

Her lips purse at my request. "What're you talking about? I'm right here."

Shaking my head, I push myself up against the headboard, the distance welcomed as I try to regain my composure. Her presence is too intense to bear. She watches me curiously, uncertain. "Let me *see* you."

She nods slowly, mulling over my words as I beg to hold on to any small bread crumb that led us here. She doesn't immediately move, seemingly debating whether to make this—*us*—real.

Her mouth falls slightly open as she steps away from the bed. As her clothes fall to the ground, her shoulders relax. Little by little, the more items she removes, the more figurative layers she peels back, slowly removing the mask she wore all night.

When she stands bare in front of me, her arms twitch by her sides, wanting to cover herself up, but I pin her with my gaze. "You're so beautiful," I whisper before she climbs into bed with me. I push her hair back and kiss her tenderly, before I devour her, removing my own clothes with her help.

And when she moves on top of me moments later, she's unrestricted and unfiltered, moaning as the pleasure takes her over, especially when I grip both her hips and move her back and forth on me, causing more friction for her.

I want to make this good for her. To take care of her needs, so she knows I'm not just here to get mine and leave.

I'm here for *her*. All of her.

I tell her with every touch, caress, and thrust that I want her.

I take my time with her, emphasizing every move while my dick aches to find its release. She writhes on top of me, aching and needy.

I lick my lips at the sight of her this way, but I can't take it any longer. I roll her over, hovering above her. Pulling her leg up to wrap around my waist, I sink into her at a new angle.

"Oh my God," she breathes.

Gripping her leg behind her knee, I pick up the pace, this angle hugging my cock tighter until I'm ready to release, but I wait. I wait until she reaches her climax and really lets go, panting with my name on her lips.

When she comes undone like this, her mouth agape and eyes wide—*open*—she really lets me see her.

And I love what I see.

CHAPTER 23

Kendall

While Sebastian cleans me up, his eyebrows are furrowed like he's drawing a portrait of me and not just wiping me off. His tongue hangs slightly out as he admires his handiwork, his eyes running up and down my body.

Growing increasingly uncomfortable lying here like this, where he can openly see all my flaws even though it's mostly dark, I push my legs together and sit up.

He comes closer, one hand on the headboard so he's inches from my face. "You are gorgeous. I don't want you to hide from me." He gazes intently at me, my eyes and lips. It's intense, and I grow even more uncomfortable than before.

Because I want to believe him.

But I know all too well not to get ahead of myself, believing he could be real.

Shifting on the bed under his scrutiny, I try to put some distance between us like I'd tried to do at the club so I can think clearly.

Although I know he can't see into my past, my poor life choices, his heated gaze suggests otherwise. I knew from the moment we met that his eyes were magic, that they see too much.

I've never been so intimate with another man. With my body and soul.

That's what it felt like. Like when I stripped bare for him, I stripped away my defenses. And for the first time, I was able to free myself from the pressure of my ex, from Lauren and my parents, to be better, do more.

Be more.

But Sebastian accepts me the way I am. Not only accepts it but adores it. I could tell in the way he worshipped my body. It was slow, sensual—personal. Right up until the end, when I didn't want it to be over.

It was beautiful and freeing. It was… overwhelming.

"I'm sorry about earlier tonight," I whisper as he lies next to me. I lick my lips, tasting the way the unfamiliar words feel on them. I'm not normally apologetic in my actions or words. Not anymore. Not since Adam. But the words just fell out—even though I didn't mean them any less. "I was kind of a bitch." I fiddle with a loose thread on my comforter.

"No, don't say that."

I meet his gaze then, drawn by his firm tone, like he actually doesn't believe I was being a rude bitch. "I have this… compulsion." I hesitate, unsure of how to explain myself. But he needs an explanation, and after what we just did, he deserves one. "When it comes to being around guys, or people in general, I find it hard to be myself."

He stays silent but doesn't remove his gaze from mine.

"Like a game. It started when I first moved here. I wanted to reinvent myself. New place, new me, and all that shit." I laugh, angry at how silly this sounds. At how juvenile I can be sometimes. It's moments like these when I agree with my family—I am a disappointment.

He still doesn't say anything, but he squeezes my hand. The gesture is all I need to continue; maybe I don't sound as ridiculous as I feel if he wants to hear more. If he wants to know me better, unlike other guys who would've walked away by now.

"I formed a pattern, a routine that morphed into this game where I play the 'cool girl.'"

I turn my attention to the window with a sad smile, remembering my ex's cursing. How he wished I was more relaxed and chill, that I wouldn't nag and go psycho on him every time he went out to the strip clubs. How he constantly made me feel guilty, even though he was in the wrong. "I like 'cool girl' because she's in control. I like being in control. The last time I lost it, I lost part of myself that I never really got back."

He kisses the side of my head, his lips lingering there, and it's so sweet, it's almost heartbreaking. I exhale, content. Content to be here with him because he doesn't make me feel ridiculous or immature or like a failure.

I open my mouth to say more, to even tell him about my ex, where the whole thing started.

But before I can say anything, the front door to the apartment opens, interrupting our conversation. "That's Emma." I cringe. Of course, it's Emma.

He nods, his gaze darting between me and the comforter and the door. "Is that my cue to go?"

I inhale deeply to steady my voice, my whole body still trembling with remnants of his touch and the way he listened to me. From the turmoil in my head and heart.

Should I let him stay or ask him to leave?

That is the question.

I want him to stay, but I *need* him to leave.

Sebastian Davis makes me feel things no other guy has ever been able to do. Even with just a fucking smirk, my knees buckle. With a touch, it all goes to Hell.

When he says I'm beautiful, the most dangerous move of all on a girl like me, I almost believe him.

When he scoots to the edge of the bed, ready to leave, I grab his arm and blurt out, "Stay with me."

His face lights up, and his eyes narrow before he starts crawling back on top of me. "Ding ding ding, that is the correct answer. We have a winner. Would you like your prize now or in five minutes?"

I match his grin and put my finger up to my chin in thought, playing along with his game. "That depends. What is it?"

He runs his hands down his bare, sculpted chest. "This." He flashes his gaze toward me as his hands continue down, wrapping around his hardening length. "Possibly this…"

I lick my lips and watch as he strokes himself. "*Definitely* this. And definitely fucking *now*."

The words barely leave my mouth before he's kissing me, bringing his tip to my entrance. He hums against my lips. "You're so wet, baby."

I nod, arching my back, ready for him to take me again.

He's inside me with one fluid motion, peppering kisses along my neck, nipping at my earlobe. He takes it slow again, kissing and touching me everywhere until I can't take it anymore.

After we both find our release, when Sebastian whispers against my lips, "Fuck, you're perfect," my heart stops with so many emotions.

He's the breath of fresh air I've been waiting for, and now that he's here, it's better than I imagined.

I have indeed won a prize.

CHAPTER 24

Kendall

It's dark, but I can see him scanning my room and the pictures lining the walls. He stops at the picture on my nightstand, the one of Lauren and me. My chest squeezes at the smiles on our faces, at what we used to have.

We're ten in the picture, looking more like twins than ever. We were even wearing the same outfit, but mine was the gray version while hers was pink. Her arm is slung over my shoulder, pulling her little sister close.

On any other nightstand, this might be an adorable picture. On mine, it's a reminder of what I used to have with my sister, my family. Only when we got older was everything ruined. It became about image and wanting more—*being* more—with her and my parents. Showing off. And since I didn't have anything to show off, it made me the bad guy.

I held my breath for him to say something, wondering how I'd explain it to him. He doesn't have siblings, so I'd only end up sounding like a bitch, as Lauren has eloquently put it so many times. And I already started the night off on rocky terms with my stupid game. Didn't work in Vegas, and I should've known it wouldn't work with him here.

"Did you and Emma go to the same college?" Sebastian's question throws me off. He points to the picture on the board next to the window.

"No, but we visited each other a lot. Been best friends since we were kids. High school was a strain, but she was always there, you know?" I admire the picture, Emma and me with pom-poms at a football game. "We lived in the same town, so she was *physically* always there, but no matter what group of friends I was hanging out with that week, I could always count on Emma."

He wraps his arm around my waist and pulls me closer to him so he's spooning me. I feel him nodding against the back of my head.

"When we went our separate ways to college, I didn't think we'd stay in touch. People lose touch, you know they change. But actually, for us, we grew closer. She was my only good friend."

"She always so quiet?"

"What do you mean?"

"She didn't say much at the club. I thought maybe she was shy."

I smile. "You just have to loosen her up, but she's not as charming as me." I poke his arm playfully.

He grips me tighter. "Charming? That's what you call

that terrifying snarl when I pay for your drinks?"

"Got you in bed, didn't it?"

He pauses. "Damn, you did. No proper comeback here."

I burst out laughing and turn to him with his arms still around me, his hand resting on my lower back. Face-to-face, I trace his tattoo as best I can since the only light comes from the moonlight outside. I exhale, relieved that the college conversation didn't go far.

"Tell me more about college. Any crazy stalkers?"

Or not.

"No. No stalkers of any kind." I smile as convincingly as I can, a large lump in my throat.

"Please don't tell me *you* stalked anyone? You did, didn't you?" He tips my chin up, and his wide grin and twinkling eyes at our banter give me pause. They give my heart pause. Even in the dark, I can tell how handsome he is.

And he's in my bed.

Wanting to know me.

To trust me, and for me to trust him in return.

"Well…" I start, holding in my giggle at the way his jaw drops open. "Channing Tatum is from Alabama, so I always had to make sure when he came to visit his roots, I was there."

"Channing Tatum, huh?"

"Oh definitely. I never did catch him—my stalking skills are rusty—but I never lost hope that we'd find each other someday in aisle three of the Piggly Wiggly."

He turns on his back and laughs at the ceiling, his hand on my hip.

"It was going to be very romantic." I shrug, taking in his playful form. How gentle and fun he can be like this, but how quickly he can turn animalistic when he's inside me, his dirty mouth whispering to me as we move together.

"Guess you have a thing for strippers, then? Is that a good thing for me?"

I search his eyes, forgetting for a second that Sebastian strips for a living. Because when I'm with him, I don't see the oiled-up dancer pulling his clothes off on stage. I see Sebastian, the warm, sexy hero of my romance novel.

"*Magic Mike* is one of my favorite movies. It's especially fun watching it with Emma, the prude." I roll my eyes, my finger still tracing the rose on his chest, the moonlight illuminating it more at this angle.

"She's a prude and still friends with you? How does that work?"

"It's called balance. Like having a salad at lunch and pasta at dinner—*balance*."

He raises his eyebrows, and his teeth show as he smiles. After a pause, he turns to me, gripping my hip more firmly, his calloused hand on my smooth thigh. Tingles run up and down my leg, but he's not being playful. His expression is more serious. "What aren't you telling me?"

"What do you mean?"

"About college. What's wrong? You cringe when I bring it up."

I fidget with a loose thread on my comforter again and shake my head. "Nope. Just nothing to say."

He squints at me, trying to see me even in the dark. To see my truth, when I'm so unwilling to share it. And I study him in return, surprised he's been so intuitive since we met.

He holds me tighter, encouraging and understanding. I touch his bicep so maybe some of his strength will transfer to me. With a deep breath, I start. "I dropped out of college after two years. Barely finished my fourth semester." I gulp. "When it was time to start the fifth, I just... didn't go."

He stays quiet, but his eyes are open so I know I didn't bore him to sleep. No, he looks interested in my words and my confession.

"It was a hard time for me leading up to that point— unhealthy relationship, problems with friends. But mostly I just didn't feel like I belonged. Not because it was hard or I was incapable, but because I really didn't feel like I was meant to be there." I swallow, my throat dry with every shaky breath I take. The only other person I've talked about this with is Emma, and that was so long ago. The words feel new now, like my truth about college is someone else's and not mine. "Does that sound stupid?" I ask to lighten the mood, but also because I don't want him to think I'm a dumb bimbo. That I'm an ignorant hick from Alabama or something.

"No," he says hoarsely.

"My parents were pissed when they found me still asleep in my room, my shit still unpacked. Of course, they compared me to Lauren like they have with everything else." I lean on my elbow to elevate myself and face him while I imitate my mom. One hand on my hip, I point with the other. "*You're never going to have a future like your sister's if you don't get your ass a college degree. Stop being so lazy and fight for something for once.*" I put my own expression back on and scoff. "Like I want Lauren's life. And I did fight for something." I keep my gaze on his. "To get the hell out of their house and out of that shithole town."

He kisses me then, his lips soft against mine. It's not hungry, just sweet. So sweet and soft that tears sting the corners of my eyes. I know he gets it—gets me—through his kiss. It says it all. And I want to cry harder knowing that I've finally found a guy who understands me.

"That's my favorite fucking thing about you."

"What? That I'm a disappointment to my parents?" I ask sarcastically, then gulp in anticipation for his answer.

"That you aren't afraid to live. You might dim your light to a world that doesn't understand, but they're the problem. Not you, not your light. So let it shine, baby."

Stunned, I don't answer. I just watch him as he gently kisses the back of my hand.

"So yes, you dropping out of college when you didn't want to be there? That's my favorite thing about you."

"Okay," I say, breathless at his words, his intense expression, *him*. His words make my eyes water again. I needed to hear those words. I didn't realize how much I needed them until he said them.

"Want to know my other favorite things?" He pulls on my lip with his thumb and forefinger. "This." He trails a finger down my bare chest, holding my breasts. "These." Then he continues beneath the covers to my lower stomach before he cups me between the legs. "And this," he growls and then kisses me, swallowing my moans.

My moans for this beautiful man. This man I've only known a short time, yet he's seen more of me than anyone else I know.

A scary thought, but also freeing.

Peaceful.

Maybe this is what it could always be like, being open. Maybe this is the reward for being honest and getting things off my chest—a sexy man with a magic tongue who's also a warm snuggler.

Feeling lighter than ever before, I exhale in relief and know that I'll sleep with dreams of nothing but warmth and freedom.

CHAPTER 25

Sebastian

She tickles me, tracing her fingers over the tattoo on my chest. It's the only one I have, unlike Ty and some of the other guys who had a brief obsession a few years back. Ty still claims he doesn't regret trying to look like Dwayne Johnson, although he makes sure to point out that he has hair, unlike the bald master of Iron Paradise, his own traveling gym.

I grab Kendall's fingers and kiss the tips of them one by one, savoring them like they're popsicles on a hot day.

She snuggles closer with her head resting in the crook of my shoulder, sighing contently, and my heart is ready to burst. That I have this girl in my arms, that she trusts me enough to be open with me. To let me see her.

"What's your tattoo mean?" she asks lazily, her eyes fluttering open to watch me.

I swallow, because of her and because of her question. "For Eric." I run a hand down my face, gathering my thoughts. It's been ten years, and it's still difficult to talk about him sometimes. "He was my best friend growing up, spent every weekend playing video games at my house. My uncle used to call us Mario and Luigi." I laugh, the sound foreign to me when connected to anything I say about my uncle anymore. "Eric died when we were in high school. Hit by a drunk driver on his way home from my house one night."

"My God, Sebastian." Kendall sits up, her hand still in mine on my chest. She squeezes my hand while she squeezes her eyes closed. "I'm so sorry. I had no idea, or I wouldn't have brought it up."

I pull her to lie back down with me, keeping our hands intertwined over my tattoo, my reminder of the world's ultimate cruelty while I hold my saving grace, the world's most beautiful thing—Kendall's light. "I want you to know me like I want to know you." I give her a tight-lipped smile, somber yet secretive, closing my lips to keep from telling her all about last year, about Joelle and everything with my uncle. I want her to know me, but I can't go there, not yet. Not until the anger subsides.

It lingers still.

Like a shadow that blends into the darkness, it remains there, unseen but still present.

"What about your mom?"

"Hmm?" Lost in my own head, I don't hear her question.

"You said your uncle used to call you Mario and Luigi. What about your mom? Your dad? Or did you live with your uncle?" She bites her lip. "I'm sorry. I don't mean to pry—"

I silence her with a kiss. "I did just say I want you to know me." I avert my gaze, not sure where to begin or how much to say. "My mom worked a lot. She's a flight attendant, so she's gone for many days, sometimes weeks, at a time and usually at a moment's notice. Her brother—my uncle—lived next door, so I stayed with him while she was gone." I give her a sad smile. "I never knew my dad. My uncle was the closest thing to it. Growing up, I thought of him as a father figure. I always made excuses for his dickish behavior but turns out he's just a dick." Grinding my jaw, my heart races at the thought, not wanting to get into it further. "But the movie marathons kept me entertained."

"Right. Good ole Sylvester Stallone."

"Exactly." I turn her onto her back and touch the tattoo on her side, a black outline of a cactus. I've traced her entire body with my hands and tongue, and aside from me, this is the only mark she has on her. It's not even two inches long. And unlike the first time we were together, I'm going to find out what it means. "Why the cactus?"

She sinks further into the pillow. "I'd rather not say... not after you just told me about your friend. I'll just sound stupid."

I place a tender yet firm kiss to her lips to encourage her to open up, to let her know she could never sound stupid. Why she thinks anything she says is stupid is beyond me to begin with. Breathless, I pull back. "Tell me."

Her eyes search mine and relent. "It's my happy place," she starts. "The cactus reminds me of the desert—calm and peaceful." She licks her lips and meets my gaze. "Empty."

My heart sinks as a darkness falls over her blue eyes, casting a shadow over her light. She turns her face toward the window, a small sliver of sunlight shining through the curtains. Next to them, pictures of her and Emma are tacked onto a board. Some are framed. Only one of her and her sister sits on her nightstand. I want to smile, but the picture looks to be ten years old at least.

And my heart hurts even more.

Her sister is difficult, but not the kind of person you want to shun. Their disdain for each other seems more like a defense mechanism because underneath it all, it seems to me they're just hurting. So they take it out on each other.

She turns her attention back to me. "A cactus is able to sustain its own life with limited resources in the desert. No help. That's just how it exists." She shrugs, her emptiness written all over her expression, the darkness still shading her eyes.

It about fucking kills me.

She thought she'd sound stupid if she said it, but it just makes me want to pull the curtains open and show her there's light in the darkness. I know the darkness all too well, and while I'm dealing with it in my own way, she hides.

She shouldn't hide.

I can't let her hide.

My tattoo may stem from a tragedy, but I won't let the same be said for hers.

I cringe when I open my eyes to direct sunlight coming in through the small window. I rub my eye with one hand while the other is trapped underneath Kendall.

As soon as I adjust to the light, I take in her sleeping figure. She sleeps with her lips slightly parted and a hand underneath her chin. I put a small strand of hair behind her ear to see her face more fully, just as I did in the middle of the night.

When she opened up to me so willingly and honestly, I stayed quiet during her confessions so I didn't spook her. I was afraid she'd stop if I interrupted her, like a squirrel you want to pet but will either run away or bite you if you get too close, so I let her talk.

The sound of her honest words was like holy music to a believer.

I inhale her vague vanilla scent before getting up. She stirs and turns over but doesn't wake up. Her sun-kissed skin calls to me, begging me to run my hands down her back. But I let her sleep. We barely slept all night, after all.

In the bathroom, I smile at the claw marks on my shoulders, thanks to Kendall's fingernails and passion.

She was incredible, letting go like she did. Letting loose for me.

Checking my messages, I see Ty sent me a few.

Ty: *Dude, where'd you disappear to?*

Ty: *Gym in the morning?*

Those were from last night, but one is from twenty

minutes ago.

> Ty: *Bro, I'm going to the gym to do deadlifts until I can't breathe. Until I can kick Phil Heath's ass. You in?*

I text him back that I won't be going to the gym until later.

> Ty: *Just tell me when.*

Moving slowly around the bathroom and her room, I sneak out before rummaging through her kitchen cabinets and refrigerator as quietly as possible. As soon as I get the scrambled eggs cooking and the turkey bacon sizzling, a door opens behind me. I turn around with a smile, only for it to be immediately replaced with a frown.

Emma.

Her hair is piled on top of her head, and she's wearing a short polka-dot pajama set. Rubbing her eyes, she remains in the middle of the living room.

I clear my throat. "Good morning."

Emma jumps back and hits her heel on the coffee table, rattling the small vase of flowers sitting on top of it. "Ouch, son of a bitch!"

I put my hands out in surrender. "I'm sorry. Didn't mean to startle you."

"Well, you did *startle* me," she spits. "Where the hell is your shirt? Why are you naked in my kitchen?"

While she shields her eyes like she's nine and an X-rated

film is on in front of her, I take note of my appearance. I am in fact shirtless, and my jeans are basically falling off me without my belt. "Guess I'm so used to walking around half naked that I didn't even notice."

I shrug, but she tilts her head to the side in confusion, then glares at something behind me. "What's burning? Is that my turkey bacon?"

"Oh, right!" I turn around and vaguely hear her groan about my ass crack. Pulling my pants up, I tend to the bacon. When I turn around, she's gone. Shrugging, I get back to work.

"You know," Emma starts as she returns, startling me this time. Jumping back like the bacon grease stung me, I face her and raise my eyebrows. She comes close and points at me. "She likes you, but I'm not convinced of your character."

"What—"

"You're cocky. I could tell from the moment I met you."

I smile. "You're not the first to mistake my charm for arrogance. I just need to win you over, and I do not shy away from a good challenge. Which I sense this is by the way you're squinting at me."

Hands on hips, her expression serious, she continues. "She's tough, but you know it's only an act, right." It's more of a statement, so I don't answer. "I don't know if she told you about Adam from college, but you better not turn out that way. I'll cut your genitalia off."

That gets me. Not the threat, but her words about this Adam. Kendall mentioned losing control with someone before but nothing more.

No longer smiling or joking, I back away from Emma. "No need. I don't know what Adam did or who he is, but I care about Kendall. A lot. I don't want to hurt her."

Emma's expression softens. Her eyes are large when she doesn't narrow them in my direction. "Let's just say he was an insecure asshole. Lied with every breath so he could make her feel less than." She looks down, and when she looks back up, her eyes have a faraway look as though she's watching a sad drama. "She's got a big heart, even if she doesn't always show it." She shakes away her memory like she's shrugging off a jacket. "Maybe I said too much. It's her story to tell. But I wanted to warn you."

"Threaten me," I correct her.

With a tight-lipped smile, she pats my shoulder and reaches for a piece of bacon behind me. Crunching on it, she goes back into her room.

I find a tray and grab the small vase off the coffee table to spruce up my display. Careful not to spill the coffee, I make my way into Kendall's room, but she's not in bed.

I set the tray on her desk by the window and jump when the door to the bathroom bursts open.

"Who did you expect, Freddie Kreuger?" She smiles at me, her face free of makeup and her wet hair over one shoulder. "He only gets you when you're asleep, you know. Not when you're already awake with—*bacon!*" She licks her lips at the sight of the tray, and I want to lick her lips too.

"Damn it, this was supposed to be romantic as fuck." I gesture to the tray as she takes a bite of the turkey bacon. "When did you get in the shower?"

"Right after you left. I thought you heard me. Should I

be concerned about your listening skills?" *Crunch, crunch, crunch.* "Because this apartment is pretty small with thin walls. I'm sure Emma never slept last night with all of our moaning and groaning." She eyes the rest of the tray. "What else do we have here?" She looks everything over, slightly bending toward it.

And my eyes are on her towel. My mind on her bending all the way over and me taking her from behind. My dick hardens at the mere thought. "Eggs, but how about more of that moaning and groaning first?"

"They'll get cold, and I don't like—"

I remove her towel and cup her breasts from behind as I whisper, "I'll cook you five dozen new eggs if you bend over for me."

She giggles, resting the back of her head on my bare chest. I kiss her shoulder and hold her close, her calming presence tugging on my heartstrings.

Her past haunts me like it's my own, angering me that anyone would treat this woman like she didn't deserve a red carpet everywhere she went.

But her past doesn't matter in this moment, because I want to make her present worthwhile. To show her she deserves the world.

The feeling grows more and more urgent as she bends over, slowly and sensually, while I remove what little clothing I had on.

I run my hand down her smooth back while I let my hard length idly press against her. She arches her back against my touch, which makes me groan.

I groan even harder when I enter her, pushing inside her

as far as I can go. She's soaked for me, the feeling too much. I bend over so my chest rests on her back. "Hold on, baby."

She nods urgently, her knuckles turning white as she holds onto the edge of the desk, and I smile against her neck as I pull out and plunge into her with everything I have, the silverware rattling against the plate to our side.

I grip her hips as I pick up my pace, wanting to become one with this woman I've only known a few weeks but has completely entranced me.

CHAPTER 26

Kendall

I officially can't walk.

Sebastian's stamina is that of an Olympic runner. What does he mix in his protein shakes, Viagra?

And God, the way he owned me this morning from behind. Gripping my ass like I was his surefire way to Heaven.

The way he fucked me was unapologetic. Yet he cherished me. Ran his hands down my body like he couldn't believe he was touching me.

I could get used to that kind of worship—and energy. To the way he makes me feel important, like he's not just attracted to my body but to *me* too. Something I've never experienced, especially with Adam.

When he asks Emma and me to go to the gym after our third—fourth?—round, I was surprised he still had the energy. That coach of his must be feeding those boys something special. The way Ty was eyeing the slutty chick in a sleek black dress last night, *and* her friend, must mean he had a long night too, but he's particularly enthused this morning as well. No sign of a hangover, morning wood, or exhaustion from these boys.

Men, I should say.

There's nothing boyish about the six-foot-plus men alternating turns with deadlifts. Emma and I stand close by, taking turns on the squat rack.

The guys like to train at Gold's Gym Venice when they're in LA, and I've only been here a couple times, so Emma and I jumped at the chance to come back. Even at twenty dollars for a day pass, it's worth it to train at the Mecca, the gym where so many celebrities work out, from actors to bodybuilders to the everyday folks like us.

And it was comical, to say the least, watching Ty try to sweet-talk the receptionist into free passes, his compliments about her pink streaks in her hair not working in the slightest.

Naturally, the first thing I did once I stepped foot inside was look for Samantha Ray. She likes to train here and posts a lot of her videos here, but there's no sign of her. Not for lack of looking… and Insta-stalking. It's too late in the day for her—she normally comes early in the morning—but a girl can dream.

Emma always teases me about what a big fan I am, but she agrees that the woman is an inspiration with her positivity and advocacy for women to do more strength training.

That's what attracted me to her and the whole fitness industry, why I wanted to become an influencer myself—to inspire people. Weight training has empowered me in a way I've never experienced before. It's made me feel strong, physically and mentally.

I shake my head, thinking about all the reasons I wouldn't be successful as an influencer, that it's all just a fantasy, and set up the barbell for my set. I breathe in and out, letting the world around me fade away. It's just me and the weight. I plant my feet shoulder-width apart and dig my heels into the ground as I lower my body. On the exhale, I raise up slowly and controlled, the way Emma instructed me when I was first learning.

I've gotten even better, my improved flexibility allowing me to sit at a right angle more easily.

My seventh rep is shaky, and sweat runs down the back of my neck. The garage door is open to the outside workout area, inviting the LA heat in to suffocate us. I take a deep breath and go for my eighth rep, while Emma spots and coaches me to do one more. Then she eggs me on to do one more.

And one more.

Until I get to thirteen and can barely walk the bar back to its place.

"Nice form, Gray." Sebastian high-fives me while his gaze trails down my chest following the line of sweat hiding there.

It's too hot, so I'm only in my sports bra like many of the women in here. But with Sebastian looking at me like that, I suddenly feel exposed and inappropriate. Shivers run down my spine before I swat him. "You're going to get me pregnant with that look."

Sebastian kisses my cheek, staying close to me as Emma gets into position. I stiffen, my body too sweaty to be this close to another human right now. But Sebastian doesn't seem to mind. He keeps his arm around my waist, even when I try to pull away.

He kisses me on the cheek again like he can't help it, and it makes me smile. The gesture is sweet and natural, like we're already at the stage in a relationship to be completely comfortable with each other.

"Did you not have enough last night? Jeez, I could barely sleep," Emma says to us, getting ready for her set. She's in her sports bra as well, her black hair perfectly in place. She doesn't even seem to be sweating. Rather, she's glowing, her bright green eyes twinkling against her porcelain skin.

"What's wrong, Emma? Sad you didn't get any last night?" Ty winks at her in the mirror, but Emma rolls her eyes and pushes up to release the barbell from its hold.

Walking backward, she breathes in as she settles down into her squat and exhales as she raises up. She squats 115 pounds for ten reps like it's five pounds, and even glares at Ty in the mirror the whole time. The woman is a badass.

When she's done, she walks past him, bumps into him purposefully, and turns her nose up at him.

I raise my eyebrow at the way Ty eyes her and then share a look with Sebastian, who just shrugs.

We stop for lunch afterward, a place the guys swear has the best tacos. It's not Tuesday, but I can never turn down a good taco, let alone the best one I'll ever eat.

We're halfway through lunch when Emma says, "So how do you guys know each other? What do you do?"

Sebastian wipes chipotle sauce from his mouth, distracting me from Emma's question with visions of me licking it off him. Ty answers, "We're dancers in Vegas. Been together for several years now."

"What, like hip-hop? Backup dancers?"

He smiles, but my whole body stiffens. The urge to throw up rises inside me, but instead, I blurt, "Yes, hip-hop. They're really good too."

Sebastian chuckles at me but draws his eyebrows together in confusion. "Well, we dance to hip-hop songs during our show, but we're part of Naked Heat." When Emma stares blankly, he lays it out more plainly. "We're strippers."

Emma chokes, and I have a flashback of the time I told her I wanted to go swimming with sharks together. Diet Coke squirted out of her nose in protest. "Strippers?" She looks at me with an expression of amusement and disbelief, like I told her they're wizards from Hogwarts.

Like she's saying, "*That's cute, but seriously, what do you do?*"

Emma recovers quickly, with the help of Ty patting her on the back. "Well… no wonder you're the best Kendall's ever had." She smirks at me, and I know it's her way of getting back at me for not telling her they're strippers. She knew her comment would embarrass me in front of Sebastian.

And it definitely worked.

As if Sebastian didn't already hold all the power, he now has another excuse to do so.

He turns to me, after hesitating with Emma's news, as if he doesn't know how to take it. "You said that? Best sex you've ever had, huh?"

I roll my eyes, playing it off. "Don't make me regret it." I nod at them then, refusing to meet anyone's gaze. "Everyone ready to go? I have to be at work in a few hours, and I could definitely use a shower. That's why you wanted to sit on the other side of the table from me, isn't it?" I tease Sebastian. "Because I smell, don't I?"

He doesn't miss a beat, but the robotic tone doesn't escape me. "You guessed it. That's exactly what I'm thinking."

CHAPTER 27

Sebastian

She tells Emma everything, but she didn't tell her the most basic thing about me—my occupation. Why I'm even in LA. Where Kendall met me in the first place.

Why would she hide that?

She's embarrassed.

I went along with Kendall's jokes at lunch, thought it'd be more polite than confronting her in front of her friend. But the truth is, it stings.

Fucking hurts, actually.

The realization sinks into me like fifty shark teeth.

And a severe case of déjà vu overcomes me, though not because of the last time Kendall and I were in Vegas.

Because of *her.*

Joelle.

"What are you going to do the rest of your life, Sebastian?

175

*Get naked for other women when you have a wife at home?"
Joelle spat. "What if we have kids? Not a chance in hell I tell
them their father's a fucking stripper."*

*"What's wrong with that? I make a good living, at least.
It's better than being a nagger. Should I tell them about you too
someday?" I returned.*

*She scoffed. "Great. That's great, Sebastian. I'm trying to
have a mature conversation. This is what stripping does—kills
your brain cells to where you can't even comprehend how to be
an adult."*

*"You're not trying to have a conversation with me. You
want me to just lie down and let you step all over me. Well,
that's not going to happen."*

*"No wonder your uncle isn't sure of doing business with you.
You can't handle even a grown-up discussion." She continued
folding clothes on the couch in our apartment that we shared.
She continued like her words didn't cut through me. Like she
wasn't voicing my fears that I'm not good enough to do anything
other than strip. "You should take some pointers from him, you
know. He's offering you a real opportunity here."*

*I nodded, knowing she was right. Running a hotel with my
uncle was one step closer to my dream—my dream of owning
one myself someday.*

*Taking her attention away from the clothes and holding
her hands in mine, I said, "I don't want to fight, okay? I have
a show in an hour. Will you just come, have a drink, and we
can talk afterward?"*

*She glanced sideways in avoidance, not just from our
conversation but of me. "I have a lot of work to do around
here, and for the wedding. I'll just see you after." She shrugged*

out of my hold, and the mature, adult conversation we were having was over. Just like that. With her avoiding what was really going on.

Real mature.

But when I kiss Kendall goodbye at her apartment, a kiss full of desire and promise, I can't believe she's the same as Joelle. Not when she smiles her genuine smile. I can't believe she'd be embarrassed by me, of what I do. She's never mentioned it before, not during any of the times we've talked, or this weekend.

I convince myself that she's nothing like my coldhearted ex.

But the nagging feeling that it might be true stays with me the rest of the day.

At practice a few hours before the show, I text her to ask one more time if there's any way she can make it. I want her there, but I need her to convince me that her absence isn't because she's ashamed, that she legitimately has to work and couldn't get someone to cover for her.

When all she says is *Sorry, have to work or I would*, I start to panic. But then she immediately sends another.

> Kendall: *But I'll make it up to you after, cross my heart.*

That message puts me at ease. For now, at least.

> Me: *Let me take you out for a late dinner, after the show.*

Immediately I get a response. She says okay, and I nod like she can see me. Instead, Ty can see me, and he doesn't miss the opportunity to make fun of me. "Dude, the bobblehead move isn't in the routine. You should pay attention."

I flip him off, then shake my head because he's right. I have to focus on our practice for tonight. It's short but important. Leo wants to go over a few things that we missed last night, and I need my head here.

Not in the way Kendall cried my name while she came for me this morning.

Not in the realization that it might be coming to an end just when I thought our relationship could turn into something real.

Leo snaps his fingers in my direction. "Ready? Let's take it from the top."

I go through the motions with the other guys, determined not to let them down. I take practice seriously, just like the shows. If I don't, then it's pointless being here. These guys, my brothers, were really there for me when Joelle left me.

They took me back in with open arms afterward, even though I was a mess and couldn't keep up as well. They were patient with me and helped me through it all. I owe them so much—the least I could do now is to stay on beat.

After practice, Leo slaps me on the shoulder and follows me to my car. "Everything cool, man?"

I nod, but I know it's in vain. Leo's known me for years, knows my past. I can't lie to him.

"Tell me the truth, Sebastian. What's going on in here?" He pokes my temple but doesn't laugh. His features are torn, his lips twisted. It looks like he wants to say something but doesn't, like he's trying to gauge my mood first.

"I could say the same to you, man. What's up?"

Leo picks at his hand, and I want to shake him to spit it out. Because I know *him* just as well as he knows me.

But when he finally speaks, I wish he wouldn't have. "They're getting married. Joelle and—"

"Jesus." I know whom he's referring to, but don't know who's worse—her or him, so I just wish a silent curse on both of them.

Leo hesitates. "My stepdad heard it from one of their mutual friends. I wasn't going to tell you, but I felt guilty knowing and not saying anything. Please tell me I did the right thing now?"

If I were a religious man, I'd pray for strength and patience in this moment to keep from punching Leo, but I remind myself that he's just the messenger. He didn't do anything wrong.

They did.

And I've tried every day since that wretched night to get away from it all.

I shake my head and grip him by the shoulder as we stop in front of my car, the LA heat beating down on us, driving the rage within me. Nothing like Vegas, though. If I can handle Vegas, spring in LA is nothing.

Joelle is nothing. As Satan's mistress, she emits more evil heat than both cities combined.

"Nah, man, you did good." I flash him a smile. "I'm past all that, anyway."

He nods. "Right. You have Kendall now. She's cute. I see

the way you smile at your phone when it's her. Everything good, I guess?"

This morning I would've told him everything was fucking perfect with Kendall. As perfect as the beginning of anything new gets. But now I hate to say that it might end here, before our story can really begin. "Yeah, everything's good," I say instead.

"Does she know? About Joelle?"

I laugh him off; he's always taking on the fatherly role with us, even though he's only four years older than me. "We're still new. Don't want to scare her off with all my drama." For good measure, I add, "Besides, I'm over all that bullshit. Haven't heard from either of them in a year and haven't wanted to. I've moved on, brother, thanks to you and the guys."

The way he studies me, unwavering, tells me he doesn't believe me, but he still says, "Glad you came back. Otherwise, I would've been stuck hiring another newbie, and I just can't handle the young people jargon anymore. What the fuck is *lit*? Why is that a thing?"

"Careful, your old colors are showing, and gray really doesn't look good on you."

He laughs and runs a hand through his black hair, his broad shoulders uncontained by his black tank. For a large guy, he's managed to find a tank that swallows him.

On my way to the hotel suite to relax by the pool with the guys before the show, I again consider being a religious man, but this time to thank Him for the guys. Even when they give me news that makes me want to vomit. Or punch a hole in the wall. Again.

I have other things on my mind, anyway.

About who will help me get over it.

Kendall and I may not have a tomorrow, but I meant what I said about tonight, taking her out and showing her a little more of me.

In hopes that she stays at least a little while longer.

CHAPTER 28

Kendall

"I can't live this life," I whine, my eyes moving back and forth between the cottage cheese and Greek yogurt. I make myself dizzy doing so, and also from trying to figure out which is worse. I toss my hands up and turn to Emma. "I want ice cream."

"It's only been a couple hours since our workout with the guys, and you're already looking for the dessert?" Emma sits on the couch with her wet hair falling freely over her right shoulder. She types away at her laptop, and I wonder what she's writing.

But I focus on the task at hand: ice cream. A cookies 'n cream masterpiece with hot fudge. I groan and go back to my options.

"You don't have to live like this, you know," Emma says after she stops typing and looks at me. "It's not a human requirement."

Even though she's right, I refuse to admit to her why I do it. That I want to be in good shape. That I like being lean. I need to stay this way if I ever decide to take the jump and attempt the fitness influencer route.

I've talked to Emma about it before, and she was encouraging. She thought I'd be great at it, actually, but we haven't talked about it since. Instead of getting into it now, I change the subject. "But if I quit, then we won't be gym hoes together. You'll just be a gym ho, and that's sad." I pout in her direction from where I stand in the kitchen. With the apartment so small, I can almost reach out and touch her in the living room area.

"We are not calling ourselves that."

"Gymster duo?" She visibly cringes and moves the laptop from her lap. "Double gymbos?"

She rubs her face, but over the next twenty minutes and a couple glasses of wine—because it's Saturday and we're young—we throw more names out, only to be vetoed. We even say Dynamos from *Mamma Mia!*—Emma's favorite—but we'd need a third person.

"Margo?" Emma suggests.

"Yeah right. I'd like to be there when you ask her to join our gym team. She'd wipe that optimism right off your face with just a glare."

We continue arguing like we're middle schoolers coming up with a name for our fake tribe.

I throw my hands up in defeat. "I don't see you coming up with anything good."

"Well, you were close with Gym Heroes, but not quite

right."

"And what is?"

She turns to me and actually smiles, something she doesn't often do, so this must be good. "How about this. I teach classes for my job, so what about Gym Class Heroes?"

"Ah, so logical. As always." I stare blankly at her as the wheels in my head turn. "Isn't that a band, though?"

"No. There's no way. Don't take this away from me."

Emma only listens to musical soundtracks and yoga tunes—mountain flutes and all—so she wouldn't know if that's a band or a cult. I run my hand through her hair in pity. "Okay, I'll let you have it."

She makes an obscene gesture with her hand, indicating a dick spewing. "Boom."

"Are you drunk?"

She rounds her back and sinks into the couch, pulling back into her shell. The couch swallows her small frame, and she looks vulnerable. "I only drank one glass of wine. I had to. Your names were embarrassing."

"That's all it takes to loosen you up?" I grab a pencil and paper from the end table, the ones Emma put there to make grocery lists.

"Are you actually writing that down?" She leans over and paws at my notepad like it's another glass of wine. "Give me that. That's for groceries only."

"And more wine is a grocery." I shrug. "I need this for future reference. You know my memory sucks." I stick my tongue out at her as I walk back into the kitchen.

Emma sinks even deeper into the couch as she mumbles, "Skank."

"Gym ho."

She giggles and reaches for the wine bottle. With nowhere for her to go today, I let her have at it. Normally, I have to force it down her throat, so this is a welcomed change.

But when I return from the shower, a towel on my head and a robe wrapped around me, I start to worry. "What's the deal here?" I ask, pointing to her head tilted back as she takes superhuman gulps of wine right out of the bottle.

Doesn't seem like fun and games anymore.

She shrugs with a mouth full of wine. I'd join her in a second glass—hell, a fifth even—if that shit didn't taste like just… well, *shit*. Her diet doesn't allow for moscato or white zin because unfortunately, it's full of sugar and not so much alcohol. So cabernet it is. There's no taste, but at least there's not so much guilt.

"Since when do you drink right out of the wine bottle? In the middle of the day?" I place my hand on her forehead. "Are you feeling okay?"

She averts her gaze out the window on the far wall by her bedroom door.

"Hey, what's going on? I thought we were having fun here."

A small smile tugs at her lips. "I am having fun."

"Then why do you look like someone died? Oh my God, did someone die?"

"Did you see me take a call or something? You've been with me all day."

I shrug. "Anything could've happened while I was in the shower."

"You do take long showers. A whole apocalypse could've gone down while you were in there." She pours wine into a glass as I take a seat next to her. Then she looks into her glass without smiling. Instead, she swirls the red liquid around like it's tea and she's reading tea leaves.

I nod, unsure whether to pry. I want to. Haven't seen her this sad since we were thirteen and her parents divorced. No matter how much they reassured her that they still loved her, that she'd always be the center of their universe, she knew better even at thirteen. But it didn't sting any less when her mother drowned herself in alcohol, especially after her dad remarried and had more kids, everyone forgetting Emma's existence in the shuffle.

Unless it's her birthday or Christmas. Then her father makes sure to wire money, and her mother sends a wrinkled card, wine stains smudging the words, three days late.

"You can talk to me, you know." I take her hand in mine just as my phone vibrates.

It's Lauren complaining about wedding things and checking in to make sure I have my bridesmaid dress ready. Which I haven't picked up yet, but I don't tell her that. With the wedding only a week away, I can't have her flipping out.

Because I'll get it before then. She doesn't understand that it's okay not to do something seven weeks ahead of time.

I roll my eyes at her incessant use of emojis. Some are unnecessary. Like what the hell did she send a shark for? Is she admitting she's vicious? Should've just used the snake.

We may only be a year and a half apart in age, but we're a lifetime of experience different. She's an old soul, but not exactly wise. I'm carefree, but not exactly level-headed at all times. I'm not too good to admit it, but I don't need it shoved in my face every minute. *Mom, Dad—*

"Are you listening?" Emma snaps her fingers at me.

"Yes."

"But what do you think about the other thing? It's weird, right? That he'd go home with *two* other girls? And the way he stared at me earlier—*God.*"

I nod, unsure of what she's talking about. And if I didn't have my judgmental family on the brain, I'd be intrigued that Emma is clearly talking about a guy and may be jealous.

No way. I read her wrong. That can't be what she's talking about. She hasn't been jealous or anything over a guy since Brant cheated on her, and that was almost two years ago.

Wait.

Two girls… and he was staring at her earlier…

"Wait, Ty? Why do you care what he's up to?"

She shakes her head and laughs, but it's not a cheery one. "I don't. That was so stupid. Forget I said anything." She waves her hands in front of her face, and she looks like she did in middle school, wide-eyed and vulnerable. Not like a grown woman living in LA with her own business.

She squares her shoulders in true Emma style and announces she's going for a walk, as though our lower body workout earlier was a joke.

When she asks me if I want to join her, I scoff. "Yeah right."

She rolls her eyes.

"But you're okay?"

She nods with her hand on the door, and I start getting ready for work.

And then… *Sebastian.*

My heart flutters at the thought of him coming over, emphasis on *coming*, but my stomach drops at the thought of his face when he left earlier. Hesitant and a little distant. And I hope it wasn't because of what Emma said, that he was the best I'd ever had.

It's true, but I didn't want him to know it for fear that he wouldn't think me a challenge anymore. That I was too easy to please. That he'd be bored.

By the time I'm ready for work, my usual insecurities have set up camp in my lower stomach, making me want to throw up. Especially when I'm helping customers at work, and they take their shoes off. It's not always a pleasant experience, but I've gotten good at holding my breath, refusing to smell the air around me.

By the end of my shift, I'm ready to call Sebastian and cancel. Tell him I had fun and that I'll catch him the next time he's in town.

But when his name pops up on my phone, I smile, my resolve to cancel forgotten. I instantly feel lighter, even though he only sent a smiley face. Makes me think it's all in my head, the insecurities Adam put there long ago coming back to haunt me like they always do.

But with Sebastian, it's different. He makes me feel *good* about myself for once.

As I type back that I can't wait to see him tonight, I breathe a little easier, thinking he could be the one to take all my insecurities away.

CHAPTER 29

Sebastian

My adrenaline races, heart pumping and legs trembling. The same high I get from working out, but I'm on stage now finishing our last show in LA.

I laugh with the guys as we head backstage. "Nice air at the end, man!" Jordan high-fives me, referring to the ending backflip.

"All you, Jordan." I shrug. "You're getting a lot better. You're going to take center stage in no time."

Ty snaps his head back at me, glaring.

I throw my hands up. "Don't look at me. You better get your shit together before you lose your spot to a rookie."

That earns me a slap to the back of my head, just before he turns to Jordan with a smile. "I don't mind some competition." Then his facial expression morphs into one I imagine the Italian mafia gives its victims before slicing their faces off. "But watch yourself."

"Good luck to you," I say to Jordan and shake free of their tension. I'd make a joke to lighten the mood, to keep the dancing on stage, but as long as I've been here, this is how we do things. It's all in good fun.

We all get along with each other—Leo makes sure of it—but spending so much time together makes us think twice about crossing each other.

Naked Heat is more like a family, something I've never known before.

Naked Heat gives it all to me.

A sense of belonging and acceptance.

Something I never had with Joelle.

This is what's on my mind when I pull up to Kendall's—wanting her to accept me too.

And maybe if I show her more about myself, like I intend to tonight, she'll be more accepting.

She answers the door in high-waisted ripped jeans, her feet bare and nails painted pale pink. They give her a girlish quality, a contradiction to the fierce woman I'm used to, but her low-scooped tank does the job.

All thoughts of Joelle, her engagement, Naked Heat—it all dissolves as I enter Kendall's magnetic field, pulling me toward her.

She takes my breath away, face glowing and hair pushed to one side like she spent an hour in front of a fan. Or driving through LA in a convertible with the top down.

I smile at the thought of driving with her along the water through Malibu, my arm around her shoulders and her laughter for music instead of the radio, her smile pierced in my mind.

With a hand on her hip, she smiles. "Are you coming in or what?"

An overwhelming need for her consumes me, as it has the last couple days. I take her in my arms and kiss her against the nearest wall, push my body against hers with the front door wide open.

A throat clears a few feet from us. When I back off, I notice we've attracted a small audience. An Asian couple across the dim hall glares while covering their young daughter's eyes.

"Show's over, Mr. and Mrs. Lang." Kendall kicks the door closed and jumps onto me like a cat pounces on a mouse.

She swallows any uncertainties I had when I walked in, and when I cup her ass and squeeze, I all but lose consciousness from the urge to be closer to her. Especially when she hugs my waist with her firm legs.

She peers down between us at my obvious hard-on, even through my jeans.

"You ready?" I say, my voice strained with indecision between taking her out as promised or locking us in her room and kissing up and down her naked body.

She catches her breath. "You sure you don't want to...?" She nods toward the bedroom.

I kiss her pouty lips. "I want nothing more than to bury myself inside you all night, but I have dinner waiting for us in the car."

"Huh?"

I kiss her one more time and set her on the ground.

Taking her hand, I call over my shoulder, "You'll see."

CHAPTER 30

Kendall

Sebastian kisses me, lingering and pushing me against his car, so close together the slight evening breeze is unable to get between us.

I smile against his lips. "This is what you had planned? The big surprise?"

"A kiss in the parking lot isn't romantic?" He smiles slyly. "Because it took my breath away."

I shove him back. "Nerd."

He clutches his chest in as dramatic a fashion as posting to Instagram without a filter.

I open the door to his car and settle inside, smoothing my jeans down and wondering where he's taking me. When he showed up at my apartment, I was giddy—actually *giddy*.

Especially when he said he had a surprise for me. No guy has done anything like this.

Sebastian Davis is indeed one of a kind.

He drives across town, holding my hand the whole way. We near downtown and keep going, past the throngs of people out for dinner and fun. This is what I like about LA and the city life in general—the fact that people are out after eight o'clock and that everything's open.

In Alabama, Walmart was the only thing open all night, and if you knew any better, you wouldn't visit past nine. It was a "proceed at your own risk" kind of thing, since that was when the shady night crawlers came out to play.

The local Walmart became the Upside Down from *Stranger Things* after dark.

"You're smiling, and I didn't put it there." Sebastian pulls me out of my thoughts. "Who is it? Who's the other guy making you smile?" He squeezes my hand and looks away when he says it, not even toward the road but out his window.

Like he really thinks there could be another guy.

When he turns back to me, he forces his best angry look with squinty eyes that make him look more like he needs a bathroom.

For now, I roll with his playful manner. "Is that supposed to be your mad face? Because you're going to hurt yourself."

His expression softens, his eyes on the road. When we pause at a red light, he turns to me, leaning over the console and placing a soft kiss on my lips.

My heart.

My heart stops at the gesture, like he's trying to tell me something too precious for words even, and only a kiss will do.

A magical kiss.

Honking behind us breaks us apart. I touch my lips as I look out the window at the blur, catching glimpses of strangers, our paths crossing for the briefest of seconds.

"I knew everyone in my hometown," I whisper.

He stays silent, but his silence is the kind that encourages me to go on. That's how Sebastian works. He silently presses to get to know me, and I've never been able to stop from sharing myself with him no matter how hard I tried.

"There's a population of ten thousand, but still, I knew everyone. Not like LA. I go weeks, months without seeing the same face here. Without people knowing *me*."

He shifts in his seat slowly while he nods.

"I love going to the grocery store, to work, anywhere. They're all new people every day, and I can just blend in."

We turn onto a gravel lot, an empty field stretched in front of us. It's dark, and the city lights are faint out here. Downtown is close enough, though, reminding me that we're not out in the middle of nowhere.

I reach for the door handle, but Sebastian stops me. "You are *beautiful*. Let the world see you. It'd be a shame for you to hide in the crowd."

That's not what people from my hometown think.

I open my mouth and close it as I stare at our laced fingers. When I look up, my mouth hangs open at the way he stares at me. Like he's hungry for me, for my beauty. He looks like he admires me, and not just physically. His gaze is trained on mine like he sees past the surface.

He watches me with so much conviction; I believe his words when I've never had a reason to believe them from anyone else.

We get out of his Jeep, and while he retrieves something from the back, I step toward the field. The gravel crunches beneath my feet, but other than that, it's quiet here. LA's downtown bustle is faint, white noise behind us like static.

The stars are bright and plenty. Tilting my head back, I close my eyes and let the breeze brush across my cheeks.

That's when I hear it.

The soft waves of the ocean.

I don't come down this way at all, so I hadn't realized where Sebastian was taking me.

"Ready for the best surprise ever?"

I turn around to see him holding a blanket and cooler. "A picnic?" I can't contain my smile.

"A picnic for my lady." He walks past me to the edge of the gravel where the grass begins. A few feet in, he sets the cooler down and lays out the blanket. "Are you going to drink your wine from all the way over there?"

I shake my head, moving my legs closer to him.

A picnic under the stars with a gorgeous man.

No, this most certainly has never been done for me before.

CHAPTER 31

Sebastian

She sways her hips when she walks toward me, tucking a piece of her hair behind her ear.

Her jeans hug every part of her, and her hair slightly moves in the breeze.

She's fucking *breathtaking*.

When she delicately sits next to me on the blanket, it takes everything in me not to pull her onto my lap and hold her there, kiss her neck, and revel in her vanilla scent.

And she wants to disappear, to not be noticed at all in the LA crowd? She has no idea how beautiful she is. No idea that no matter how hard she tries, she'll always be noticed. Even in LA, where she's surrounded by models and actresses, she'll always stand out.

She has a soul that attracts even the most brokenhearted, the most undeserving of us. We want to be in her presence for even just a glimpse of her light.

"This is it," I say, holding my hand out to the empty lot, gulping in anticipation of her reaction.

She looks around with a shy smile, confusion hiding there. Her eyes dart back and forth over the emptiness.

It makes me chuckle as I pull out the small boxes of personal pizzas and the bottle of cabernet sauvignon. "This is the lot I told you about. Where I want to build my hotel."

Her mouth falls open as the realization settles. Bringing her hand to her chest, she says with reverence, "It's..." She keeps her gaze out into the distance. "It's perfect."

She places her hand on mine, stopping me from getting the food ready. She studies me, not in confusion or hesitation, just awe. Like I told her I found the cure to cancer.

And I feel it. The feeling tugs at my heart, opening it up to this woman on this blanket in the middle of a field full of dreams. Instead of letting it swallow me right now, I shrug, playing off the whole thing while I sift through the cooler.

Kendall smiles. "What're you waiting for?"

"I'm trying to find the damn cups I brought for this wine. Hold your panties."

She slaps my arm and moves closer to me. "I meant the hotel. Why not go for it? Buy the lot and open your hotel. It's your dream." She hesitates, then says, "You found your dream, and you shouldn't waste it."

This is where her light dims. Her hesitation in herself. Her inability to acknowledge that light of hers exists.

I've gotten more than a glimpse of that light, but only spurts. I want more. I want to do everything possible to keep her light there because as much as I want to keep it for myself, it's not something to hide from the world.

"It's not that easy." I shuffle the items around once more in the cooler with no sign of the cups.

But when I turn around, Kendall is drinking straight from the bottle. "I don't like to wait." She takes another sip before handing it to me. "What's not that easy? I mean, what's wrong with this land? Seems like this would be a good place to do something, but why hasn't anyone snatched it up already?"

"It's haunted, for one." I maintain my deadpan tone and expression. "Yeah, Freddie Kreuger actually buried his victims' bodies here after he was done with them."

"Oh my God!"

I don't break character, even though she looks adorable with her cheeky grin and I want to join in on her laughter. "It's true. When anyone tries to buy this land, the souls haunt them in their sleep."

"Freddie's army!"

"Exactly." I crack a smile at the way she plays along. Then I look around, putting on my most scared face. "We probably shouldn't stay long. I think I feel rumbling below us. It's almost time for them to rise."

"I think that's just your ego coming out to play. Even the Earth can't hold it down for too long."

"One, two, Freddie's coming for you. Three, four, better lock your door," I chant, but can't contain my laughter. My shoulders shake as I take a swig of wine from the bottle. Barely swallowing it down through my laughter, I take a deep breath. "I had you going, though. Tell me." I lean closer, facing her head-on, and wiggle my eyebrows. "I had you going, right?"

"Yes," she replies, matching my seductive tone, "I'm so wet from your joke that I just can't stand it."

She meant it as a joke, to play along with mine, but her saying she's wet makes my dick twitch without control. My throat suddenly dry, I do my best to swallow. "I knew it."

"Seriously, why don't you buy it? The beach in the distance, the city—this is the perfect location."

"It is." I pass her the bottle. "I've looked into the owner of this land. He's had it for a while but hasn't done anything with it. I could try to convince him to sell, I guess." I exhale roughly as I continue. "I don't know about the rest. My investment-to-profit ratios aren't impressive enough to get outside funds, and a loan would be impossible by myself. I wouldn't get to keep any profit for at least five years, and it'd be another thirty before I was free of debt. Not sure it's a risk I'm willing to take at the moment." She raises an eyebrow in disbelief. "What? I didn't lie when I said I have a business degree. Nor did I sleep through my classes."

"No, that's not what I was thinking. I, uh..." Her eyelids flutter, and she pulls at her hair nervously.

"Yeah?"

"Hearing you talk all professional and formal... it's kind of hot."

"Yeah?" I repeat, but this time it's more of a whisper.

"I'm actually wet now. Talk dirty business to me again."

"Profit margins. Inspections. Collateral. Lo—"

She cuts me off with a kiss, her lips smashing against mine without holding back. Crawling onto my lap and straddling me, she continues kissing me, tugging at my lips.

I pull back to catch my breath. "You keep doing that and I'll think it's leading somewhere."

"That's the goal," she says breathlessly as she slips a hand between us and rubs my length.

I bite back a curse and rest my head on her chest as she moves her hand up and down, but she brings my face back up with her other hand and continues kissing me.

I'd be afraid someone would see us, but we haven't seen any cars pass by since we pulled up. Normally this spot wouldn't be so empty, but being so late, it seems everyone's either going home or would rather walk around downtown in hopes of seeing a celebrity.

Kendall doesn't seem concerned in the slightest as she pulls my dick free, then pulls her own jeans down. "Should've told me we were having a picnic. I would've worn a skirt."

"I won't be so stupid next time," I say as I help her out of them. I check around one last time but don't see anyone, though I still cover her ass with my hands as she lowers herself onto me. With a gasp from her and a growl from me, she moves up and down at a steady pace, kissing me greedily.

I hold her close, her soft breaths vibrating through me as I help move her ass up and down more quickly, bringing us both so close to release. So close to the edge of bliss as she rides me here in the open, in a place so special to me.

Sharing it with her makes it even more special.

The warmth radiating from our bodies joining keeps us unaffected by the slight breeze. The surrounding beauty nothing like the beauty of her shaking in ecstasy while I'm still inside her. Nothing like her beauty in this moment as she pulls back to meet my gaze with wide eyes and a small smile.

I pull her down as I find my own release, gripping her ass to push as far as possible inside her while I kiss her, hungrily tasting her with all the energy I have left.

Drained, we stay this way for a moment, our breathing synced. The city noise and small waves from the ocean slowly infiltrate our senses once again the longer we stare into each other's eyes. Like our souls are recognizing each other for the first time.

My throat goes dry, the feeling inside me begging to be let out again. "You know what goes good with sex?" I ask instead.

"Tell me."

"Pizza."

"Mmmm… yes, please."

As she scoots off me to put her jeans back on, I reach for the small boxes that are less warm than when we began our picnic, but warm, nonetheless. "If I didn't know any better, I'd say you're more excited about the pizza than the sex."

She looks at me as she zips her pants up. "Maybe. Haven't had a cheat meal in weeks." She shrugs and sits next to me, snatching a box. "What kind of pizza is it? I've never had Angelo's before."

"And you've lived here how long?"

"Hey, cut me some slack. I've been trying to stay away from this stuff because, you know, carbs."

"And that is why I got cauliflower crust and asked for

no cheese. It's still pizza, but we don't have to feel *as* guilty, at least."

"Yeah right. You could eat an entire pizza, regular crust with extra cheese, and you'd still have a ten-pack."

I beat on my chest and yell into the quiet night, my voice echoing in the distance and scaring the birds.

She covers her face like we're in public and I embarrassed her. Like I scared more than just the birds. "Just eat your pizza, will you. Which, by the way, is fucking amazing," she says with a mouthful, which makes me laugh harder.

"Save some for me."

Once our pizza is eaten, we settle onto our backs and watch the sky together, talking about the hotel. About the size and style I want. How I want it to be comfortable for families but formal enough for small events. How I want a large pool and big fitness center.

"You should add a full-service spa and sauna," she suggests. "Then you should give me discounts."

I smile at her, thankful for the suggestion and for the way she includes herself in the future. That she thinks she'll stick around long enough to see the project to the end.

That she's dreaming with me—because that's all this is, a dream. The chance that I build my hotel is slim. It would take too much money to get there.

And I'd have to leave Naked Heat again.

As I wipe pizza sauce from Kendall's chin with a wink, I wonder if she'd be okay with that. If I continued being a stripper.

Judging by the way she hid it from her best friend, I don't feel good about those chances, either.

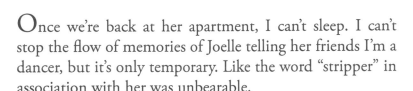

Once we're back at her apartment, I can't sleep. I can't stop the flow of memories of Joelle telling her friends I'm a dancer, but it's only temporary. Like the word "stripper" in association with her was unbearable.

With a deep breath, I whisper to Kendall, partially hoping she doesn't hear me so I don't have to deal with this. So I can avoid her rejection. "You didn't tell Emma about me... about what I do?"

Her eyes flutter open, briefly meeting my gaze before casting them back down. She idly traces the rose tattoo on my chest with her forefinger. "No."

I gulp, my voice shaky with my next words. "If me being a stripper is going to be a problem, I need to know."

She stills, and when she doesn't answer, I shake my head, the weight of it all coming down on me. Sitting up, I start putting my shoes on, but just as I'm about to say something, she tugs on my arm. Her small hand is unable to cover my whole bicep, making her look so fragile when I know she's anything but.

"It's not," she pleads. "Honestly, I never thought I'd see you again, so it didn't seem to matter at the time if I told her."

I nod, unsure if there's anything else.

She scratches her head and sits against the headboard while I watch her over my shoulder. "I told her I met a guy in Vegas, but anything more seemed futile since it was

Vegas. Not like I thought I was special enough for you to come looking for me." She looks away.

I drop my shoe and fall back into place with her against her headboard, cup her face in my large hands, and kiss her. "You *are* special. That's why I had to find you. To see you again."

She returns my kiss but does so hesitantly. I don't know what else I can say or do to convince this woman that she's worth so much. So much more than I can give her. But I'd be happy to try.

I want to try.

I kiss her again more forcefully, begging her with my lips to believe me. Begging her to return the favor and accept me as well.

"It's really not a problem," she says again more firmly, but I'm not sure if it's for her benefit or mine.

I'll take it, for now. I'm ready to take anything she gives me at this point. "Good, because I make like six figures a year doing what I do," I joke, though I actually do.

"Really?" She taps her chin with a delicate finger, and I want to kiss her there. Everywhere. "I could use some cash. Maybe I should start stripping."

I whip my head around, and we almost bump foreheads. She sits back, stunned, her eyes wide like I've scared her when she's the one who scared me with her comment.

The thought of her taking her clothes off for other men sends a rage through my whole body unlike anything I've ever known. Trembling, I take deep breaths and try to control my primal need to claim her, for her to know she's mine.

I growl and decide to unleash the beast within, anyway. "I don't think so."

When I smash my mouth to hers, her moans bounce off the walls. She's not stunned anymore. No, she meets my every movement with her own eagerness, her nails digging into my shoulders. Instead of wincing, I welcome it. Because it reminds me that she wants me.

At least for now.

There was hesitation in her words and kiss before, but for now, it's enough for me. I'll convince her I'm real and falling for her in time.

That's all I need—*time*.

CHAPTER 32

Kendall

The next morning, Sebastian and I wake up to his alarm going off at five o'clock. And Ty's text. I snort when he reads it aloud, even though it's so early in the morning and my eyes hurt.

"From Ty—*I felt strong doing heavy deadlifts yesterday but woke up as a ninety-three-year-old geriatric. Pick me up a walker on your way to the hotel.*" Then Sebastian turns to me. "See what I have to deal with every day? A baby."

Sebastian leaves soon after, with several kisses to my lips, cheeks, and temples, and I need a week to recover from his visit.

Because holy *fuck*.

That *man*.

I stretch out on my bed, delightfully sore in every spot. Cabinets open and close in the kitchen, and the sink

207

starts running. I stumble only a little and smile at how Sebastian tossed me around last night like I was nothing.

And everything.

The way he couldn't get enough.

It felt good to be wanted. Needed. Accepted.

"Cardboard pancakes or mushy oatmeal today?" Emma asks without turning to me.

I sit in a chair by the window and put my elbows on the table, resting my head on my hands. "Why do the Insta athletes always make food look so *yum*, and our only options are cardboard and essentially puke?"

She barely giggles. "It's their job."

Too early for joking, I guess. She's always up early even though she hates it, but it seems like she has to start the day at dawn to fulfill some kind of lifelong path—some yogi shit she discovered on her journey to find herself after Brant. "As I said yesterday, you don't have to eat this shit. Why are you even bothering if you're miserable?"

"Healthy dinner food options are usually delicious." I shrug. "I may not have a great breakfast, but you better believe I'm ending the day on a good note with a spring salad. Or honey-glazed salmon." I raise my pinky up like I'm in a mansion and not a small apartment that's barely able to contain the two of us. It's on the outskirts of LA, wedged between a hotel that I'm pretty sure is a brothel, and an Asian restaurant owned by the family across the hall, who I'm pretty sure kill their own food over there. The smell never goes away. Seeps into our apartment little by little every day until I'm sure one day I'll be living in that restaurant and not know it.

Emma doesn't laugh.

"Okay, my dinner joke wasn't funny. It's early, give me a break."

"Maybe if you would've gotten more sleep last night instead of Sebastian's lovin', you'd be on your game today." She grins over her coffee mug, small waves of steam radiating from it. She drinks it black, no creamer, and I want to hurl. Black coffee? Only soul-crushers drink it that way.

"You're just mad you aren't getting any *dick*." I flip her off, and she shakes her head.

"Are you taking him to Lauren's wedding?"

My face flushes. *Will I? Should I?*

Sensing my hesitation, she teases and pokes my side. "He could be Lauren's entertainment at the reception. Who needs a band?"

I know she's kidding, but that's exactly the reason I shouldn't ask him. People will wonder who he is, what he does, and I can't have my family knowing I'm seeing a stripper. Especially not this early. I let out a weak "Right" and smile for Emma.

But my mind races.

"Easy." She holds up her hands. "Looks like you're about to vomit."

"How can I tell my mom that I'm seeing a stripper?" Between this and the impending tasteless breakfast, I do actually feel the urge to vomit.

Emma blinks at me. "Are you seeing him? I mean, are you going to see him again? Realistically, he lives several hours away, travels a lot, and flirts—*a lot*."

Voicing my worries makes this all real. *I'm seeing a*

stripper. And even though it's not serious, he makes me think it *could* be.

I want it to be.

I exhale and let my head fall on the table. She's right—all those things are true, especially the last one. It's part of his job. And although that would make many women jealous, it's not something I've ever been guilty of. I don't tend to get jealous at all, unless my boyfriends frequent strip clubs like Adam used to.

"You're right." I throw my hands up. "It would never work, logistically."

Emma winces like she does when she uses the "p" word, *penis.* Like she's guilty of something I'm not aware of. "Look," she says while I brace myself for her next words, "I may have misjudged him and let my own trust issues with guys get in the way." Her expression softens, as much as her tight ponytail will allow. "Sebastian doesn't flirt so much. Definitely not as much as Ty. My God, did you see the way he slapped my ass yesterday? The nerve."

"Huh?"

She shakes her head. "What I'm saying is… when have you ever been logical about anything? College, moving out here, riding the waves of life's ocean? So you add falling for a stripper to the mix."

"Should I be offended? Not sure how to feel about this right now."

She shakes her head again and rests a hand on mine. "You know what makes you happy. You've always gone after what you wanted, and from what I heard last night? You want that hunk of man."

"Don't say shit like that." I shake my finger at her. "It just sounds dirty coming from your prissy mouth."

She grabs my finger and bites—actually *bites*—it.

"Hey!" I screech. "I always knew there was something feisty buried in there, but *Jesus*."

She shrugs and starts humming the tune of what I think is ABBA's "Dancing Queen," then sets two plates full of pancakes and eggs in front of us. "Oh, and Gym Class Heroes *is* a band." She pulls up an image on her phone.

"I told you." I scrunch my nose up at them. "And not a hot one, either. Unless you're into the whole 'I'm high and I own it' look."

"You're not into that? Just strippers, then?" she says sarcastically.

I mimic her words in my best childish voice like I used to do when we were in elementary school. Oh the days of "I'm rubber and you're glue," or my favorite, "That's my name, don't wear it out."

"Real mature."

I stick my tongue out but pieces of pancake fall out, and when I burst out laughing, more small speckles of dried oats decorate the counter between us.

"You're disgusting," she says, trying to hold in her own laughter. "I don't know why I ever let you move in."

"Because you need me to keep things interesting around here. Who else would agree to be your lesbian lover to the neighbors?"

"Please stop." She final loses her battle and snorts.

I hold up another forkful of pancake. "Remember when Pop-Tarts were acceptable?"

"When we were ten, yes."

"I wish I had a strawberry one right now." I stuff a large bite in my mouth. "I'll just pretend," I say while more pieces of pancake fly out of my mouth.

"That's it." She throws a towel my way and takes her plate to the couch while another fit of laughter consumes me.

I've laughed more this weekend than I have since I moved to LA, and a long time before that. And not because of LA itself. I fell in love with the city immediately, with its vibrant life and lack of tractors like you'd find on every highway back in the South. It's been an unbelievable dream come true.

Being here with Emma, with Sebastian this weekend, I'm finally settling in. It even feels like home.

But when Sebastian's name lights up on my phone with an incoming text, Emma's words of caution nag at me and tug me back down a hole I know all too well from when my parents constantly told me what to do.

And most importantly, what *not* to do.

Don't get that tattoo.

Don't go out with those friends.

Don't drop out of school.

And now all I can hear them say is *Don't date a stripper.*

Now that it's getting too real, that I'm contemplating leaving the confines of my bedroom, I panic.

I panic that it's too much, and I'll have to let Sebastian go.

The one man who makes me feel wanted, cherished, and sexy.

The one man I could actually fall for.

CHAPTER 33

Sebastian

The day after I leave LA, I miss Kendall immediately. Ty called me a pussy this morning on our way to San Diego to continue the tour along the coast, but I don't mind.

Especially when I get a picture of Kendall at the gym.

She's very noticeably sweaty, with armpit stains and all, although it does look like she's trying to hide them with the way she angles her body. Loose strands of hair stick out to one side, and she's making a duck face that makes her squint.

She's not doing anything purposely sexy, and that's exactly why it turns me on.

Her face is glowing, probably from sweat, but to me, she's simply glowing.

If we weren't on this tour right now, I'd stay buried inside of Kendall Gray for the next couple weeks straight, letting her laugh and terrible shower singing consume me.

"Weekend was good, then?" Leo lies down on the chair next to me. We're by the pool, resting up before tonight's show. "You've been smiling nonstop."

"Yeah, it was good." *Good* is an understatement, but my pride can't handle being called a pussy for the second time today.

"Glad what I told you didn't stop you. Deciding whether or not to tell you was tearing me up inside." He sits up and leans over. "Not to bring it back up again unnecessarily. Sorry, man."

I wave him off, even though my jaw tics. "It's fine, but no, I'd rather not talk about it."

"But if you need to, you know you can come to me."

I fist-bump him to end the conversation, but he's not done. "You talk to your mom?"

Leo is only a few years older than I am, but the way he fathers us makes him seem much older. And as much as I appreciate it, I was on a good high—a Kendall high—before this conversation started bringing me down.

Because truthfully, I haven't thought much about Joelle and the news of her engagement. Haven't thought about my mom. Haven't thought about anything but Kendall's vanilla scent and sun-kissed skin, my new happy place. Even better than the gym. Hell, at this point I'd say better than the beach, and I *love* the beach.

"I haven't," I manage. "She didn't answer my call yesterday, but that's not unusual. She'll probably call back. Even if it is in three weeks."

"What're you ladies gossiping about over here?" Ty

interrupts. "Do I need to bring the mimosas? Maybe have them put a tiny umbrella in it for you?"

"Sounds like someone's been hitting the alcohol already."

"Nah, just happy you're finally getting some on the regular." He slaps my knee. "Is that what you're talking about? That sweet thing you spent all weekend in bed with? Because I do not want to miss this."

"I already told you everything, douchebag."

"Yeah, but hearing it a second time is even better."

"Says the guy who hooked up with, what, three different girls this weekend? And my story with one girl is juicy?"

"But it's the first girl for you in over a year, dude!" he says rather loudly, which attracts the attention of a small group of girls to our left who just arrived. They make eyes at Ty first and continue to Leo before landing on me. Not having seen them or being so used to it that he doesn't notice anymore, Ty continues with his hands under his chin. "This is what girls must feel like when watching Oprah or the Kardashians. Like they're on the edge of their seats with their hearts ready to burst." He scoots to the edge of the chair for emphasis and rests his head on one hand, giving me googly eyes.

"It's not that big of a deal. I just met her a few weeks ago," I say as my own heart is about to explode. "Besides, I've been with women since Joelle."

Ty scoffs. "What, that one girl you didn't even spend the whole night with?"

I roll my eyes, wanting to correct him, that there have been at least three one-night stands, but there's no use.

"Don't play this down now, Sebastian." Leo rolls his

eyes to Ty.

I swing my legs around the chair, not wanting to get into this right now. Kendall is great, and while she's got me by the cock, I still haven't won her over.

I can't get too excited over this. That's what happened with Joelle, and look at how that ended.

She's getting married.

And not to me this time.

"Don't leave," Ty pleads. "We'll stop. We'll behave and not ask about her ass."

"Okay, Ty," Leo steps in once Ty crosses the line. "Let him be."

"I'm just fucking around guys." Then Ty drops his tone lower, dropping the humor too. Eyeing me, he asks, "Obviously, it's more serious than just looking at her nice ass."

I make a noncommittal sound, unsure of where he's going with this.

"Have you told her about Joelle?"

My jaw tics again as a natural reaction to her name, like she's cursed me. Being the witch she is, I'd believe it.

"You haven't told her yet?" Leo's self-righteousness drips from his words.

"It still hasn't come up." I shrug as they both give me doubtful looks, my guilt slowly eating at me. "I'll tell her next time I see her." And before they can ask, I add, "And I don't know when that'll be."

"This *is* like the Kardashians," Ty says dreamily, and I roll my eyes again.

But the nausea building in my stomach stays there for

the rest of the afternoon. The sun is high, and a cool breeze rolls in every now and then for a good balance. The universe seems to know how to balance.

Like when one bad thing happens, it balances out with the good.

When it's hot, it sends a cool current to give you relief.

When Joelle left me, it sent me Kendall. Sweet, sexy Kendall.

Which is why I can't tell her about my past, not yet. Not when I'm still trying to win her over. Telling her I was engaged before, lost a business to my uncle, and barely speak to my mother?

That would not win over a small-town girl with big eyes and lips, and even bigger dreams. Because she might act like a city girl with a big attitude, but deep down, I know she still has some small town in her. A part of her that wants simple and sweet, not my drama.

No, my drama would scare her.

CHAPTER 34

Kendall

Sebastian and I have texted frequently the last few days since his visit, so much that I've come to expect a good morning and good night text from him. But I don't expect it when he calls me one night later that week.

And I definitely don't expect the casual way he does so, and the casual way I answer. Like it's normal for us. The thought of it being a regular thing excites me.

"Hey, baby," he says, and at the sound of his gruff yet cheerful voice, at the way he calls me *baby*, I want this to be our normal. I want to talk to him on the phone when he's away.

I want him to call me *baby* again.

"I'm sorry, who is this?" I tease.

"Ouch," he says, and I can imagine him clutching his chest dramatically in the only way he knows how to be.

"Moved on already?"

"Well, what's a girl to do around here without a certain sexy stripper to entertain her?" As soon as the joke leaves my mouth, I attempt to correct it, unsure of whether or not this is a sore topic since we last talked about it. "Er... I..."

But he bursts out laughing before I can form whole sentences. "I'll fly back right now to keep you from being lonely."

"I keep myself busy with thoughts of you, especially at night when I touch myself."

There's shuffling on the other end like he dropped the phone. "That's... fucking *hot*," he growls and exhales.

"Oh?" I manage, the only thing I can say. The change of tone in the last ten seconds has me reeling, losing control as always when Sebastian is involved.

"Where are you right now?"

I gulp. "At work. Took my break when I saw your call."

He curses. "Call me when you get home. I want to hear you come for me."

I gasp lightly, then hang up with my hand over my mouth at the sultry edge to his otherwise humorous tone.

I'm ready to run home right now.

I go through the motions during most of my shift, only snapping out of my trance when Margo blurts out at me, "Is that *you*?" She fumbles with her phone to show me what's on it. I can't decide if her face is one of terror or shock, but then she grins mischievously and nudges George in the side.

I peer over both of their shoulders, leaning between them to see what's on the phone. "What the *fuck* is that?" I grab her phone and zoom in to make sure I'm seeing this correctly. And sure enough, it's Emma's Instagram post with a picture of me at the gym, sweaty and taking my shirt off with a sports bra underneath. I'm looking somewhere in the distance, and I remember wearing that outfit last weekend when Emma and I went to the gym with the guys. Underneath her post is *#WomanCrushWednesday*.

When did Emma even take this?

"You look hot, Kendall from Alabama." George booty-bumps me. "Shed that conservative southern skin real quick and exchanged it for an LA tan and legs for days."

I'm still speechless as he and Margo exchange comments about how perfectly my ass is sticking out, emphasized in my pink spandex capris. My abs are even showing with the lighting from the sunlight shining through the open door.

I couldn't have posed better if I'd tried.

If I'd seen this on Instagram elsewhere, I'd think it was a sexy-as-hell yet tasteful picture. But it being me, I panic and immediately turn away before I can read the comments. I'm sure they're all wondering who the skank is and why she's on there like that, when I wasn't even consciously posing.

I didn't even know she took it, let alone that she was going to post it.

"Holy shit." Margo giggles. "You have like thirty comments, and it's only been up for less than an hour."

I don't want to know what vicious words have been thrown my way. I've had enough of them my whole life.

I nod, heading toward a customer who just walked in. "I'm sure they're all super kind too," I call over my shoulder, making sure to emphasize the sarcasm.

My fingers itch to dissect each and every comment, but

I continue toward the customer and plaster a smile on my face when I get close.

When the customer leaves with two pairs of sandals, ones I myself will have to buy with summer approaching, I grab my phone and hover over the Instagram app. I fight with myself like I do when I approach a stop sign at the same time as another vehicle and can't decide who goes first.

I end up texting Emma instead, but I rein in my crazy because the picture is actually a good one and shows how much progress I've made. Deep down, I know I just want reassurance that others thought so as well, but I can't come out and ask her. That'd be conceited.

I get a response immediately.

> Emma: *Isn't it cute? I took it when you weren't looking. More natural that way, like Samantha.*

She follows with an emoji rolling its eyes, but I know she's laughing.

And as I leave work, I send her a thank-you text. Thanks to her post, I've gained several new followers from those who know her through her yoga studio.

Even though my stomach still feels queasy, I'm smiling when I get home, not only because of Emma's post, but also my call with Sebastian.

When he answers, he skips the pleasantries and says instead, "Are you in bed with your clothes off yet?"

"Yes," I breathe into the phone, already turned on by his eagerness. His hunger for me. "Are you? Fair's fair."

"Of course. I've been waiting for you since we hung up

last."

"Mm-hmm…"

"Are you touching yourself?"

"Yeah, but I wish it was you," I whisper, closing my eyes as I slide my hand into my panties. I picture Sebastian leaning over me, smirking as I unravel beneath him, his length against my inner thighs as he works me to my release.

"You still with me? You have to share in the fun."

"Mm-hmm." My voice raspy, as I'm unable to form coherent words, let alone full sentences.

When I moan his name into the phone, he demands, "That's right, say my name. Picture me with you, *worshipping* you."

"Yes… yes," I say as I work myself faster, hearing him shuffling.

"Faster, baby. Come for me," he grunts. "Come for me."

"Fuck, Sebastian," I say around the same time he also curses and grunts again. I know he found his release as well. *He was ready for me indeed.*

A slow smile spreads across my face in the darkness, and I wish he was here to spoon and hold me against his hard yet warm chest. So I could fall asleep to the sounds of his soft snores while tracing the tattoo on his chest.

Heavy breathing and our soft sighs of pleasure fill the phone line and room.

No one gets me off like Sebastian. Even when he's hundreds of miles away, he has a stronger effect on me than anyone I've ever met. Not even the screenshot on my phone of Channing Tatum, shirtless and sweaty, has ever been able to get me off.

I'm elated, spent from the day and our sexcapades. My eyes remain closed as I blurt out, "Come to my sister's wedding with me."

Silence.

Then, "Really? To Alabama?"

I sit up and wipe my hand down my face. "Yeah, but if you don't want to, I understand. I know you're busy and—"

"I'd love to," he says softly, in reverence even.

I smile at his answer but panic the minute we hang up.

I'm bringing a stripper to my sister's wedding.

A wedding where all my conservative, traditional relatives will be in one place, suffocating me.

I'll no longer be able to hide him and this part of my life. I'll be on display, yet again, to be judged.

And I don't know if I'm ready for that.

CHAPTER 35

Sebastian

She asked me to be her date at her sister's wedding.

I've been desperate to keep her, to claim her as mine, and the fact that she wants me to meet her family means she wants me just as much.

I've won her over. Didn't think this would happen again after Joelle, but I found someone who accepts me, unlike Joelle did. Unlike my uncle or my mom.

Unlike my dad who was never around, who left before I was born. I didn't even get a chance to show him who I was before he decided he didn't accept me.

I used to think all I had were the boys at Naked Heat, but now I have them—my family—and Kendall. My city girl with southern charm.

The rest of the week, I'm in the best mood, counting down the days until the wedding. It's right in the middle of our tour, but Leo gladly gave me the weekend off.

Anything to get me to have a life again.

At the hotel, I step out of the shower and grab a towel when my phone starts vibrating on the counter.

Mom.

I answer, "You called sooner than expected."

"What's that supposed to mean?" She yawns on the other end, and I imagine her with a cup of coffee in each hand because she can't drink it fast enough. "Listen, I called to tell you I'm home helping Sid and Joelle. I assume you heard?" Without waiting for an answer, she continues, "They decided to move the date up to next weekend. God, like they can't wait another couple months. Now they're inconveniencing everyone with this short notice. Did you know I had to take off this week and lose my vacation later this year? It was so last minute, I couldn't plan accordingly. Sid was always selfish."

"You're telling me." My teeth grind together so hard I might chip one.

Silence answers as I get lost in my anger at Joelle and Sid—the guy she cheated on me with. If only he was a normal guy—it would've hurt, but what she did was even worse. My teeth grind harder.

I think my mom has finally run out of things to say for fear of putting her foot in her mouth again. And here I thought she'd forgotten about the whole situation.

"How long have you been home?" I ask, focusing on us instead of the she-devil and her demon king.

"A week or so. Are you—"

"A *week*? And you're just now telling me?"

"Don't be so dramatic. I know you're busy, anyway."

"Right." I shake my head, not at her but at myself, for being disappointed when I know better. She didn't know I was on tour. I never told her, and there's no way in hell she looked up our tour schedule herself. She avoids the topic of Naked Heat at all cost. The mere thought of her only son growing up to be a stripper is enough to give her crow's feet that she can't afford to keep Botoxing. "Speaking of being busy, I have to go. Got plans."

"Before you rudely cut me off, I was trying to ask you a question. You'll be able to get off this weekend, right? We'll ride together up to Lake Tahoe for the wedding and—"

"You're joking, right?"

"Stop cutting me off. I raised you better than that."

"Really? Because I don't remember you ever being around."

"Sebastian, what has gotten into you?"

"I'm not going to that fucking wedding."

"Watch your tone! Remember who you're speaking to."

Suddenly I'm ten years old again, and she's scolding me for getting crumbs on the couch.

The problem is that I do remember who I'm speaking to—my mother who was never around when I grew up. A woman I haven't seen in several months now, which isn't uncommon for us. A woman who never came to my school plays even when I played the lead or attended my college graduation where I graduated with honors.

I study my reflection in the mirror now that the fog from the hot shower has cleared, and I laugh. A humorless laugh that changes my usually friendly exterior. With my dark hair sticking out on all sides, I'm looking at a possessed version of myself in the mirror like I'm in an episode of *Supernatural.*

"I repeat, no way in hell am I going to that wedding to watch a piece of trash marry a fucking bastard. Besides, I have plans this weekend." With that, I hang up and punch the mirror, shattering pieces of my reflection across the counter.

"Oh my God, yes!" Joelle jumped up and down, clapping and smiling. I'd never seen her so happy, and in that moment, I loved her even more. "I'll marry you, Sebastian Davis."

She didn't wait for me to put the ring on for her, just grabbed it from the box and slid it onto her slender ring finger. She studied it while I pulled back her black hair so I could study her face. She was so beautiful, with a million stars in her eyes that matched the sparkle in the diamond ring I spent weeks picking out.

We were in the middle of the Strip with a cheering crowd surrounding us. I only noticed them when she looked up and waved her ring finger around for all the strangers to see, while I waited my turn for her attention.

After she circled around, she grabbed my face and kissed me without warning. I had my eyes open and saw that hers were too.

I send a quick text to my mom to apologize for cursing. It's not her I'm angry at, although she hasn't helped.

I run my bloodied hand through my hair and lean my back against the counter, thinking about all the signs I missed with Joelle.

Or worse—misunderstood.

She was wrong for me to begin with, but what she did to me toward the end? It gutted me.

And no matter how much I've tried to convince myself and others that I'm over it, that I'm moving forward with Kendall, and that I'm better with her, I'm starting to think that maybe I'm not.

CHAPTER 36

Kendall

I open my old bedroom door, and it looks the same as it did when I was thirteen. I was obsessed with Britney Spears even then; her face and lyrics decorate the walls. Only thing missing is her face from my comforter, where I went for the plain black to match the curtains.

I never redecorated when I moved back as a college dropout for that short time. I didn't expect to live here forever, so I never made it *mine*. At one point, when we were all a big happy family, it felt like mine. I was included in the family instead of cast out just because I wanted to do something other than settle in this small town with a boring husband.

I wanted something different.

"God, you were such a dork with all this Britney." Lauren huffs, looking at my room with her lip twitching. Disgusted like I told her I'm wearing torn jeans to her wedding.

"At least it wasn't Hanson." I smile sweetly.

Lauren wraps a trembling arm around me. "Mom and Dad are driving me crazy."

I draw my eyebrows together, partly in shock that she didn't have a retort or eye roll for me.

She slides away, still avoiding eye contact, but continues, "They want all this extravagance, but Rhett and I only wanted a simple ceremony and intimate reception. Somehow we've ended up with two hundred guests."

I snort. "Probably worried this will be the only wedding they'll throw, so they have to go all out."

"Why do you always do that? Deflect and put yourself down in the process? It's annoying."

"And I should be more arrogant and self-obsessed like you? Is that right? I'll do my best."

Now Lauren rolls her eyes and crosses her arms before stomping away.

What the fuck just happened?

Nothing is ever good enough for her, apparently. Not even when I give her something to make fun of me for. Guess she likes to have original material; it doesn't mean as much to her if I put myself down.

But that's also why I do it, to protect myself. If I tease myself first, she won't have as much of a chance.

The rehearsal goes swimmingly. A couple of the single

groomsmen were the only ones to say more than two words to me, aside from my mother who kept telling me to walk slower and straighten my back.

Afterward, I go back to the house to change for dinner, as do Lauren and her friends. I hole up in my room, anxious to see Sebastian. He should've been here by now, but it's probably for the best that he wasn't. The rehearsal would've been boring for him.

Once I'm dressed in my full-length bold red jumpsuit, I pace around my room with a sinking feeling that he's not going to make it.

I check my phone, but no texts.

I move my hair to one side and rub my hands up and down my exposed arms like it's thirty degrees and not eighty-eight. Alabama this time a year is always a bitch, the humid air so thick it suffocates you and traps you in its clutches. It's not as bad as mid-summer, but it's still hot.

I decide to put my hair in a low ponytail, mostly to keep my hands busy. My makeup is already done. I even took extra time to make sure the wings on my eyeliner came out flawless. Now I part my hair down the middle, tying it back and pulling it over one shoulder.

Then my phone vibrates with an incoming text. I jump to the bed for it and almost face-plant into the wall in my vintage wedges. I found them in LA and immediately had to have them. The buckles on the straps are everything... except practical in this moment as I leap for my phone.

Sebastian: *I'm running late. Meet you at the venue.*

No smiley face or anything? I feel like I missed something, like I'm not in on the inside joke and soon I'll really be face-first into the wall.

But in order to be the cool girl my subconscious still wants me to be, I don't ask. I'll wait until he gets here to gauge his mood. We're always better in person, anyway. Better with body language instead of words.

Me: *Sure thing <3*

CHAPTER 37

Kendall

At the venue, my friends and family immediately disperse when I walk in the door. I'm left holding my clutch and shoulders high with tension. I've only been back in town once since I ridded myself of this place, and now that I'm here, I'm a stranger.

My family and Lauren's friends are huddled around one another, laughing like they don't spend every minute together. And I'm alone, wondering if I ever felt at home here. I grew up here, so I'd think I'd feel some connection.

But I feel nothing.

I felt nothing as I pulled into town, passing my old high school on the way. I spent four years of my life there, had my first kiss in the gym after cheerleading practice, spent hours practicing our cheers on that football field.

But it's tainted with the bad memories as well. Just like

this town.

I've never been inside this country club, though. Which is a relief—no memories of who I was before here. But I might as well be at Grand Central Station among zillions of people. Just like I'd go unnoticed at the busiest train station on the planet, I go unnoticed here. Slide by people I've known for years without so much as a nod.

An arm wraps around my waist from behind, and I immediately relax. Leaning my head against Sebastian's warm chest, I sigh. "You're here."

"Sorry I'm late." Kissing the top of my head, he turns me around and holds my arms out, drinking me in with nostrils flared. "I *like.* I like very much."

Before I can do a twirl to give him a better look, he pulls me in for a greedy kiss. And as much as I like it—I haven't seen him in almost a week, after all—we're at my sister's rehearsal dinner with all my family around.

A throat clears a foot from us for an extra reminder.

"If I'm not interrupting, I'd like to get my rehearsal dinner started now." Lauren crosses her arms over her chest, wrinkling the top part of her off-white, off-the-shoulder, A-line dress. "And jeez, Kendall, can you be any sluttier? First, the cut-out jumper showing your boobs, and now sucking this guy's face off. Who even is he? I didn't know you were bringing a date."

"Sebastian Davis, at your service for face sucking, among other things." He winks at me while extending his hand to her. His crisp baby blue button-up strains against his bicep as he does so. During the whole exchange, he holds me flush against his side with his other hand, and his warmth keeps me safe. Grounded. Makes me feel like I'm not so lonely for once among these people.

Lauren chokes but shakes his hand limply like she does when she takes the trash out, holding it far away and taking care not to get the "icky" on her. Then she turns to me. *Oh great, we're not done.* "Seriously, at my bachelorette party, you couldn't bother to dress up, and now you've decided showing off the goodies was a good idea at my rehearsal dinner. Rhett's ninety-year-old grandma is here, not to mention his two nieces."

Sebastian's jaw flexes, and I swear his teeth might chip from how hard he's grinding them. The warmth I previously felt instantly chills.

I place a light hand on his chest to keep him back. I can handle my sister. That's one thing in my life I've had no problem with. "Speaking of Rhett's family, shouldn't you be over there kissing their asses by now? You're about twenty minutes late for your brown-nosing."

She visibly rears back, a comeback on the tip of her tongue to throw at me, but she stops and points at Sebastian. "Where do I know you from?"

"Hey, honey," Rhett calls to Lauren from the other corner of the room.

"Ah, duty calls. Run along." I shoo her away with my hand and she goes, albeit reluctantly. Once she's gone, I turn to Sebastian and say, "She's unbearable—"

Before I can finish my sentence, he's back to sucking my face off, holding me close like one of us has been off to war and we're finally back together again.

That's when I notice the hint of whiskey on his tongue

as it swirls with mine. I push him back slightly to put some distance between us and search his eyes. He looks sober—delectable for sure. His beard is trimmed and proper, like the rest of him. He's even wearing black slacks and dress shoes.

"What're you smiling about?" He rests his forehead against mine like we're not in a room full of people, let alone a room full of my *family*.

"Didn't realize I was."

He lifts my chin up and greedily kisses me once more, almost like he's trying to convince himself of something.

And as much as I like kissing him, as much as I'd like to find a quiet broom closet to lock ourselves in, something's off. He's been drinking, and he's particularly handsy for this occasion.

"Oh my God." Lauren rushes back to us and points again at Sebastian. Lowering her voice to a whisper-scream, she turns to me. "He's the *stripper* from Vegas!"

Sebastian tenses again, not at Lauren's words but at my silence. He watches me, waiting for an answer. An explanation. Something.

But I can't find my voice. Even though I thought the whole way here about how I'd tell my family that I'm seeing a stripper, I have nothing. My mouth simply hangs open.

"You've got to be kidding." She throws her hands up like now she's seen it all from me. I've done everything possible to humiliate and disappoint her.

Only a matter of time before she runs off to tell Mom and Dad.

I brace myself for more shaming, but right now I'm

mostly concerned about Sebastian. He's even more off now, his smile forced.

And when Rhett announces the food is ready and everyone should sit, I hope Sebastian doesn't crack.

Next to me.

At my sister's rehearsal dinner.

On our way to find our seats next to my parents, I squeeze his hand, trying to convince myself that it'll all be okay.

That I'm just reading him wrong.

But I can't deny the smell of alcohol on his breath, or the way he squeezes my hand throughout dinner as though if he lets go, he'll never get to hold it again.

CHAPTER 38

Sebastian

After a few beers, then whiskeys, on the flight and at the small bar close to the venue, I finally loosen up enough to avoid ruining Kendall's bitchy sister's dinner. And, of course, it's at their pretentious country club. A couple guys in bow ties—grown men in bow ties, like this is the nineteenth century—asked me when I got here what my putting game looked like.

What I wanted to say in return was that I'd like putting my foot in their asses, but instead, I smiled and swallowed that down with a large gulp of Jack Daniels.

Her sister seems the type to want to show off, like tonight is the actual wedding. She and Kendall could not be more opposite. Thank fuck for that, because otherwise, I wouldn't be here.

Although, for a minute, I think I actually saw Lauren

flinch. Like it hurt her to fight with Kendall.

But I was probably seeing things, the alcohol fogging my vision.

When the dinner is finally over and we get to Kendall's parents' house, my head clears and my thoughts sober up as I settle onto her bed. Looking around the room, I take in all the Britney Spears posters and pictures of Kendall with her sister. They're all pictures from when they were kids.

"What happened between you and your sister?" I ask.

"Nothing happened tonight. That's just how she always is." She swipes at her makeup in the bathroom, the door positioned so I can only see half of her. "Before you got here, we tried having a normal conversation, but she went all apeshit when I didn't answer properly—whatever that means."

I stay silent until she comes back in the room and crawls into bed next to me. "That's not what I meant. I mean, why don't you get along?"

"Um…" She gulps. "It happened forever ago. It's going to sound ridiculous."

"Try me."

"Well, when we were in high school, I made out with her boyfriend at a party one night. And before you say anything, it's not what you think." She leans up on her elbow, facing me. "Jeremy was a cheating bastard, and she didn't believe me when I told her he'd been flirting and texting half the cheerleading squad. So that night at the party, I wanted to prove to her what a piece of shit he was, and she just couldn't handle the truth."

I kiss her hand.

"I know it sounds so immature, and I was, back then. We were best friends before, but ever since that night, we just haven't been the same."

I nod in response, unsure of what to say. Unsure if this is a good reason not to be friends with someone so close to her. But I don't want to meddle.

And the way Kendall's lips part has me distracted.

Her red jumpsuit from tonight is still on my mind. Lauren may have hated it, but I found it sexy yet adorable. Very Kendall.

All I want right now is to taste her. To bury myself inside her in order to convince myself she's mine. That this is all real. But I can't. Her parents' house is big, but not big enough to contain Kendall's screams.

And when I try kissing her, she can't stop giggling, thinking how ridiculous it is to have me in her childhood bedroom surrounded by Britney Spears posters. Her eyes follow us every time we move.

It's actually pretty comical, and I'm spent from the day drinking and the extra whiskey from dinner, so I don't mind simply holding her close to my chest, ignoring all the dark thoughts in my head.

As I look in the mirror the next morning, a few hours before the wedding, I wonder what I'm doing here. I'm not in a celebratory mood.

As I get dressed and ready to meet Kendall at the

church, where she's getting dressed, I can't help but think about Joelle.

It's her wedding day too.

Her wedding day that was supposed to involve me, and now I'm nowhere near her. Months and several states separating us.

I pull up to the church with a couple of Kendall's cousins, who ignore me the whole ride over because they're in deep conversation about the University of Alabama's rowing team. I would've joined in but don't have anything to add to the topic, not even a sarcastic comment.

My stomach is in knots, so I can't worry about what the team will do this year without last year's seniors. Hands trembling, I take the steps up to the front of the church toward the floor-to-ceiling doors surrounded by columns. Reminds me more of the Parthenon than a church.

"Sebastian, this venue is perfect!" Joelle said, twirling around in the center of the reception hall with her arms spread wide—the most stress-free I'd seen her in weeks. Right outside Vegas, plenty of dancing room, and reasonable price for our budget. Since her parents weren't involved—not approving of someone like me—we had to do it ourselves.

Joelle and me against the world.

I turned to the coordinator and shook his hand. "We'll take it."

"Really?" She smiled with her hands to her mouth like she was praying.

"Anything you want, baby. That's what I promised you when I proposed."

"I love it!" she squealed and twirled some more while I

watched her, elated and determined to make her that happy for the rest of our lives.

Even at the cost of my own happiness.

Kendall's cousin nudges me. "You going inside or just going to admire from the outside?" He chuckles at his own joke, and I try hard to refrain from rolling my eyes.

He has no idea the turmoil going on inside me as I walk inside the church, damn near shaking as I picture myself walking down the aisle ahead of my bride.

For three months while we were engaged, I imagined Joelle walking down an aisle decorated with flowers much like this one. Of being dressed in white and smiling at me like she did when we first met, full of wonder and clarity. Like we *clicked*.

People say the wedding is for the bride, that the groom just shows up for the day and doesn't dream about it for a lifetime like the bride does. While the latter might be true, the rest isn't. I was excited to get married, to vow to be together forever in front of a small group of friends and what little family supported us and our relationship.

I wonder if her parents will be there for her today, if her mom will help her put her dress on and if her dad will walk her down the aisle.

If they're more accepting of a man who's seventeen years older than she is simply because he runs a successful business. A man who doesn't strip for a living.

"You're shaking," Kendall whispers, wrapping her small arms around my waist from behind.

I turn around and inhale a calming breath at the sight of her in her one-shoulder lilac bridesmaid's dress. Her hair is parted to the side and pinned back on the other.

My heart rate slows as I take her in, instantly giving me peace. That's what Kendall does to me. Her presence always mesmerizes me, calming me when I spiral. Yesterday I threw back beers like I found out Coors Light was going out of business, but when I got to the rehearsal dinner and saw her, I relaxed. As much as I could, anyway.

I'm still attending a wedding. On the same day my ex-fiancée is getting married.

Some shit just can't be fixed, no matter how badly we want others to take away that pain. But Kendall makes me think less and less about it, especially when she delicately wraps her hands around my neck and stands on her tiptoes to kiss me softly.

I meet her halfway and whisper against her lips, "You look great."

She pulls back and hides her smile, but I catch her before she can look down.

"Don't hide from me," I say, my voice raspy. "I need to see your smile."

She draws her eyebrows together in confusion. "Are you okay?"

"Kendall, get back here!" her mother demands, running from the altar. "Your sister is getting married. Can you pay at least a little attention to her?" She smiles at me impatiently. "Sebastian, she'll be out in a minute."

I smile and back away from Kendall.

She squeezes my hand. "She's stressed. Also, upset that I didn't tell her I was bringing a date."

"You didn't tell anyone about me?"

"Well, it was last minute, and I—"

"Kendall! We need a group picture." One of the other bridesmaids waves her over.

When I release her hand, it feels like I'm releasing her from being with me. Letting her off the hook, because why else would she not tell her family and friends about me other than she's embarrassed by me?

Other than she doesn't see us having a future.

As I watch Kendall go, uneasiness settles in the pit of my stomach.

CHAPTER 39

Kendall

I lift the bottom of my maxi dress and walk toward Sam, who's frantically waving at me like I can't see her from ten feet away. As she leads me to the dressing rooms, I can't rid myself of the nagging feeling that I'm losing Sebastian. I need to explain why I didn't tell my family. He doesn't know them and doesn't understand.

I need to explain their judgmental habits, that I don't want them ruining my feelings for him.

That I want to keep him all for myself.

I started to explain it to him last night, but his sour mood seemed to dissipate when we got back to the house. He held me close to his chest while we talked into the night, sharing stories about high school.

"Okay, smile!" The photographer, a girl we went to high school with, takes a few shots, pointing and telling us to switch and squeeze together and make silly faces.

But I'm not in a silly mood.

My mother stands behind the photographer, smiling at us like she's in the picture herself. "Kendall, smile, please. Act happy."

"I am happy." I roll my eyes and put on the realest smile I can fashion. Except I'm not happy—I'm worried. Worried Sebastian is sulking somewhere and making this a bigger deal than it is.

"Okay," the photographer says while clapping her hands, "let's get some shots by the altar!"

Again, I smile as we stand at the front of the room, facing the pews that will soon be filled with guests. I smile as wide as I can while we take shot after shot, my mom pointing out all the angles she wants and how she wants us like she's the photographer.

But when I watch Sebastian walk toward the door with the phone to his ear, rubbing his head, my smile goes from wide to tight-lipped.

Then frowning at his disappearing figure.

CHAPTER 40

Sebastian

"You're in Alabama?" my mother screeches. I have to pull the phone away from my ear. "What the hell are you doing there? The wedding is today. Did you forget?"

I chuckle heartlessly. The fact that she thinks I could forget is laughable. Her thinking I was actually going to go is even more ludicrous.

That's Mom, though. Unaware of anything or anyone other than herself. Careless about anyone's feelings, believing we should bury them because it does no good to act on them. The world will always deal us bad hands like the dealer at a blackjack table. Sure, there's a lucky one here and there, but the dealer—the house—always wins.

Since Joelle, I've chosen to be happy with my rules and routine. This way the house—life—can't get me.

But right now, this last week, I'm ready to go back to my

angry tendencies and snap my phone in half. Partly because my mom is unbelievable, and partly because I shouldn't be here, with Kendall and her family. Not when she's clearly embarrassed by me.

After she walked away, her cousin asked me what I do for a living, and when I told him, he laughed. If he had just taken a drink, he'd have spit it out all over me.

When he saw I was serious, his laugh purposely turned into a cough, his hand to his chest like a little voice inside his head was yelling, *Abort! Abort!*

He walked away quickly and, I assume, told others, as they stared with wide eyes of disbelief at me until my mother called. I've never been ashamed or embarrassed by what I do, and these small-town rich kids can fuck off, but at that moment, I was glad my mother called.

For once, she rescued me.

"Why would I want to attend my ex-fiancée's wedding, Mother?" I hiss. "The same ex-fiancée who cheated on me with my—" I whirl around at the sound of a gasp behind me.

A gasp that at any other time I'd find endearing and sexy, but it's full of fear now.

Fear and shock.

"Sebastian, stop being a child," my mother continues while I stare at a wide-eyed Kendall. With the large church doors so expansive behind her, she looks small. Fragile even. Especially with that look of surprise on her face.

Unlike the strong woman I've come to know. And I've done this to her.

"Mom, I'll call you back." I hang up before I even finish

GEORGIA COFFMAN

the sentence and step toward her. "Kendall, I can explain."

"You were engaged before?" she whispers.

My heart stops at the way she shrinks into herself, wrapping her arms around her waist. "It was a long time ago, and that's not even the whole story. I never brought any of it up because it doesn't matter anymore. She's out of my life and mind. You're all I've been able to think about."

"Except now this woman is getting married, and it's bothering you. That's what's wrong, isn't it." She says it more like a statement, understanding washing over her. "That's why you were drunk last night when you showed up. Because you *haven't* been thinking about her," she spits, twisting her full lips in disgust and narrowing her eyes at me before she turns to leave.

I grab her arm. She has every right to be upset that I didn't tell her, but her tone and judgment piss me off. I'm not the one who has explaining to do. Joelle has nothing to do with what's really going on here. "Don't give me that look. You look like the rest of your family when I told them I'm a stripper."

She exhales and looks away like she's annoyed with this conversation.

"Why did you even bring me here? To make yourself feel better standing next to a stripper, make yourself feel like you have *your* shit together?" My jaw might finally break, along with the rest of me. History's repeating itself right in front of my eyes, and I can't stop it.

I can't stop what I know is coming.

She whips her head toward me, a strand of hair sticking to her lip gloss. She pulls it back so hard I think she might

250

rip it off her head. "If that were the case, I don't think having a stripper next to me would help."

"You can say what you want, but I actually like what I do." *Exactly what I said to Joelle only a year ago.* "That's why I went back to doing this. I did the corporate thing, the nine-to-five bullshit. Wasn't for me."

"Oh, cut the fucking crap already. Like your dream has always been dancing and getting naked for desperate housewives. You got slammed, knocked to the ground, and couldn't fucking get back up in the business world. Stop pretending everything's fine when—"

"You're right. I should stop seeing the good in everything. Especially you. I'll save myself a lot of heartache, right? Because you'll always be this stubborn, so stubborn you can't even muster up an apology to your sister, to finally fix things between you that happened, what, seven years ago?" I shake my head at her, looking down on her for the first time out of anger. "Instead, you've spent your whole adult life arguing with her like you're still in high school. Grow up."

The crack of her hand meeting my cheek echoes around us, suffocating us.

With one hand on her stomach like she's going to throw up, she covers her mouth with the other, tears in her eyes.

I watch her intently, trying to decide what else to say, but my whole body is shaking from anger. I turn away from her, done with the conversation. Done with this town that doesn't even have a CVS or a decent bar.

Done with Kendall, the girl I thought was different but wasn't. Wouldn't be the first time I've made the mistake of

trusting women I meet at shows.
But it'll damn well be my last.

CHAPTER 41

Kendall

I've never seen Sebastian so angry, but it was more than that. *Disappointed.* He was so disappointed.

In me.

In *us.*

And what's worse is that he's right. I'm twenty-three years old but still can't manage to have a mature conversation with my sister who used to be my best friend. Still haven't managed to find a career or anything I'm interested in, and I dropped out of college three years ago. Haven't even had a real boyfriend since Adam, which wasn't even a relationship, something that's never been clearer than it is now after being with Sebastian.

None of what I had with Adam was real, no matter how much I wanted it to be or how much I tried to convince myself it was.

The only real thing about it was the aftermath.

And the shell of myself that he left behind in his path of destruction. Even my shell is now cracking the longer I stare after Sebastian.

I've trapped myself in a cycle of self-destruction, and I can't find my voice or feeling in my legs to chase after him and make things right.

The door behind me creaks open as Sebastian essentially runs down the steps and rips his tie off, his back straining against his shirt. Even his muscles are angry at me.

"Kendall, there you are!" Elaine pulls my arm. "We're about to start."

I nod and walk robotically back into the church, not wanting to take my eyes off Sebastian. Not wanting this to be the last time I see him.

I make it through the ceremony and halfway through the reception with a forced smile on my face. I only run to the bathroom twice to cry, which took off half my makeup, but everyone's so focused on Lauren—as they should be— that they haven't noticed me.

At the reception, the bartender graciously hands me a cigarette, so I sneak off to where my mother won't find me. She'd actually strangle me if she knows I'm smoking, then try to get me to move back because "LA is a toxic environment." As if LA is the problem here.

Then I watch my sister and Rhett share their first dance, smiling at each other like they're the only ones in the room.

The sight makes me want to puke.

And the more time that passes, I move from devastated to flat-out pissed. Pissed that Sebastian didn't tell me about a major life event, then ditched me, and now I've had to deal with my family asking where he went, plus my extended family asking me why I'm still single with no kids at twenty-three like I'm actually sixty. I'm *pissed* at their small-town thinking that everyone should be married by now.

This small-town thinking is why I'm in this mess, why I felt the need to hide Sebastian in the first place.

And Adam. Stupid, fucking Adam, who still torments me long after he's gone. We haven't spoken in years, yet his presence still lingers, his harsh words playing on repeat in my mind.

Sam has checked on me four times like I found out I have some life-threatening disease, and I hate her pity. I hate all their pity.

Sebastian was supposed to make this weekend bearable, fun even. Play interference with the questions and pats on my shoulder with variations of "Don't worry, you'll find someone."

Instead, I get pity. Pity from everyone as they admire Lauren in all her lacy glory while I'm puffy-eyed and barefoot because even my Steven Madden strappy heels can't make me feel better.

Probably because my parents bought me those shoes, and now I can't enjoy them. They're tainted.

I exhale roughly, trying to release some of the tension and anger built up. Trying to be happy for Lauren.

Our feud isn't all my fault, contrary to what Sebastian might think. He doesn't know me, and I clearly don't know him.

He was engaged? And didn't think it was important to tell me, to share with me about his life?

For someone who's been so hell-bent on me sharing myself—mind, body, and soul—with him, he sure kept a lot to himself.

The thought angers me further.

"Whoa." Sam comes up and takes my bouquet from me. "There won't be any flowers left if you keep that up."

I look down at the petals falling around my feet like snow and realize I was picking off the petals in an angry game of *he loves me, he loves me not.*

He definitely loves me *not.*

"You making it?" Sam says, rubbing my back and frowning.

I grit my teeth. "I'm fine."

But all I can think about is Sebastian. It's my sister's wedding day, and all I can think about is that my own relationship—one that could've been the real thing—is over.

Over after only a few weeks.

This is why I don't get serious with guys. Why I never let them get too close. It always ends in heartbreak. And for the first time, I know what that feels like, to be aching from head to toe in complete devastation.

I angrily text him, but he doesn't respond. I go through the motions for the sake of my sister, dance with the other bridesmaids, take shots with the groomsmen. All my favorite songs play, and if Sebastian was here, he'd playfully tease me for my terrible rendition of "Havana" by Camila Cabello.

Toward the end of the reception, he still hasn't texted me.

A part of me didn't think he actually left, but he did.

Never came back, probably walked back to the house for his things. That's how badly he wanted to get away from me.

The longer he doesn't text and the more my mother smooths down my hair but coos at Lauren even though her hair is falling down at the sides, I want to explode.

"Where's your date?" Camden, Rhett's college friend and groomsman, asks. When we walked down the aisle together, he held me close and winked at his friends watching us. That irritated me, but him bringing up Sebastian is even worse in this moment.

But I smile as sweetly as I can, as I would've pre-Sebastian era, when things were just fun with no strings or feelings attached. "What date?"

"That's what I like to hear." He takes my hand and spins me around toward the dance floor. He scans me up and down, and I realize my mistake.

I'm angry at Sebastian, but I don't want Camden to take his place. "Actually, I had too many tequila shots. Probably shouldn't be spinning." I giggle like I used to when playing up my femininity. Guys love it, and Camden is no different. Only Sebastian was immune.

Camden begs me to stay longer, but I pull away.

I'm still close enough to hear him mumble, "Tease."

I drop the sweet-as-honey smile, place my hands on my hips, and feel the familiar rage rumbling in the pit of my stomach. "What the fuck did you say?"

He holds his hands up and backs away from me without explanation.

I stare him down the whole time, the rage building inside me.

I need another shot.

Except I take three and wink at the bartender when I'm done. He's smiling at me, and in another life, we'd be making out in the back, groping each other before the night was over.

Instead, I slide off the barstool on wobbly legs. I put my shoes back on when I got off the dance floor, but they're not worth it. The minute I take them off again and set them on the floor, my mother orders, "Put your shoes back on. We're not animals."

I blink at her. "Where did you come from?"

"What?"

"You're like a ninja. Were you actually waiting in the bushes for me to take my shoes off? To let me know that you're disappointed yet again?"

She grabs me rather firmly by the arm and turns me to face her head-on. "Are you drunk?"

I throw my hand up, still holding my shoes. They shine midair, and I'm mesmerized by them. The shining lights in this dark night.

My mom shakes me again, so I answer, "It's a wedding, isn't it? Don't people drink here? *Jesus.*" The last word comes out more like *cheez-us*, which makes me laugh.

But my mother doesn't think it's funny. "Do not use the Lord's name in vain." She grits her teeth but strains a smile to the guests. A few come up and thank her for a wonderful night, but they have to take off since it's getting late, and "Mary Jane just *has* to get to bed, bless her heart."

I wave at them princess-style, fingers glued together and cupped. Then I giggle like I did in middle school when

Emma and I got caught sniffing markers because I'd seen a guy doing it on TV. At the time, the guy seemed cool in his leather jacket, so I thought sniffing markers was cool. Emma didn't forgive me for a whole week for getting her in trouble.

"Go splash some water on your face." My mother keeps up appearances as she manhandles me behind her back.

Nod.

Wave.

Tight-lipped smile.

It's almost enough to tell her how I really feel. "What I need is to splash my face with more tequila." I wave at the hot bartender with wavy hair. He nods at me and smiles, and I move toward him like his dimples are calling to me.

But my mother follows and glares at him.

Worst wingman ever.

Shaking her head so hard her hair flaps around her shoulders—as much as the hairspray will allow, anyway—she says to him, "Do *not* give her any more. Can't you see she's hammered like a teenager at prom?"

That makes me laugh. *Hard.*

I snort and lay my head on the cool surface of the bar. More guests come by to say their goodbyes, while my mom basically lifts my head up by my hair like my body isn't attached to it.

Although several guests have left, there are still plenty littering the dance floor. "We have to do the sparklers before everyone leaves. Then you're going home to sleep this off." My mom licks her finger and wipes at my mouth. "Your lipstick is smudged." Then she smooths my hair down *again.* For the hundredth time, at least. "That hairdresser should've curled your hair with a smaller curling iron, and she definitely should've used more hairspray. When was the last time you got a trim?"

Now that's enough to make me snap.

I swat at her hand, ready to explode when Lauren comes up, pulling us to the side of the bar and through the hallway where we can't see anyone.

Or more importantly, where they can't see us.

"What're you two doing?" she hisses. "People were staring!"

Lauren's been dancing and kissing Rhett like they don't have the rest of their lives to do that. Like if she doesn't kiss him nonstop right at this moment, she won't survive. And yet, she still looks flawless.

Her lipstick isn't the least bit smudged. Hair is perfectly pinned in place, save for a few strays on the sides. And she smells like she just walked out of a spa, fresh and citrusy.

She looks perfectly put together, while I apparently look as though I ran through a car wash without a car.

That pisses me off even more as I run my fingers through my matted curls.

"Honey, everything's fine," my mother coos again, gripping Lauren gently by the shoulders. "Go back and enjoy dancing. I'm just helping Kendall freshen up. We'll be out in a jiffy."

Lauren exhales and relaxes at my mother's soothing tone. But then her rage returns when she looks at me. Her eyes narrow, and she grits her teeth. "While you're physically freshening up, can you check your attitude at the front desk too? You've been a moody bitch all night."

"Now, Lauren," my mom starts, and my shoulders relax, relieved she's here to mediate. That finally, my mother won't go along with everything Lauren says and does. That she'll stick up for *me* for once. "No need for language, but Kendall, honey, you have been moody. I know that boy left, but this is your sister's wedding. You can pretend to want to be part of this day and this family for a couple hours, mm-hmm?"

So much for sticking up for me.

No, instead she twists the knife in my heart that Sebastian left me just hours ago.

That he's not returning my texts.

That I'll probably never see him again.

My mom and Lauren watch me, searching my eyes for any sign of cooperation. Or for any sign that I'm a bomb about to go off.

This family always gangs up on me like I'm a train wreck in need of their assistance, like I can't handle myself. And it all fuels my anger further, something I've gotten used to tamping down since the incident that ended Adam and me for good.

The alcohol, the anger that Sebastian abandoned me, my mom and sister ambushing me about *my* poor attitude when all they do is point out my flaws?

Oh hell *no.*

Then I do something I haven't done since Lauren and I were in middle school and she stole my favorite hoodie.

I lurch forward and take her down by her pretentious updo.

CHAPTER 42

Sebastian

On the plane back to San Francisco, I order three drinks and stare out the window at the dark sky. Only thing visible is the light flashing on the wing.

I take another sip of my Jack Daniels and let it burn the back of my throat unflinchingly, the same way I did on the way to Alabama. Except that had been for an entirely different reason. I at least had Kendall's smiling face and soft skin to look forward to then.

Now I only have a hotel room shared with Ty waiting for me.

While my ex is happily married by now, with many of the same guests we would've invited to our own wedding to witness it all. She probably even used the same list.

I finish the rest of my drink in one gulp and fight the urge to bang my head against the window.

I can't believe I was so stupid to fall for it again. To fall for a girl from the show. To get clobbered like I'm the mole in Whack-A-Mole. I'm quick, but I can only outrun the same scenario so many times before the hammer comes down on me, embarrassing me for not getting away quickly enough.

For getting attached to someone who's ashamed of me.

Guess I can't beat myself up too much. It's easy to get lost in eyes as big as Kendall's and her girl-next-door southern accent.

Images of having her on top of me, coming undone unhindered and unapologetically, invade my senses. Her whimpers, vanilla scent—everything consumes me.

I should be going through round 457 with her right now in a secluded corner of that reception.

Instead, I groan and hide my growing hard-on before I order yet another drink, alone.

I'm alone.

Just me and Jack Daniels.

I'm barely able to request an Uber from the airport, my phone screen blurry.

And still on airplane mode. I switch it off, then pull up the Uber app once more.

As I climb into the car moments later, my phone vibrates with incoming messages, but instead of checking them, I let the driver make mundane conversation about his kid starting Little League in the fall.

When we get to the hotel, I knock and then wait outside Ty's room, but no one comes to the door. I pace down the hall with my duffel bag, ready to set up shop on the paisley carpet, when the door flies open.

"Hey, man—" I stop when I see Ty's naked with a pillow over his gems. "I can come back, or maybe I'll just shack up with Leo."

Out of breath, he looks up and down the hall. "Dude, what're you doing here?"

"I texted you I was on my way back hours ago. You answered me!"

He shrugs, closing the door behind him when we hear a soft plea from inside for Ty to come back to bed. Ignoring it, he asks, "What about Kendall? I thought you were both coming back, like maybe the wedding was a snoozefest and you wanted to have some real fun." He wiggles his eyebrows. "Away from her family's prying eyes."

I give him a tight-lipped smile and change the subject. "I'll just call Leo. Have fun tonight."

"Whoa, whoa. Talk to me, player."

"Don't think I'm the player here." I point back and forth between us and tilt my head toward the room.

"She's a flight attendant. You know how I like my women in button-ups and tiny scarves." He winks, making me feel gross. The idea of a one-night stand depresses me at this point.

"Night, man."

He fist-bumps me and flashes his bare ass on his way back in the room. Squeals follow me onto the elevator next to his room. My finger hovers over Leo's name on my phone, but instead of dialing, I close out of it and lean my head on the elevator wall.

When the door opens, I continue through the marble

lobby, past plush cream couches with gold throw pillows. One wall is full of mirrors, where my disheveled hair and bloodshot eyes reflect back at me.

I hoist my duffel bag farther onto my shoulder and request another Uber to take me out of here.

When I reach the beach, I set my bag on the sandy ground and take off my shoes, Kendall's words echoing in my head as I walk along the cold water.

I had dreams once.

They didn't involve me taking my clothes off for money.

I wanted to be a businessman—that's why I got my business degree. I'd known it since I was in high school. Although they tend to have long hours, businesses are more stable than stripping.

I wanted a stable life for a family.

To provide a stable life that I never got growing up.

Kendall doesn't understand. Her family may give her shit, but they do it because they care. They want the best for her.

Pisses me off that she doesn't get it.

But it pisses me off more that I didn't admit to her that she was right, about more than the stripping. She was right about Joelle too, but not for the reasons she thinks.

I want to own my own hotel. I meant it that night I took her to the empty lot. I made love to her in the middle of it. I had everything that night—a bright future.

But it's all crashing down.

And I know where I need to start to put it back together.

CHAPTER 43

Kendall

On the plane back to LA, I rest my head against the back of my seat, scrolling through my Instagram newsfeed. Trying to escape. Wanting to forget about this weekend.

Except I find Samantha Ray's new posts I missed from the last hellish few days.

They're all of her at the gym and videos of her workouts. She's naturally beautiful, with the body to match. But what I like about her isn't that she's just cute and fit on the outside, but she's honest and open about her struggles. How she falls off the wagon with her diet sometimes, how she often goes through a rut with her workouts. It's all part of the process.

Her post now is of her at Venice Beach with a caption that talks about doing the fitness thing from the inside out. Exercising for the mental and emotional benefits as well as the physical.

That's what being a fitness influencer is about to me: being inspiring to others. Which is why I haven't fully pursued such a thing.

I'm not inspiring.

I'm a fuckup with nothing to offer.

I turn my phone off and close my eyes, my heart sinking at the familiar voice in my head telling me I'm not worth shit, especially after this weekend. After ruining my sister's wedding.

Rhett had to pull me off her, after which a few guests rushed over to the embarrassing scene. In my drunken state, I'd found satisfaction in the fact that I finally smudged Lauren's lipstick, tousled her hair, and scratched her arms. She looked more like a zombie bride for Halloween than a princess on her wedding day.

But now? Now I want to vomit from the hangover and from my behavior. Both of which I got a good lecture for from my parents. My dad's a quiet man, hardly speaks since my mother does enough talking for the both of them.

But he wasn't quiet last night. Far from it.

"When are you going to grow up?" my parents said, repeating the same words Sebastian spat at me before he walked down the steps of the church and out of my life.

Those words play over and over as a drink cart bumps into the back of my seat. I scowl, thinking that could've been my elbow, but the flight attendant lightly touches my shoulder. I turn and see her red hair twisted on top of her head. She's an older woman with high cheekbones and red lipstick, a nostalgic vibe in her soft expression. "I'm so sorry, sweetie. I didn't get you, did I?"

I shake my head at her, regretting that I wanted to say "fuck you" just seconds before. "I'm fine, really."

She nods and asks if I want anything to drink. I order a Diet Coke, still feeling guilty as she continues down the aisle.

It was an accident, and I was rude about it.

What happened to me?

I used to be nice, right?

I think back to high school, before my bad choices got me thrown in jail for a night, before I made out with Lauren's boyfriend, before Adam tore me down and left only a shell in its place. Before he took away my self-esteem and confidence, both of which I've been searching for in all the wrong places ever since then.

I think back to when I had friends—real friends who looked out for me instead of plotted my demise. When I got asked to dances by the neighbor's son who wore a bow tie and opened my doors.

Fast-forward to after the incident with Lauren's boyfriend. Being so close in age, we hung out together and with the same friends. After she caught me making out with her boyfriend, they picked sides, and only Emma stuck by mine.

The others didn't believe me when I said I had good intentions, to expose the lying bastard.

After that, I only got asked to the dances by guys in leather jackets and Converses who asked to borrow a cigarette, then left the dance with other girls.

Lauren and her minions would laugh, but Emma was always there to pick up the pieces.

Even though she was dealing with her mother's alcoholism after her dad remarried, she stuck by my side and listened to me.

I need her now, so when I find her waiting at the airport for me, I all but run toward her. I'm ready to take her small frame down with me, but she holds me upright.

Like she always does.

For whatever reason, the sturdy hug she gives me, which is rare for her and her aversion to physical contact, makes me cry the tears I was holding onto the whole way here.

She doesn't say anything, just helps me carry my bags toward the car. And when I get out into the LA sun, cars whizzing by, palm trees swaying in the light breeze, I'm home.

It feels more like home than entering my small Alabama town with the deteriorating Welcome sign. The letters for "Small town with a big heart" are fading and sad, not inviting as the slogan might suggest.

But as we pass the large metal LAX letters surrounded by plush greenery, I know I'm home.

All that's missing is that I was supposed to be coming back with Sebastian. He was supposed to stay the night here before meeting the guys in San Francisco.

We were supposed to have one more night together, one to ourselves.

Emma doesn't ask about him, which I appreciate. I told her before I got on my flight that he left early. Instead of talking about him, she tells me stories of her Pilates class, of a guy who attended to impress his obviously new lady friend. He watched her the whole time with the look of puppy love and missed the next move. Fell right on his face.

I chuckle but feel a sting that this guy would go through a Pilates class for a girl he barely knew. Sebastian couldn't even make it through a whole day with my family and me.

When we arrive at our apartment, I toss my lilac leather backpack onto the floor and face-plant onto the couch.

Emma shuts the door and sits at the kitchen table. "Are we going to talk about it now or later?"

I inhale and strain my neck to see out the window at the setting sun. "Let's go out. I have the night off already, anyway."

"So later, then."

"I'll tell you on the way." I jump up and head toward my room, muttering, "I need a drink."

CHAPTER 44

Sebastian

I jog around the corner and head back to the hotel, sweat dripping from my hair onto my bare shoulders.

"Congratulations on your wedding," I said to her last night.

I'd pulled my phone out and dialed a number I'd called too many times to count, one I knew by heart, even though I didn't want to admit it.

And when she answered, I wasn't prepared to hear her voice.

It was happy.

Joyful.

Like that of a newlywed.

While I sat on the empty bench with waves crashing a few yards away. The occasional car honking in the distance. Alone.

Her happiness was a punch to my gut.

"Hello?" Joelle said again, in her singsong voice that I hadn't heard in months.

When I congratulated her and she realized who I was, she scoffed and cursed me. It stung, but I wasn't surprised. Not at all surprised that she'd forgotten my number and me altogether.

I put my shirt back on as I enter the lobby, careful not to run into the small family of four as they roll their luggage out. We have a show tonight, and I need to be on my game. I can't let the guys down, but the jog wasn't enough to clear my head.

I knew it was a bad idea to call Joelle last night. I almost said as much, but she cut me off, as usual. I could never get a word in with her around. "Why are you calling, Sebastian?" Her voice was soft, taking pity on me even.

I exhaled and paced in front of the bench. All I could hear were the waves crashing behind me, like the blood rushing to my ears as I figured out how to say what I needed to say. Why I felt I had to call her to begin with. "Why did you leave? We were happy at some point, right? Tell me the truth."

She didn't hesitate, like she had the words sitting on the tip of her tongue all this time, just waiting to unleash them on me. "We were happy, Seb. Until you lost your drive."

"What?"

"Your drive. You lost your will to do anything worthwhile. You left the hotel business you had with your uncle when it got tough. When you had to make hard decisions, you went running back to Naked Heat. It's always been your comfort zone."

"You always hated that I was a stripper." I shook my head at the surreal feeling to be having any conversation with her. I never thought I'd see or hear from her again, even if she did just marry someone very close to me.

Someone who *used* to be close to me, anyway.

"No, I didn't like you being a stripper. Sorry, I thought you were better than that, but—"

"Don't talk down about it. Those guys are the best I've ever known. At least they're decent human beings, unlike the bastard currently sharing your bed."

"Is that why you really called? You're still mad about Sid?"

"I don't give a fuck about him."

"That's convincing." I imagined her rolling her eyes. "What I was going to say was that I thought you were better than to purposely steer away from a challenge to go back to your comfort zone like a child."

"I didn't steer away. Your jackass of a husband fucked me over."

"You talked about going back to stripping long before the incident."

"That's what you're calling it now? An incident? Or is that what he said to make himself look better? What a tool." I chuckled humorlessly.

"My fucking point is that you're the one who lost interest in the business, even though I knew you really loved it. Instead of being the responsible business partner, you'd go in late after being out all night with your stripper buddies, like you never left. You clung to them and your safety zone like a security blanket. It was sickening."

I get in line to order a smoothie now, my gut tightening as nausea consumes me. Joelle's words replay in my head like there's no stop button.

She was right.

Everything she said last night—she was right about me.

The realization hits me like cold water splashing my face.

I did steer away from a challenge. From a change. I got used to Naked Heat after five years with them. I didn't know how to be anything other than a dancer, so I went back.

Last night, when I didn't answer, Joelle continued, defeated, "Sid saw it too. Got worried you'd be a liability instead of an asset. You should really talk to him."

"He should've talked to me first like a man, instead of fucking my fiancée behind my back." I hung up, never taking my eyes off the water.

I was scared—*terrified*—of taking a risk on my own business. When Sid offered to help, I jumped at the chance. I trusted him. But the fear never went away that I was failing, even after almost a year of running our small hotel. Naked Heat was the easier option, and I was good at it. It was easy.

And when I saw Sid and Joelle kissing in our driveway, I didn't hesitate to resume my old dancing position.

Nor did I hesitate to punch him in the nose and never speak to him again.

Although I was to blame for my own insecurities, Joelle had no right to do what she did. I don't forgive her for that, but I'm starting to forgive her for calling off our wedding.

She did me a favor, anyway, in more ways than one. We were wrong for each other in the end. The way she made the decisions without me should've been my first clue that she was more concerned about making wedding arrangements than life plans with me. We would've realized it sooner or later that we weren't meant to be.

With smoothie in hand, I walk back outside. Opening my phone, I read the texts from Kendall I got last night, cursing me to Hell. Instead of being angry, I smile at her audacity. Her intensity when she lets go is something I'll always admire about her.

After talking with Joelle, I feel lighter. Lighter than I have in a long time, like I needed that closure. Her reasoning as to why I wasn't good enough.

Why I wasn't enough for her.

That's what was holding me back. I needed the closure in order to move on with Kendall and go all in.

I'm about to call her, this overwhelming need to hear her voice consuming me, but Jordan jogs up with Leo in tow. "Hey, we need to do some last-minute prep. I have an idea how we can amp up the excitement for the ending of tonight's show. Come up with us."

I clutch my phone tightly as I reluctantly nod.

On the way up, my fingers itch to dial Kendall's number, my body on fire knowing I have to wait.

To wait to tell her I'm over my ex.

That I'm over the past and want a future.

With her.

CHAPTER 45

Kendall

I take a sip of my third drink and bob my head to the music. Resting my elbows on the bar, I stick out my chest as I scan the crowd. I wasn't planning on rebound sex tonight, but my buzz has me considering those options.

Emma advised me against it because, of course, she knew what I was thinking before I even said it.

She at least agreed with me that Sebastian was an asshole, but she wasn't too eager to defend me. Instead, she had "I told you" written all over her smirk. It was visible even in the dark Uber.

Which pissed me off.

"Margo and George are on their way," Emma shouts at me over her martini. "They'll make you laugh."

Eyeing a hot guy on the other side of the bar, I answer, "But I have you to do that."

She snorts. "Yeah right. Now I know you're drunk." She points to my drink. "Maybe you should slow down."

"Maybe I'll speed up and run over to that hot-as-fuck guy." I smile at him and take a sip through my straw, taking extra time as I close my lips over it. Which gets his attention.

And after all my texts to Sebastian have gone unanswered since last night, I need some attention.

"Hey," says a deep voice to my side, but it's not the guy I was flirting with from across the room. "You never called."

"Excuse me?"

"I gave you my number weeks ago, and you never called."

His smile and bald head look familiar, but I can't place him.

"From the gym? I'm Rob." He steps closer to me as people move around us.

I shake his hand and suddenly remember giving his number to Emma when I got home from the gym that morning. "Of course." I put on the charm. I've been out of the game for only a few weeks. A few weeks where I let my guard down with Sebastian. But I can do it. I reverted to my old ways at the reception so seamlessly, I can do it again now. "I'm such a stupid, stupid girl." I place my empty glass on the bar. "Let me make it up to you?"

He opens his mouth, but nothing follows.

Now I remember him very clearly—the beefhead who can't flirt.

But he's sexy in a Joe Rogan kind of way, so I lead him to a quiet corner where I'm hoping to test his kissing ability. And hoping he doesn't fail.

"Thought we could use some quiet." I wink as I lean my back against the wall.

"Yeah… I like… quiet."

"I bet you do." I run my hand through my hair, waiting for him to make a move, when my phone goes off in my hand. It's Emma calling.

"You need to get that?"

"No. It's just my roommate." I play it off with a wave of my hand, but a sinking feeling overcomes me. Especially when she calls a second time.

But I ignore it again as he pulls me closer—she's probably just trying to stop me from myself.

Before he can kiss me, I panic. Placing both hands on his chest, I push him back. "Maybe we should just talk some more." But I didn't even want to do that. Suddenly I felt icky. Even being in his presence made me nauseated.

Then Margo appears as if out of the walls and grabs my arm. "We need you! Emma just left."

Confused, I let her walk me away from… *what's his name?* "So what if she left?"

"She ran into her ex-boyfriend or something? Got all flustered and stormed out." She shrugs, but her eyebrows are furrowed, concerned for our mutual friend.

There's only one ex she could be talking about, but I ask to make sure. "Brant?"

She shrugs again. "That'd make sense. I don't think anyone else could've gotten that kind of reaction out of her. She was almost in tears."

Understanding settles deep in my chest. If Emma ran into Brant, after all this time of no word or interaction from him, she'll be a mess. I need to get to her.

I nod at Margo. "I'll go home and check on her. You stay with George, have fun." I give her a small, reassuring smile before calling an Uber.

I call Emma on my way home, but it goes to voice mail. I kick at the floor of the car like it's Brant's face. The motherfucker broke up with her after she caught him in bed with a woman from his real-estate agency.

After Emma moved across the country for him. Gave up everything for him. And then, not even two months after she got out here, he left her broken.

Even the thought gets me angry, so angry for my friend and her broken soul.

And I'm even angrier that I wasn't there to smash his skull into the ground and squeeze his nuts off.

I clench and unclench my fists the whole way to our apartment, my temper ready to explode like it did at my sister's wedding, which was the first time since Adam. I try to control my breathing, my nostrils flaring to the point of physical pain.

By the time I make it inside, I'm still riled up, adrenaline coursing through me at a much higher rate than it does while I'm at the gym. Breathlessly, I open Emma's bedroom door without knocking. "Emma? Hey, it's me."

"I don't want to talk to you." Her voice is muffled by the comforter raised up to her eyes.

I'm just about to close the door to give her some privacy, but the way she said "to you" makes the hairs on the back of my neck stand up. *What does that mean?* "Emma, what happened?"

She sits up like a vampire in her coffin after coming back to life. "I'll tell you what happened. Hmm." I can see her, even in the dim lighting, put her finger to her lips sarcastically. "My so-called friend—that's you—asks me to go out with her. Asks me even though she knows I have an early class tomorrow, and I want a good night's sleep because I'm responsible. But she begs me to anyway like she always does, and I go because she needs a fun night out." Then her tone changes to a very serious, non-sarcastic one. "Then she disappears completely to go stick her tongue down a random stranger's throat."

Shocked that she didn't mention anything about Brant or anyone else, just *me*, that *I'm* her problem, I start stammering. "What? That's what... you're upset about?"

"Yes," she seethes. And if the light were completely on, I bet I could see her red cheeks, like the way she gets angry when the TV is left on all night. Or when I don't clean the blender right after I use it.

I hold my arms out in my defense. "I was only gone for a second."

"*Please*. You ditched me the minute we got there. The only reason I went was to try to cheer you up. So much for a girls' night."

"Oh, cut the shit. We were out to have fun. Sorry, if my idea of fun actually involves hooking up and doing grown-up things." Pissed, I storm out of her room in a huff and into my own, slamming the door behind me. All my anger toward Brant, Sebastian, my life—it's all redirected toward the one person I thought was on my side no matter what.

And now she's turned on me.

I hear footsteps stomping before my door swings open. "Grown-up? You want to talk about being an adult? *Ha!* Like you know anything about that. You can't even wash a blender on your own."

"Get over the damn blender, seriously. I wash it when I get home from work. Not a big deal."

"So typical of you. Nothing is a big deal to you. Just continue going out, having a bunch of sex, and forget about responsibility. Go on living your easy life while the rest of us are, in fact, adults."

"I don't know what the fuck your problem is, but get out of my room. Go take a fucking Midol, or better yet, a tequila shot. Make it seven." I fold my arms across my chest. Can't believe I rushed home thinking she needed to be consoled for running into her own nightmare. I wouldn't have bothered if I knew this shit storm was waiting for me.

Emma walks out, but just as quickly comes back in. "You know, this is what your mom, Lauren, Sebastian— what everyone is talking about. You think the world revolves around you, and it doesn't."

I open and close my mouth, the anger inside replaced with hurt.

Because that stings.

The words about my family *sting*.

Emma knows better than anyone what my family is like and the hell they always give me. So for her to take their side now?

It fucking stings.

And mentioning Sebastian's name makes it all worse.

"Too far, Emma."

"Oh, did that hurt your feelings? That they actually have a point? That it's not them, it's *you*?"

Tears prick my eyes, ready to spill over, as she slams my door shut. The horrid weekend, my family, Sebastian, and now Emma? The way she looked at me? It's all too much. I have no words. I have nothing to say to her.

Because she's right.

They're all right about me. I'm a disappointment.

And the realization has me crawling into bed like a wounded puppy.

Defeated.

When my phone lights up with incoming texts and calls, I don't bother to look. No one and nothing can change the way I feel at this moment.

Not even Adam made me feel this low. Not even all the times he made fun of my outfits or my accent.

Not even when he repeatedly called me a psycho.

Not even when he said he wanted nothing to do with me, after I told him I loved him.

No, I'm at my lowest point now. And as I let the tears fall, my pillow soaked, I don't know how I'll resurface.

I can't sleep. I can already feel a headache settling in.

I can't stop thinking about the way Emma's voice cracked and the way her eyes watered while she looked at me as though she didn't recognize me.

I turn over so I'm facing the window, the moon nowhere

in sight, the streetlight outside too dim.

Darkness surrounds me.

I check my phone and see it's almost 4:00 a.m. I have several missed calls and texts from Sebastian, but my stomach rolls at the thought of talking to him.

At the same time, my heart lurches toward the phone, needing him to comfort me. He's the only one who can, the only one who makes me comfortable enough to do so.

But the way he looked at me in front of the church sinks in. His cold, dark eyes that sent cold shivers down my back like I was the worst person he'd ever met.

I spent my whole adult life trying to make sure I did everything I could to make my parents proud. Turns out, not only have I disappointed them, but I've also made my friends and Sebastian—someone who could've been my future—hate me.

The need to yell at him mixed with wanting to hear his soothing laugh have me calling him back. Even now in the middle of the night. The worst that can happen is that he doesn't answer.

Or worse, he does.

"Hello?" His voice is clear, and something else…

Pained.

I inhale, imagining his cologne washing over me like it did so many times when he slept with me in this bed. "Stop calling me," I whisper, and I hate my own weak voice. It doesn't sound like mine at all.

"Kendall, let me explain," he pleads as shuffling sounds from the background, and then I hear silence. It's so silent on the other end, I think I hear his heart beating. He sounds desperate, yet his voice is firm and confident, like him. No matter the situation, he's always been confident, something I'm not. "I was a complete jackass. I shouldn't have lashed out at you."

After having been yelled at earlier, it's a relief to have someone speak gently and apologetically. I burst into tears.

"Kendall, please forgive me. Please forgive me, and believe me when I say I didn't tell you about Joelle because it was a fucked-up situation, and I didn't want to bring you into it." He pauses, my involuntary hiccup filling the gap. He mutters a curse. "I want to see you. I want to hold you and explain and apologize profusely with my words, my mouth. I want to kiss you everywhere."

"Stop calling me," I repeat, unable to say anything else. I can't let his words take hold of my heart. I have to distance myself from him if I want to do what he and everyone else thinks I need to—grow up.

He's an unrealistic future for me.

Everything is against us—our distance, our pasts, our present demons.

"I'm going to call you tomorrow. I'm going to keep calling until I can convince you we're meant to be together."

Another sob escapes me, and I sink farther into my pillow with the covers pulled over my head. Before I run out of here and drive to San Francisco to see him, before I can take seven steps backward when I should be moving forward, I say something I know will get him to back off, no matter how immature it might be. "We're not meant to be. None of it was real. It was only good sex. That's all."

"You don't mean that."

"It was the best I ever had. And now I know what it should be like, thanks to you." My voice is distant, the words not registering. Like I'm not speaking them. And the minute they leave my mouth, I want to take them back.

To apologize and beg to see him.

But I end the call instead.

I only want to run to him because everyone else close to me isn't speaking to me. They're all mad at me, and I'm alone.

And it seems I'm going to be that way for a long time.

Because I need to grow up. To stop making excuses for my failures, when I'm the only one to blame.

But tonight... tonight I wallow in my tears. For now, I allow myself to grieve, from the heartache of what was and what could've been.

CHAPTER 46

Sebastian

The line goes dead, and my heart stills along with it.

I lost her.

The one girl who made me want to love again. And she's gone.

The girl on the phone just now didn't even sound like my Kendall, my feisty, confident Kendall. The girl I knew who fought passionately.

She sounded off. Defeated. Like a lightbulb that gives out, no more electricity running through it. I could hear it in her voice, the way it whispered with fear.

How badly I want to take away her fear and give her light once again.

"It was only good sex."

Her words rip me apart, and I have a hard time believing them. She always seemed to have fun even when we weren't in bed, with our laughs and conversations.

I refuse to believe she meant it. That it's over.

I refuse to believe I misjudged the situation once again.

I'm going to keep my promise and call her tomorrow. The wounds are too fresh right now from the hectic weekend. A good night's sleep for both of us will provide the clarity for her to see this isn't over.

It can't be.

CHAPTER 47

Kendall

My phone buzzing on the nightstand wakes me out of my stupor. I lift my head from where my face is planted in the pillow. At first, all I can think about is my headache from drinking and not going to sleep until after five o'clock.

The ache reaches every part of my body.

The buzzing persists, like Lauren's screeching when she gets her Mary Kay products in the mail.

Lauren.

Emma.

Sebastian.

All the people I've disappointed in my life, not to mention my parents. The worst of the worst disappointments. Is there a Guinness World Record for the number of disappointments you can achieve? I need that award. It'd be the only award I'm capable of.

Emma's words attacking my immaturity surround me like my comforter. It's a hundred degrees in here, and this blanket is suffocating me.

I kick it off just in time for my phone to ring again. I snap it off the nightstand and sit up. "What?" I growl with more rage than I did when Dr. Shepherd was killed off *Grey's Anatomy*, my reaction to that about as bad as when I purposely cracked my ex's windshield.

"I was engaged before."

I rub my eyes at the familiar low voice on the other end of the line. The one I still imagine humming against my inner thighs. The sound and subsequent feelings haunted me all night. "I got that, Sebastian."

"I was engaged before, and she left me because I was a stripper, so I overreacted when I thought you were embarrassed by it. Well, that's not technically the main reason she left—"

My patience wears thin with every word. "I don't care why you overreacted, okay? I need you to leave me alone." I breathe in and out the way I learned in yoga, the whole reason I started it in the first place   to calm my temper.

He exhales in frustration on the other end. "I wish I was there. I need to explain."

"Don't you get it? There's nothing to explain or to work out. We were never meant to have more than that one night in Vegas. Never should've tried to make it more than that. It's all been fucked up since then." I fall back onto my bed with my legs dangling off the edge.

"Don't say that. I don't believe it."

"God, Sebastian." I cover my face with one hand, my

anger turning into despair. Despair that he's trying so hard. I can hear the sincerity in his voice. He believes in us, but we were doomed from the beginning, from the first night we shared.

I rummage through the drawers of my nightstand, sure that I have half a pack of cigarettes in here somewhere. "I'm a small-town girl, you know? I know I try to tell others differently, but I am," I say, defeated, embracing my past as my fate with every word. "I'm a small-town girl. I don't date Vegas strippers. Guys who make a living out of undressing and teasing women. Who live this crazy fucking lifestyle touring the country, appearing in women's calendars, in their fucking wet dreams. This is all on another level for me, and I can't do it."

"You might be from a small town, but you're not the small-minded person you think you are, the one you believe your sister to be. You moved to LA. You wouldn't have done it if you were okay with living the small-town, average life. Don't give me that bullshit. Tell me what's really bothering you, why you're pushing me away."

I squeeze my eyes shut, a single tear running down my cheek. I picture him holding my hands as if he were here, pleading with big eyes.

I find the pack of cigarettes and lighter as he says, "You're scared. You're scared of something real in your life, of someone accepting and loving the real you. You haven't had that, and you're fucking scared because I'm offering all of that to you." He exhales and softly speaks. "I know what that's like. I've lived my whole life that way. Give us a chance. Accept us."

He had me there—all of it. Everything he's saying is true. I *am* scared. Scared of my strong feelings for him, of letting someone really see me because I've never felt that I could before. I'm scared he won't want the real me, the one who got into fights, dropped out of college, and now has no future.

I'm exactly what everyone says: *a failure.*

"You're right, I am scared," I say, lighting my cigarette with trembling fingers, then sit at the desk by the window. Emma hates when I smoke in here, and I don't need to give her another reason to yell at me. "I have a lot to figure out for myself, and that doesn't involve you. Not right now, and I don't know if it ever will."

Instead of getting defensive per usual, I give up.

I just give up.

Then I hang up and wonder if that was the first sign of growth.

But the ache in my chest suggests it's still a sign of my immaturity, of being unable to face my insecurities and be honest with him about them. All of them. He's been nothing but welcoming when I open up to him. He even encourages it.

Yet I push him away. I find any excuse, real or fake, to push him away.

Instead of calling him back and apologizing, begging him to take me back like I really want to, I put out my cigarette and curl into a ball on my bed.

I close my eyes, closing myself off to him and the rest of the world.

CHAPTER 48

Sebastian

I send my mom's call to voice mail. It's the first time she's called since the wedding, but I don't have it in me to talk to her.

Pacing the living room, I eye the hole in the wall and recall punching it after Joelle came to pick up her things.

I want to punch it again now.

I tried for almost two weeks to get over losing Kendall. Her smell. Her taste.

I've gone almost a whole month without feeling her skin against mine. Without making love to her. That's what it always was, even when it was raw and hungry.

But I convinced myself that she was right—I wasn't supposed to have her in the first place.

We weren't supposed to see each other after we met in Vegas. It was only supposed to be a one-night stand.

But I pursued her.

I found and added her on Facebook.

I'm the one who pushed her to make us an *us*.

I did it again. Made myself believe a woman was into me for *me*, when all the signs suggested otherwise.

She didn't even tell her best friend about me other than *I was the best she'd ever had.*

That's it. That's what she said to her.

Then she said it to me too, as a reason *not* to be with me.

And it fucking broke me.

I open and close my fists by my sides. The urge to insert a matching hole next to the one already on the wall overwhelms me the more I think about her. Grinding my jaw, I continue pacing, watching the hole as it mocks me, needing to make another one so all the Pinterest fanatics out there will be happy I have a matching set.

Instead, I clasp my fingers together across the back of my neck while another familiar urge creeps to the surface.

The urge to drink. A lot.

Enough to block the image of Kendall's bare ass sticking out as she bent over for me.

I'm going to need a shit ton of Jack Daniels.

Picking up my phone, I call the one person I know will be up for a drinking contest on a Wednesday night.

"What's up, bro?" Ty answers on the second ring.

"Meet me at Pete's in five." I hang up and grab my keys off the counter, but my trembling hands drop them. I pick them up, but my phone slips out of my pocket and falls to the floor. Instead of picking it up, I squeeze my eyes closed, jaw clenched, and stomp on it.

The screen cracks like the pieces of my life.

The smell of stale leather assaults me as soon as I walk into Pete's. The step at the door has caused me to stumble a time or two, but it doesn't fool me this time. No, I step over it with caution, taking extra care to make sure I don't fall on my face.

I scan the bar, its familiarity surrounding me. Like Hakaasan and other clubs on the Strip, I haven't been here in a while.

Tonight, though… tonight I drink.

I laugh.

I *forget*.

I relish in the old country music, welcoming me. This is the only time I'm okay with country music. Right now, with this country-style bar that reminds me nothing of Kendall, I'm okay with it.

I even welcome the small group of sweaty bikers whose whiskey breath I can smell from seven yards away.

Ty is already sitting at the bar when I enter, not surprising. What is surprising is that he brought Leo too. Not that he doesn't go out with us sometimes, but he usually needs more than a thirty-second notice. His whole getting ready routine is worse than a college sorority chick's.

Leo takes note of my surprise and lifts his beer. "I couldn't resist."

"We were just playing poker and drinking, anyway." Ty

takes a big gulp of his own beer as well.

I raise an eyebrow at him while I ask the bartender for a Jack and Coke, then take a seat at the barstool, leaving one foot planted on the floor as though I'll need a quick escape. From the look of the empty bar tonight, I only need to worry about getting drunk and trying to fight the grizzly bikers.

That and Leo's furrowed brow. *That can't be good.*

But he doesn't say anything, simply smiles as Ty shrugs innocently and says, "What? I play poker."

I make eye contact with Leo, who smiles down at the counter, obviously knowing what I'm thinking. "Strip poker, maybe, with a group of women while you sit in the middle with a crown on your head."

Leo laughs and wipes at the spilled beer on his cheeks. His bright smile is a direct contrast to his black hair. Which is usually slicked back, always straight and slicked back, but tonight, his hair is curly at the ends and hangs down on both sides, no gel or other hair products. Perhaps this is why he needs more notice to hang out in public—because otherwise, he ends up looking like a country lumberjack. Especially with his cutoff plaid shirt.

Ty nods with a tight-lipped smile before flipping us both off, swiveling in a semicircle on his stool.

I chuckle down at the counter before taking a large sip. The liquid burns the back of my throat but doesn't bother me. At this point, it's medicine. Might as well be Tylenol, Extra Strength.

But I need several doses to rid myself of these aches.

My chest is tight, and my head is pounding with images

of thrusting into Kendall before holding her tightly through the night.

But the more I drink, the more numb I become.

Being here with the guys makes me feel better too. I'm not alone like I was in my apartment.

I have the boys and whiskey. Whiskey is my buddy too, my cure-all that helps me forget.

On my fifth drink, I forget about Leo's concern—I forget about any concerns at all—and start to believe whiskey was actually made for me. That it should've been called "Sebskey."

"Sebskey?" Ty throws his head back in laughter, and Leo joins him, slapping the bar.

I turn my lazy gaze toward them, joining in on the fun, not having realized I said that out loud.

What else did I say?

We've avoided any talk of Kendall, which I appreciate. They know we ended whatever we had, that she pushed me away, even though I technically started it. I started the argument that led to our downfall.

But right now, I don't care who started it. I don't care if her crazy sister started it.

Now there's a theory. It was Lauren. Maybe I was talking to Lauren that whole time. It sounds more like something she'd do. She'd definitely only be with me for the sex, because she's probably never had good sex.

I laugh into my dwindling drink at the thought.

"Okay, 'Sebskey' wasn't that funny, dude," Leo says. I think it's Leo, anyway. He talks over me while I order another drink, so I don't quite catch who's speaking.

The guys order as well, but there's no way they're keeping up with me. Leo even ordered a water—when did he switch to water? *Weak.*

I'm the only fucking man around, giving girls the best they've ever had.

With gulp after gulp of whiskey, the thought consumes me.

The best fuck around.

Gulp.

If I have to only be one thing, I'll take that title.

Gulp.

I'm almost to the point of standing on the bar and beating my chest, although I'd probably hit my head first. The ceiling seems low, unless that's my drunkenness closing in on me, the walls tightening around me like the walls in my chest.

My head sways, my foot still on the floor, or so I think it is.

Ty waves his hand in front of my face. "Remember the first time you had whiskey? When you turned nineteen? Fuckwad over here gave it to you."

He points at Leo, who flashes another one of his perfect smiles. "I knew he could handle it."

"He threw up after two sips."

"Now look how far he's come."

I hold my empty glass up. "Look how far I've come, indeed. I'm Sebskey, otherwise known as the best fuck around." I clink my glass to Ty's beer bottle and hold it up to Leo before taking a sip.

But the glass is empty, only a few ice cubes refusing to

melt. I have the urge to hurl it at the wall. Instead, I clench my jaw, tamping down the anger, and calmly—at least I think it's calm—ask for another.

If Ty and Leo are worried about me, they're not showing it. Instead, Ty snaps his fingers in remembrance. "Speaking of fucking, Leo, when was the last time you, you know"— he wiggles his eyebrows and says sarcastically—"spent a *sensual* night with a woman?"

I nudge him and look over at Leo, who's still smiling but not looking at us. At least one of the Leos in my line of vision isn't looking—I see two.

Then Leo smiles mischievously like he stole the cookies out of the cookie jar before dinner.

Mmm… cookies sound good.

"Dude!" Ty covers his mouth in shock. "Who is she? And most importantly"—he cups his hands close to his chest in a crude gesture—"does she have big tits?"

Now Leo drops the smile and cuts his eyes toward Ty the way he does when Ty misses his cue on stage, throwing everyone off. I swear Ty does it on purpose because he likes to see the new guys scramble. He never does it when I'm on stage.

"Kendall had great tits." My head bobs back and forth as I speak to no one in particular.

There's silence to my right, but the bikers in the corner erupt in laughter, slamming their beers down.

The sound seems to be in response to what I said since they're looking right at me. "Hey, mind your own fucking business," I slur, attempting to get out of my seat and stumbling into Ty.

He mumbles something to Leo before he grabs me. "Okay, man, I think it's time to go home." He waves at the bikers. "Guys, enjoy your evening. Just going to get my friend here into a toilet to throw up now."

"I'm not fucking drunk. Don't treat me like a baby." I turn my attention back to the bikers as Ty pulls me over the godforsaken step at the door. This time I trip. If Ty wasn't holding me, I would've chipped several teeth.

Instead of moving forward, I step back in and point my finger at the small group. "I can kick your ass, you know. May not want to mess with me!"

The biggest one stands up, spilling his beer on the other one, who gets up with his hands out and yells, "What the fuck!"

While they clean up their mess, I make my way toward them—the perfect time to jump. But instead of jumping, I'm jerked backward and almost fall on my ass, unable to stand on my own two feet. "Fuck!"

"We're getting you home," Ty says, not looking at me.

"I'm not going with you. You probably drank more than me."

If I weren't drunk, I'd think Ty's smile is sad, more like a frown. But that's not Ty. He doesn't get sad in front of others. Only twice has he been sad in front of me, both of which were on the anniversary of his sister's death. I'm functional enough to know it's not February.

I brush the thought away, which is easy to do since my head feels so heavy on my shoulders. I focus instead on not letting my head come loose, then laugh at the image of a head rolling across the street as Ty and Leo carry a headless guy to their car. All I'd need is a horse.

I laugh more at the thought of being a Headless Horseman.

A couple passes us on their way to the car, and I immediately get angry at the way they're snuggled together. How it was only a few weeks ago that Kendall was nuzzled next to me, tracing the tattoo on my chest.

Now my chest cracks, my heart shriveling inside it. "Assholes!" I yell at the couple just as we reach Leo's Jeep. Ty shoves me in the back seat before I can yell at them some more.

Without turning toward Ty as he settles in next to me, I say, "I wasn't done in there."

"You had plenty." Leo starts the engine and stays silent the whole way to my apartment.

"You're not the fucking boss of me. I wanted more whiskey."

"Don't you mean Sebskey?"

I squint at Ty, searching for any trace of humor, but my head is too fuzzy to differentiate his tone. Running my hands down my face, I look up at the night sky since the Jeep has no roof.

Blank.

The sky is blank, the city lights and pollution covering up the stars.

Empty.

With all the whiskey I drank, I still feel empty. Only an empty apartment to rush home to. No hopes of filling it with blond hair and laughter.

Empty.

An empty soul resides inside me, but I won't let it give up. Part of me can't. It holds on to her, begging the universe to bring her back to me.

"I know, man," Ty says as we pull into a parking spot. "And maybe she will."

I look at him, confused, as we come to a stop. I walk slowly up to my empty apartment with the hole in the wall resembling the hole in my chest.

But the hole in my chest clings to the possibility that she's not lost to the stars, that I can still find her someday.

CHAPTER 49

Kendall

A knock on the door wakes me.

I don't move, my face still planted in the pillow with my covers thrown off the bed. I don't know what time it is or how long I've lain here like this in my solitude. My heartbreak. How long it's been since I've taken a peaceful breath.

I squeeze my eyes shut again, hoping the knocking will go away. It's Emma—who else would it be—and I'm not ready to face her, not yet.

We rarely fight, and when we do, it's mostly over me being late or forgetting to pay my half of the rent. Because, of course, I'm irresponsible, as she pointed out many times before.

But we've never fought like we did two weeks ago. She's never fully gone Hulk on me like she did that night.

Now we're on speaking terms, but there's still tension. And she avoids me, even in our small apartment where we're bound to run into each other.

The coffee maker sounds from the kitchen, and plates are moved around. I put my other pillow on the back of my head to block out the sounds.

To block out the world.

My pillow cocoon around my head works to block out the sounds, but I can't sleep. I couldn't sleep to begin with, mostly tossed and turned all night. Nightmares haunted me of my mom calling me, disappointed that I ruined my sister's wedding, how she didn't raise me to be a monster.

Lauren won't speak to me. I tried calling several times to apologize, but all I got was a text from her saying she was on her honeymoon. She'd get back to me when she was home.

She's been home for over a week now, but I still haven't heard from her.

Another knock sounds, but this time it sounds more like a bat being swung at my door. There's more banging until my door finally swings open.

But I still don't move.

Emma sets something on the desk and raises my blinds before she opens a window. I can't see anything, but I can hear the rustling. I can also hear her frustration and feel the tension. She doesn't say anything through more shuffling and spraying of what I assume to be Febreze.

A spring scent fills the room.

I refrain from groaning, not wanting to make the first sound. She's the one intruding, so she can be the first to explain what she's doing.

I squeeze my eyes shut, thinking those are the kinds of things that make me sound less than grown up—why I'm so annoying to all those around me.

"Get up," she finally says like a teacher disciplining a third grader. I half expect her to spank some sense into me with that tone.

Now I let out my groan but stay put.

"Kendall, get up," she says more softly.

I turn with the pillow still on my head, but I can see her through a small sliver under it. She's got her hands on her hips and her ponytail intact, like she hasn't been upset at all about our fight.

"I'm sorry, that I'm so immature that I barged into your room while you're asleep and started demanding shit. Oh, *wait…*"

"God, you're impossible sometimes."

"Feel free to see yourself out." I turn my face into the pillow again.

After a heavy pause, she pulls on my feet and drags me off the bed until my ass lands on the floor with an *oomph*.

"You bitch!"

Before I can get up, she climbs on top of me with a comb and hairspray. "You have to be at work in thirty minutes, and you are *not* calling in sick again." Straddling me, she starts pulling at my hair.

"What the fuck, Emma. Get off me!"

"No," she persists. "You're pulling yourself together and going to work. With my help."

"I don't want your stupid help," I protest, but can't stop the laughter bubbling deep in my throat at this ridiculous scene. "I definitely don't want a stupid ponytail, which is all you can seem to do."

"Oh, you're getting a ponytail."

"Ow!"

"Not my fault you slept all day and now have a major rat tail. Dear God, this is tangled! Like worse than that night you fell asleep in the bathtub because you were drunk and thought there was a tornado."

"It was the worst thunderstorm LA had ever seen!"

"It barely rained, but you were too drunk to know the difference," she says absentmindedly as she works on my messy hair.

We're silent for a moment as she lifts my head to get the rest of my hair up for a ponytail.

When she secures it, her hands fall to her sides, but she still doesn't move from on top of me. "I'm sorry about our fight."

Her features are as perfect as they were on the day of our high school junior pictures, except for the dark circles under her eyes that makeup couldn't quite cover. I'm hesitant to answer, surprised she apologized first.

"I overreacted, okay?" She slides off me and lies beside me so we're both staring at the ceiling. "I saw Brant that night. I just wasn't ready to talk about it."

"Are you ready now?"

She glares at me and then returns her gaze to the ceiling. "He showed up with his fucking fiancée. And it wasn't even the girl he cheated on me with."

"Brant is engaged?"

"Yeah, I had no idea, either. Until that night when he

paraded her and her ring around like he had two dates. That rock was the size of my head and more expensive than both our cars put together."

"Fucking Brant."

"Fucking Brant," she repeats, and I'm reminded of when they first broke up, of when she called me sobbing harder than ever. Even harder than when she fractured her ankle and couldn't dance for months. Dance was something she'd discovered during her parents' divorce. It gave her an outlet for all her anxiety of that time.

But when Brant cheated on her—that broke her. Broke her worse than anything her parents put her through.

In dealing with it, I tried joking about Brant's big nose. What would their kids look like with his tree trunk of a nose? And his pretentious khakis and polos like he spent all his time on a golf course when in reality he couldn't shoot better than a hundred even on his best days.

So "fucking Brant" was born. Every time we'd see him doing something on social media that upset her, I'd say "fucking Brant," and we'd talk about his outfit of the day. Until we both finally blocked him on all sites and from our memories.

Until two weeks ago, anyway.

"I'm sorry too," I say, still staring at the white ceiling. Nothing to trace or keep me occupied on the smooth paint, but I keep my gaze there, nonetheless. "I was a dickhead. I've been a dickhead since I moved here. You've done nothing but try to help me, and I push you away."

"Maybe I try too hard."

"I don't know what I'd do without you."

"That's the thing. I don't want you to think you're not strong enough to do things for yourself because you *are*. I'm just used to taking care of people. My mom, she lost her mind after the divorce and started drinking. I was the only one there to take care of her. With my dad, I actually thought he'd pay more attention to me if I ironed his clothes or cleaned the house any time I stayed there. And especially Brant. God, he didn't even know how to put Netflix on the TV without me, that jackass."

"Fucking Brant."

"Fucking Brant." She sighs. "I'm better off without him."

"Amen, sister." We both cup our hands around imaginary glasses and clink them together between us. "I appreciate everything you've done for me. It's not your fault I'm a fucking loser."

She exhales and gets up, pulling me with her. "My best friend is not a loser. She's strong and smart and very fucking capable. I haven't seen her in a long time, though. Would she care to join us?" She watches me, searching my eyes for this best friend of hers.

"I thought I was your best friend." I crack a slight smile at my obvious sarcasm. Of course, she's talking about me, and of course, she's right. I haven't been myself in a long time.

Because I don't know myself anymore.

She smiles at me, and as though she reads my thoughts, she says, "I know you feel lost. We've all been there. When I started the yoga studio, my God, I was a wreck. I was so nervous and doubted myself every step of the way, through the setup, getting the loan, and during the opening. I dreaded every day, thinking it would be my last. That I wouldn't have enough clientele to stay open. I still get nervous even now."

I'm shocked to hear her say this. I don't remember any panic from her—distracted, maybe, but never panicked. She always seemed collected, unfazed, very unlike me.

And always with a plan. Once she took over the studio, she added Pilates and Zumba. I still see her scribbling notes for other things she can do to bring people in. She's never without ideas or the drive.

I hesitate with my response. "But you never showed that. You always seem so confident with the studio and basically everything. Like you have life figured out."

She scoffs. "Are you kidding?"

"No." I look around, searching for the joke. "You seem about as put together as your slick ponytail and clean sneakers—which, by the way, is weird. Sneakers should be torn apart and dirty, so stop cleaning them after every time you go running."

"*Anyway...*" She glares at me. "You now have eleven minutes to get to work, but I want you to know that I don't. I don't have everything figured out. There's still so much I want to do and goals I have, and I don't know if I'll ever achieve them. But at least I have them." She takes my hands in hers. "Think about your goals while you're at work tonight, and write them down when you get back. Then we can go from there."

She shrugs like it's that simple, but inside, I'm panicking. *What fucking goals?*

She looks down almost shyly. "I'll help, if you want, but I won't cross boundaries anymore. I'll let you take the reins."

I pull her in for a tight hug, thankful that she cares enough to help me. "I don't deserve you."

She's stiff for the whole hug, which has never stopped me before and doesn't now, either, until she rigidly moves backward out of my embrace. She's a lot stronger than me, this wizard yogi. "You definitely don't, but I'm here to stay. With breakfast and all, even at four fifty-one p.m."

"I do *not* deserve you, you beautiful soul," I repeat as I run to the desk where she has yogurt and an egg sandwich for me. I go for the steaming cup of coffee first, but she slaps my hand before I get to it. "Okay, what was that for?"

She looks down again. "Sorry, that was unnecessary." When she meets my gaze, she says in a stiff attitude, much like Angela from *The Office*, "But you need to take that to go. You're late."

I nod and turn toward the closet, then turn back to take a quick bite of the sandwich. I end up doing a small circle, trailing my indecision between needing to get to work and needing that heavenly sandwich.

She pushes me toward the closet and takes the food while I get ready. "I'll drop you off so you don't waste time trying to find parking. And you can do your makeup on the way."

I smile as I pull a clean shirt over my head, glad we're back to normal.

Better than normal. Like this is a new beginning for us. And me.

I smile all the way out the door, filled with a hope I haven't had in a long time.

I had a glimmer of it with Sebastian, but there was always a sense of gloom stemmed from a void deep within me. Setting goals for myself might be a way to fill it.

And with that, maybe I can find my way back to him— if he'll take me.

CHAPTER 50

Sebastian

Buzzing around my head makes me jerk awake, and I realize I'm in my bed. Wiping at the drool on my chin and waving off a damn fly, I lie back down and groan.

Why did I have to drink so much last night?

Oh right, because Kendall ripped my fucking heart out.

The first girl I date seriously since Joelle, and all she has to say is that I'm the best sex she's ever had.

Fuck that shit.

Any thought of her coming back was stupid. I was out of my mind last night, but sleep gave me the clarity I needed.

Reaching for my phone to check the time and coming up empty, I vaguely remember smashing it to pieces last night.

I exhale and swing my legs over the side of the bed, but when I try to stand up, I fall face-first onto the floor like my legs suddenly forgot how to work. Like the way they got shaky once I landed on solid ground after skydiving for the first time.

I groan again, loudly, as though anyone is here to help. *Alone.*

I'm alone.

With fucking blue balls.

"Hey, sunshine. You get your beauty sleep?" Ty slumps against the doorframe with arms crossed and a smirk the size of his ego. *Okay, so maybe I'm not super alone.* "Not enough, I guess. You look like shit."

From my spot on the ground, I do a push-up and stand on trembling legs. My head screams at me like a teenage girl yells at her phone or *The Bachelor.* "What the fuck are you doing here?"

"What? You didn't think I'd miss the aftermath of a sad white boy's whiskey marathon, did you?" He places his hand on his chest and sarcastically asks, "Don't you know me but at all?"

Once I make it through a much-needed hot shower, I'm ready to begin the day. To try and stop wallowing. Especially after I walk into the kitchen and Leo has a plate of bacon waiting for me.

Which reminds me of the time I cooked bacon for Kendall, then had her bent over the desk before we could take a bite.

Fuck, I'm pathetic.

I scold myself as I sit with my plateful of eggs at the table where Leo and Ty stare at me. They're silent, the only sound coming from forks scraping the ceramic dishes, and they exchange glances here and there, avoiding me. If they think I can't see them, they'd make terrible spies.

"I don't want to talk about it," I say, relieving them of their games.

"But you can, if you want," Leo says as he crosses his arms on the table in front of him. "We can talk about anything to take your mind off of her like we did last night, or you can talk about her. We're here for you for whatever you need."

I nod, my way of thanking them, but I don't say anything. We continue eating in silence, even when Ty gets up for seconds and stumbles on a stray sneaker.

Ty finally breaks the silence. "So, you remember that time we were in Seattle and that Uber guy fell asleep at a red light?"

Leo and I look up and smile, thankful for Ty's change of subject, even if I don't remember what the hell he's talking about.

He continues with the story, and I'm surprised it doesn't involve drinking or a naked chick—two of his go-tos when he starts a conversation.

I watch them around my kitchen table. They stuff their faces with eggs and bacon, small speckles getting stuck on the sides of their mouths and some falling off their forks. They slurp their black coffee like Neanderthals and all but slam their mugs back down.

They may be messy guys, but they're my family, my brothers. I look at them and listen to them tease each other and me, and I realize I was never alone, not since I joined Naked Heat. They're the ones who have always had my back. The ones here to cook me breakfast and make sure I don't put my head through a wall.

Kendall may have left, and it still hurts like all hell, but I'm not alone.

And for now, this is enough.

CHAPTER 51

Kendall

Taking deep breaths as the sweat drips down my nose and onto the floor, I stand up after my set of bent-over dumbbell rows and wipe at my face with a towel.

I have the *Mamma Mia!* soundtrack blaring in my headphones, courtesy of Emma. She claimed last night that this should instantly put me in a good mood. I laughed like I always do because I don't understand how she listens to this while working out.

ABBA's "Dancing Queen" isn't exactly a song to get me pumped up. Or so I thought. This is actually working for me. I even do the disco fingers as I walk to the cables for lat pulldowns.

No one's paying attention to me, so I angle my body to the side and snap a selfie in the mirror. Then I add it to the collection of gym selfies on my phone. A small hint of my hamstring shows, and I silently pat myself on the back that my clean diet is finally giving me the results I've been looking for.

The diet has been torture, but the abs and hamstrings are nice rewards.

But the longer I stare at the picture, the more I acknowledge that it's more than that. More than the physical benefits. I enjoy working out because it makes me feel good. My energy has increased, and I'm feeling stronger now than I ever have.

Last night, Emma asked me to write down my goals when I got home from work, but I didn't have any.

I felt like I was asked to declare a major again. It didn't go well the first time, and it certainly didn't go any better last night.

Emma helped me brainstorm. Teaching classes at her studio, going to get my associate's degree, getting an exercise science degree. It all had to do with fitness, and she kept circling back around to becoming a fitness influencer on social media. To get paid to help others work out and model workout apparel to make them feel good while doing so. I could get sponsors and even compete in bodybuilding down the road, if I wanted.

"You already like to buy enough gym clothes to wear a different outfit every day for two months, so you might as well get *paid* to wear it," Emma said while we sat on the floor with our backs against the couch last night.

I crunched on carrot sticks and answered with my mouth full. "That's not exactly practical."

"Who said anything about being practical?"

Instead of answering, I reached for a piece of celery.

"Look, you're going to have to face the facts." She scooted around to face me. "You have to stop worrying about what your parents will say. It's not going to help. And it's certainly not going to make you happy."

I nodded, knowing she was right but afraid to admit it. Afraid to go after it because I didn't think I was good enough or capable of doing something so unconventional, especially with my parents breathing down my neck.

"Just think about it, okay?" Emma suggested as she went into her bedroom.

I thought about it all night. I thought about it all morning. And I'm still thinking about it now as I drive home after my workout.

I have so much on my mind that I want to tune it out, so I turn the radio on and lower my window, even though it's hot as balls out here. LA in June during midday is brutal.

But it feels good having the wind blow across my face, even if it is hot wind.

When the guy on the radio asks listeners a question, I turn it up. "What one thing is absolutely crucial on the first date to make you want to go on a second? Call in with your answers."

I mull this over, but only one thing comes to mind—to make me feel comfortable.

To be comfortable with someone and them think it's sexy.

And when I make that declaration to myself, all I can think about is Sebastian. The way he made me feel comfortable from the very first night we met. The way I couldn't help but open up to him.

Unlike the other guys I've ever gone out with, Sebastian listens intently, even when I don't say anything particularly intriguing. And although he has a tendency to check me out—something he's unapologetic about—he *listens* when I speak.

My chest aches as I pull up to our apartment.

I haven't heard from him in over two weeks, and I miss him.

I miss his kind eyes and easy smiles. Miss tracing his tattoo as we chatted about anything from favorite movies to life.

I miss the way he made me feel.

And I don't know if I'll ever find that again.

But what's more terrifying than that is the possibility that I might never see Sebastian again.

"Again, I have to ask. Why do you do it if you hate it and don't plan on doing anything useful with it?" Emma challenges with her hands on her hips in the middle of our kitchen. "What's the point if you're just going to complain about it the whole time?"

My spoonful of yogurt halfway to my lips, I put it down and answer, "I don't complain about it. I like yogurt." I shove the spoonful in my mouth and offer a tight-lipped smile for added effect.

She releases an exhausted breath. "You're a child."

"Why do you care if I like yogurt or not?"

"Because that's not what I'm talking about and you know it." She pins me with her glare. "Yet you always, *always*, deflect any time someone asks you a question you don't want to answer."

"I don't—" I stop myself, quickly realizing I was about to deflect again. To deny any aversion to being honest with my best friend. "Maybe I do sometimes…"

More glaring.

"Okay, a lot of times." I set the godforsaken yogurt on the table.

"You know what I'm asking," she repeats. "Why do you keep up with a clean diet when you don't like half the food? When no one's forcing you to do it?"

"I work out really hard, so I don't want to mess it up by eating junk." I stick my tongue out at her as I pick at the yogurt container.

"Why do you work out really hard?"

"Because it makes me feel… alive." I pause and expect Emma to be surprised or have any reaction other than what she's doing now. She's watching me like I didn't tell her something she already knows. "I used to do it because I liked the way it made me look, but then… I don't know, something changed? It became more about my increased energy, self-esteem, and confidence. Like lifting weights and getting stronger makes me think I can do anything."

I shrug, on the verge of tears, because I've never told anyone that. Not Emma, Sebastian, or anyone. The gym has always been my time to strengthen my muscles and my mind.

My time to shine, even if no one's watching.

Especially when no one's watching, because it's for *me*.

Emma smiles, all her perfect teeth showing. "That. That is what your first post should be, with a picture of you at the gym. Not a cute staged one, but a *real* one. To encourage other women out there struggling with their diets and workouts, to tell them that you know what it feels like, but it's so worth it once you push through. How inspiring, right?"

"That's the thing—I'm not inspiring. I don't have anything to offer people."

"I thought we were making progress," she mutters as she pulls me over to the couch. "Sit."

Confused, I take a seat opposite her. "Look, I appreciate your speech back there, but that's why I haven't committed to doing the Instagram thing. I don't know what I could say to them. You, on the other hand, you could help them."

"Is this about Adam?" she asks as though she doesn't hear me.

"What? No. Where did that even come from?"

"Kendall, it's okay. You can talk to me."

"We broke up like three years ago. He's never even crossed my mind." The lie falls off my lips effortlessly.

She gives me a sad smile but doesn't stop digging. "He still has a hold on you."

The tears build, but I fight them back.

"I see it in your eyes a lot." She shifts in her position on the couch, her nose twitching as she tries to find the right words. "How much he not only hurt you, but he took something so valuable from you. Your spirit. Your light.

Your drive. He made you feel like you weren't good enough."

A solid tear falls down my cheek. More tears fall with every word she emphasizes. Every word reaches my soul and cuts through me with the truth.

Because they're all true.

Adam broke me.

He broke any ambition, confidence, any spirit I ever had with every insult he threw at me.

I nod as she takes my hand, and I speak through my tears. "You're right. About everything. As always." I roll my eyes with a smile. I gulp, looking around the room for relief. Something to make these confessions easier. My shoulders deflate, and I decide that I've been silent enough. That I need to get it all out there. "You know, he used to 'borrow' money from me all the time. He'd get angry if I refused, so it got to the point where I just started giving any allowance my parents gave me straight to him. I told myself he needed it more than I did, anyway, since he couldn't find a job—or so he told me." I wipe at more tears that fall. "I always made excuses for him, for everything. I was so wrapped up in him, you know? I would do anything for him, and somewhere along the way, I lost sight of myself because of it."

She squeezes my hand.

"I never told anyone or talked about any of what made him so toxic. I never dealt with any of it, just carried it around with me all this time."

"Well," she hands me my phone with Instagram already pulled up, "now's a good time to start. It's time you stop focusing on your flaws—on what Adam or your family thinks of you—and embracing them as your strengths. It's time you really move on."

With shaky hands, I take the phone like it's a bomb. I'm scared of it. I'm scared of what I'm about to do.

But I'm also excited in the same way I was scared, like riding a roller coaster for the first time. The dips and turns were terrifying, but the feeling of flying and the adrenaline coursing through me were, above all else, freeing.

The excitement builds as I start typing, the energy pulsing through me like I drank an extra shot of espresso.

I'm finally going to do it. To use my Instagram for more than posts of my food and drinks with the girls.

And I know exactly what I'll write. I take Emma's advice to write something honest and *real*, even if it might not be attractive in the general sense.

As I inhale deeply and type, erasing and rewriting to get it just right for what I want to say, I slowly realize I'm more than okay with that because it's real.

And *real* is beautiful in its own way.

CHAPTER 52

Sebastian

I gather my bag out of my locker and stretch my back. I need to stretch more and get the kinks out to stay loose for future shows.

I've gotten into a good routine the last couple weeks—wake up, work out, eat, and practice. I've started going to the gym twice a day most days, and my muscles have been tighter than ever with the extra exercise.

I stretch my arms over my head as the music still rings in my ears, joined by the slamming of my locker door.

"We need to talk," Ty says, holding his hand on the locker like he's about to shove me into it and steal my lunch money.

Leo follows behind him, his hair sticking out on the sides. He tried to tame it with gel, but the dances don't exactly call for tame.

Jordan and another guy I don't recognize snicker as they pass us, but I flip them off. "Might want to keep walking, amateurs."

They hold their hands up in innocence, an innocence I once had myself. One that's mixed with arrogance. I was just like them, before I was pummeled to the ground by life itself.

But life around you continues like the subway. It doesn't stop for anything or anyone. We just have to hop on and ride it to the end.

"What's up?" I say, rubbing my chest, too nervous to look them directly in the eyes. I stare down at the cracked floor, my shadow darkening the space around me from the dim light.

Ty steps aside to let Leo grasp my shoulder and do his thing. He's done this a lot. He's more like a Godfather figure to all of us, steering us one way or another.

Which means he thinks I need steering.

That there's something wrong with me.

He sits us on the wooden bench by my locker, the thing looking like it belongs in a middle school gym. And right now, the way Leo pins me down with his hand and stare, I feel like I'm about to get scolded like I'm in middle school too.

Although I don't know what I've done.

My dance? Did I miss a step?

I even danced with girls, picking different ones every night. Ones without blond hair or shapely legs.

Just the opposite. Brunettes. Redheads. Anyone else to make me forget the time I picked a blond and it changed my life.

"You're miserable!" Ty exclaims, throwing his hands in the air, exasperated like he's tired of holding this outburst in.

Leo grinds his narrow jaw before turning toward Ty behind him. "What the fuck? I told you to be cool and let me do the talking."

Ty's eyes bulge and refuse to look at me. With his arms still out, his tank unable to contain his muscles, he waits for Leo to continue.

My lips form a tight smile, not liking where this is going.

Leo turns back to me. "What he means is... we've noticed lately that you aren't yourself."

"Is this some kind of joke?" I try to stand. "Very funny, now fuck off."

He pins me down again, his eyes softening in apology and determination. "You need to hear this." He searches for the words, his gaze never leaving mine even though I try to look anywhere but at him.

The paint peeling off the black walls leaves the white underneath to show. The pattern almost resembles a constellation, white stars against a dark night. Like the night I met Kendall, when we walked underneath the stars, our hands brushing. Nervous. Excited.

A tease for the possibilities to come.

Now she's gone, and the white spots on the wall just resemble bullet holes.

"Hear us out before you doze off." Leo drags my attention back to him. "This is what I'm talking about. Your lack of focus, energy, everything. I don't think we've heard you laugh in two weeks."

"I laughed yesterday at three oh three p.m. I wrote it down for you."

"Cute." Leo frowns at my attempt to be sarcastic.

Ty sits behind us, so we turn toward him. "He's right, Seb. When you dance, we can tell you're just going through the motions without fire, without anything. You used to love to dance! Now we get asked when *The Walking Dead* joined Naked Heat."

I rub my calloused hands together, picking at them, unsure of what to say. I've been throwing myself into Naked Heat, the only thing I have going for me in my life. And now they're telling me I suck at it?

Fan-fucking-tastic.

Leo levels with me. "That's right. You *used* to love it. You were young and needed the money. You enjoyed it then, but you've been done with this phase of your life for a while. Long before Kendall. And not even because you think Joelle made you quit. You've just been fighting it, and we want to know why. What're you afraid of?"

Ty leans forward with his elbows on his knees, his black hat turned backward. "Is it because of us? You think we wouldn't be okay without you?"

"Quite the opposite," I whisper. "You guys are all I have."

Ty and Leo exchange glances. They know I haven't spoken with my mom since Joelle's wedding, and they know we've never been on good terms even before that. I haven't spoken to Kendall, either, although Ty's caught me stalking her Instagram on occasion.

Strip FOR ME

She posts pictures of the beach with Emma, but today she posted the picture she sent me weeks ago. The one where she's making a duck face, her sweaty face glistening.

The one where she looks free.

And the caption underneath was the most honest, most beautiful thing I've seen her post on social media:

Things are changing around here, Instagram family! I haven't always been honest on here. But I'm going to start, first with this post. This is what I look like when I go to the gym. Sweaty armpits, hair a mess, exhausted. I'm not ashamed of it because it just shows I work hard! And while we tend to think about fitness as a way to look good—that's how it was for me too, at first—I have found that it's much more than that. It makes me FEEL good. It makes me physically, emotionally, and mentally STRONGER. I feel beautiful for once, when I never have before, sweaty armpits and all. So from now on, I'll be posting more about my workouts and diet to encourage you all to take that leap into working out for a better YOU. Better mind, body, and spirit. We're living in the age of the strong woman. Let's join in together! #strongwomen #femaleempowerment #inthistogether #strongeryou

I read the long post so many times that I have it memorized like it's the equivalent of a Bible verse to a Christian.

I'm so proud of her. I know it must've been difficult to get out of her comfort zone like that. To post a picture that wasn't staged, perfect, and pristine.

And then to write her heart out? Amazing.

She's gorgeous, inside and out, and it kills me.

Kills me that she's doing so well without me. That I'm

327

reading about the change in her life on social media like the rest of the world.

Over the last couple weeks, I've begun to accept that she was serious, that what we had was only good sex and nothing more. No shared connection that only comes around once in a lifetime.

And it pisses me off every time I think about it.

Ty looks away, his jaw working back and forth. But Leo leans forward, a hand gripping my shoulder. "Sebastian, you know we'll always be here for you. Just because you don't dance with us doesn't mean we can't or won't be friends. You left before, and we still hung out, talked, everything like we do since you've been back."

"It's not the same."

"No. It was better," Ty says, his back turned slightly to us.

"Ouch, dickhead. What's that supposed to mean?"

Ty and Leo exchange glances again.

Looking between them, I ask, "Am I missing the Morse code or something? Blink more slowly so I can catch up." My blood boils at their shared language. This is what I'm talking about. If I leave, I'm cast out. I'd have to miss out on their experiences, having to find out about it all through Facebook or their website. Like we're strangers.

Leo speaks up. "It was different, but what Ty means is that you were happier. You were happier running the hotel because that was your dream. Naked Heat isn't your dream. It's why you left in the first place. Not because of Joelle, your mom, or the fucking Easter bunny. You left because this was always temporary for you. It's time you embrace your dream."

I fight the lump in my throat.

I love Naked Heat, but being in a suit and tie—not a suit with snaps on the side for easy stripping but a real one—handling numbers and putting together proposals, it gave me a whole new perspective. A new world that I enjoyed being part of.

I got a taste of that stable life, and I left because I was scared.

Having Leo and Ty come to me, to set me free, helps relieve the stress I feel for leaving. I know I'll still have them no matter where I go.

"And we're going to help you do it right this time. No uncle, no magic fairy dust. Just pure determination and hard work," Leo says while Ty nods. "We're going to be with you every step of the way, starting with your first meeting at the bank and possible investors. Your first meeting is Monday morning at eight."

"Wait, what?" My brain has a hard time processing that I'm quitting a job I've had since I was nineteen, but investors? Banks? Meetings? "Monday is three days away. This is too fast. I wouldn't know what to say to them."

"You have an open lot picked out and a business plan you've been tweaking unnecessarily for over a year. Whatever else you need, you'll figure it out."

"How did you even arrange this?" I ask, still dumbfounded.

"Maybe I used a little magic fairy dust after all," Leo says, but when I glare at him, his demeanor changes. Fiddling with his thumbs, he exhales. "I called my stepdad."

I jump off the bench. "Are you fucking kidding me? You asked that prick for a favor? You're never going to live it down."

They both stand while Leo answers, "I don't care about any of it. It's worth it to call that jackass if it means getting your foot in the door. He's got the connections with investors that you need, so I made the call."

"It's too much. Too fast."

Ty comes up behind me. "And we're not even stopping there, but first things first, let's get you ready for Monday. I'm thinking new suit, maybe like a Conor McGregor-style one with the little 'fuck you' pinstripes down the side. No?"

I laugh, but I can't stop thinking about him saying we're not stopping there. Can't help but think he's referring to Kendall—a door I'm not willing to open just yet.

"And for a loan, I'll cosign with you," Leo offers.

"What?" I don't think I've heard him correctly. I'm shocked that they've been planning everything without my knowledge. A loan this size is not going to be easy to attain, much less pay back, and he's willing to take that chance on me? "You can't do that."

"I have a sizable trust that my dad left me before he passed."

Now Ty and I stare at each other in shock. This is the first we're hearing of this. "You've been holding out on us?"

Leo shrugs like it's no big deal.

But if he has enough that he can cosign on a loan with me, it's a big fucking deal. I have so many questions. And from the look on Ty's face, so does he.

"Dude, you're loaded, yet I still have to cover your ass

when we go to lunch? What's that about?"

Leo gathers his things and makes his way out the door. "That's how I stay rich." He winks and nods toward the door for us to follow him, and I feel like I'm truly following the Godfather toward the light.

The three of us walk out the back door to the club as we've done many times before. The only difference is that I'll leave soon for good, but I know we'll remain friends.

Brothers.

And when I get to my apartment, I feel lighter than I have in a long time. Kendall may not be here, but having my family for the long haul is its own kind of relief.

As I walk by the large hole in the wall above my couch, I take a deep breath as I decide it's time to let it all go. In my bedroom, I find a framed picture of Leo, Ty, and me, along with a hammer and nail, and walk back to the living room. Placing it over the hole, I stand back and nod.

Nod at the past, for it led me to Kendall.

And a nod at the future for all that's to come.

CHAPTER 53

Kendall

I step out of the car like I'm stepping on a frozen lake that could cave at any moment. Crossing my arms in front of me, I walk toward Lauren. She's in a red sundress that brings out her tan, probably from the honeymoon.

I cringe as memories from the wedding, of how I attacked my sister, flood my mind.

But I take steps forward to reconcile whatever small piece of us there is to salvage.

She wouldn't answer my calls or texts, so with Mom and Dad's help, I flew out here to force her to talk to me. I didn't want to call them, but they were eager to get us talking again. Ready to move forward, even though they're still pissed at me.

They were proud of me for making the first move, which relieved me of my guilt for asking them to pay for my airfare.

The whole flight out here, I thought about what I'd say, how I could possibly make up ruining her wedding reception to her.

Lauren doesn't hug me or say anything when I reach her on the porch. Instead, she merely leads me inside. I take in her living room decorated with rustic décor—a windowpane hovering over the fireplace, distressed coffee table, and cotton ball bouquets in vases scattered around.

I haven't been here before, to see her new house. Her new life.

One I want to be part of.

The house is nestled in a small neighborhood close to the small downtown area where they have a farmer's market every weekend. Being in a small town, it's also close to a good school where Lauren and Rhett's kids will one day attend.

The thought makes me tear up.

She's growing up and getting a life of her own, married with a stable job and a bright outlook.

I'm jealous of her.

Jealous of her being so put together, but the feeling isn't as strong as it would've been before my revelation. Before letting Emma talk me into a more optimistic, confident mindset.

Rhett comes around the corner and into the kitchen that's next to the living room. I'm still standing in the middle of it, looking at their pictures lining the fireplace mantel. He's in his gym shorts and T-shirt, very different from his usual button-up and slacks. He does a double take when he sees me.

"Hey…" he starts, as though he's forgotten my name. Or my sister banned its utterance from this house. I can't blame either one of them for it. "How are you?" He puts his hands on his hips like he doesn't know what to do with them. He shares a look with Lauren that I can't read. It's their own language—the kind you develop from really knowing someone and letting them know you in return.

Lauren kisses him on the cheek. "It's fine, Rhett. Go on to the gym. Kendall, you want some water? Sweet tea? Maybe a soda?"

She peeks around the refrigerator door, watching me, asking me politely if I want refreshments like we're strangers. Like I'm a guest in her home and not someone she grew up with, snuggling together in the bed two feet from hers and calling it a "sleepover."

I'm still new at turning my life around, at being unsure of where it'll take me, but the one thing I know I want is for Lauren to be in it. As my sister and friend, not my enemy. I want to be part of her new life, to be present for her and Rhett. To one day know her children and their favorite colors, TV shows, and even what they like to stick up their noses.

But there may not be any hope for us, after what I've done.

I burst into tears, having held them in for the last forty-eight hours. Rhett stops with his hand on the doorknob, and Lauren gently sets the pitcher of sweet tea on the counter. They're both waiting for me to do something, scared of approaching me. I'm the reason they fear coming close to me—who knows when I'll snap.

I hold my face in my hands while I full-on sob, what little makeup I had smearing down my cheeks.

There's shuffling behind me, and then the front door opens. When I look behind me, Rhett's gone, and Lauren comes around the counter to stand in front of me.

"Sit," she says.

Taking a seat across from her on her cream-colored couches, I don't know where to start. While I search for the right words in the intricate lines on my palms, Lauren takes the lead. "Why are you crying?"

Confused, I search her eyes for an explanation but come up empty. The answer seems obvious. "What?"

"Why are you crying?" she repeats. "We don't talk for weeks, and now you're here sobbing in my living room. Don't get mascara on that couch, by the way." She reaches for a box of tissues from the end table and hands it to me.

"Do you always have to be such a bitch?" I dab at my eyes with a tissue, wondering why I came here. Every word from her has me feeling like this was a mistake.

"*I'm* the bitch?" She scoffs, looking away from me. "Yeah, I'm the bitch who attacked my sister at her wedding. The one who missed my sister's bridal shower without so much as an explanation. Who disappeared from my sister's life even when she lived across the hall." She glares at me, her gaze unwavering. Her jaw clenches in anger—rage, actually. Her face is as red as her dress, her neck breaking out in red splotches the longer we stare at each other. "So I'll ask again, why the *fuck* are you crying?"

My chest is heavy as I inhale, desperate for more air to

fill my lungs. Unable to stop myself, I jump into defensive mode, pointing at her. "I may have done those things, but you didn't exactly make it easy to be your friend. Your snobby friends couldn't wait to pick me apart every chance they got. And you joined right in. Every time."

"Maybe if you wouldn't call them—and me—names, we wouldn't give you such a hard time. You realize you started it, right? You started this whole thing between us."

"Because of Jeremy? In high school?" I laugh humorlessly. "Get the fuck over it already. He was such a douchebag. He's got a nasty mullet now and washes cars over on Fifth. I did you a favor."

She pauses, studying me, all humor—fake or otherwise—gone and replaced with tension. "Sure, I was mad at you in high school, but I didn't hate you. Jeremy made out with another girl that night too, not just you. I knew he was a douchebag. But *you*," she continues, her eyes sad, "you avoided me afterward for months like that time I had chicken pox."

"I did not avoid you. You're the one who wanted nothing to do with me. I believe your exact words were, 'Don't ever talk to me again, you fucking skank.'"

She throws her hands up, her body bouncing off the couch. "I was mad! In that moment, in *high school*, I said a lot of mean things. I made a random sophomore cry when she tried to congratulate me for being prom queen. Shit, I didn't hate you. I never wanted this." She points her finger back and forth between us.

I fidget, knowing I'm to blame once again. That I might not be able to fix it now.

She whispers, "I'm not even talking about Jeremy. Not really. It's what happened after. After you broke up with Adam and dropped out of college. You disappeared on me." She angles her body toward me. "Adam turned you into this zombie. You wouldn't let anyone close to you. Even after you broke up, you were never the same, and it was hard to talk to you. Now it's years later and you still avoid me."

I flinch at her mention of Adam, hoping we didn't have to talk about him. Since Emma mentioned him a couple weeks ago, I haven't been able to stop thinking about him. Trying to deal with his effect on me, to really move on. With deep breaths, I tell myself that maybe talking about him with my sister might be another way for me to get over it.

But before I can say anything, she asks, "Want to know why I had my bachelorette party in Vegas?" She doesn't let me answer, her frown reaching her eyes. "It was so close to you that you wouldn't have an excuse not to come, like with my bridal shower. But you still didn't want to be there. And you found every excuse not to hang out with us." She looks down, her honey hair falling over her shoulders as a tear falls. She quickly wipes it away like she hopes I didn't see it.

I inhale, willing my own tears to stay locked inside. I've cried enough, but fuck if holding them in doesn't hurt worse than my pride would if they fell.

As soon as my voice sounds, the tears follow. "I had no idea," I whisper through the tears now falling on her couch. I grab a handful of tissues and bury my face in them. "I'm so fucking stupid."

"Yes."

I glare at her, a small smile spreading across her face. Which is now glowing, a contrast from the pained expression thus far. "I'll still kick your ass like we're kids again."

The pained expression is back, but not full force.

I place a hand over my chest, remembering that I did actually try to kick her ass at her own wedding. My heart sinks at how I hurt her, how humiliating it was, and how it'll be an unwanted memory she'll never get rid of. "I'm so sorry about what I did at your wedding. I was so drunk." I shake my head, not knowing where to begin or how to make it up to her. "Sebastian had just—"

"Don't blame him for your actions." Her jaw clenches, and she seems older now. Still glowing, but we're not kids anymore. And I should stop acting like one. Before she continues, I know what she'll say. "Don't blame him or the alcohol. Just... no more excuses. If falling on your ass at my wedding was what you needed to get your shit together, so be it."

Okay, not what I expected her to say.

I search her eyes, her demeanor, her sofa—anything to find the catch. The message between the lines. But I find nothing other than sincerity. She watches me intently, and I'm suddenly afraid of her, like I'm one of her patients knowing I've never flossed and she's about to lay into me.

"I'm serious." She nods. "If that hadn't happened, you might not be here now, and we might not be having this conversation. You might not have finally embraced yourself and what you really want."

"What do you mean?"

"I follow your Instagram. I see you making positive

changes that might not have happened had you not hit rock bottom." She shrugs, then glares at me. "And maybe now we can get to the bottom of why you're pushing Sebastian away."

"You don't even like him. I thought you'd be thrilled I broke it off."

"I might not have liked him at first. He was a random guy we met in Vegas—a stripper no less." She pauses. "But he seemed to really care about you. Even the morning after that first night, he watched you with excitement. The way Rhett looks at me, even."

Her words make my tears well up again.

"When you brought him to the wedding, I know I gave you a hard time, and I'm sorry, but I was actually glad he was there. You liked someone enough to bring him around the family. You hadn't done that since Adam, what, three years ago?"

"That's why I was scared."

"Of what?"

"Of how much I liked him, but I didn't think you guys would accept him."

She purses her lips. "You didn't even give us a chance."

The wind is sucked out of me. If I was standing, I'd fall to the ground.

She's right. I never gave them a chance, just like I never gave him a chance.

"Yeah, like you would've accepted a stripper as my boyfriend if I had," I say weakly.

"We might've. It wouldn't be the weirdest thing you've ever done."

I laugh at the way her teasing has changed. It's no longer malicious, just good sisterly teasing. The way we used to be.

"Well, he wasn't who I thought he was, anyway," I say.

"Oh? What could he have possibly been hiding? He literally puts himself on display on a regular basis." I toss a pillow at her, and through her giggles, she manages, "Come on. You can't date a stripper and not expect those jokes."

"He was engaged before and didn't tell me. He has this whole other life that he kept from me. Like he's not over it or *her*. And to top it off, I don't think he's happy doing what he's doing, but he won't admit it and change his situation."

"You know, when Rhett and I first started dating, I knew I wanted to marry him." I roll my eyes, and now she tosses the pillow back at me. "I kept trying to find reasons why I shouldn't, because falling for a guy by the second date is weird, but nothing stopped me. Until the fifth date, when he told me he got a DUI when he was twenty-one." Her face twists, as she becomes lost in the memory. "Only then did I pause, because suddenly he wasn't perfect. That one thing stayed on my mind for days, and I didn't see or talk to him during that time. I thought, 'My perfect future husband has a criminal past. His clean slate is tainted.'"

I wait for her to go on, surprised that perfect Rhett had anything but gold stars on his record. I've never even heard the guy curse. At the wedding when I pulled his bride's hair, he actually very gently pulled me off her.

"I was looking for excuses not to love him from the beginning, and the minute something came up, I freaked. Of course, a DUI isn't a joke, but he learned from it. It made him more cautious and determined to be better." She meets my gaze then, making me feel her every word down in my soul like she's planting them there, making sure they take root. "But then I realized that I was just scared. Scared of falling hard for a guy I'd just met. Scared that I already knew what wedding dress I'd get because getting married this young wasn't part of my plan." Her lips twitch in a grin. "And I was actually disappointed that I found a guy Mom and Dad would love."

"Yeah right." I scoff. "You subconsciously picked him *because* of Mom and Dad. They conditioned you to find a man like Rhett."

She's serious when she says, "Did you know they didn't want me to be a dental hygienist? They wanted me to be a teacher or something that would give me more time off, especially during the summer, for when we have kids."

"Doesn't surprise me."

"But I did it, anyway. You might not believe me, but I'm not afraid to hurt their feelings. Deep down, they just want us to be happy, no matter what they say."

I know she's directing that at me more than she is to herself.

"As for Rhett, I'm glad they like him, but at first, I didn't want him to meet them because he was the perfect gentleman for them. I've usually done everything the way they wanted me to, not *because* they wanted me to, but because what made me happy just happened to also make them happy." She shrugs like it's no big deal, like we're not clarifying seven years' worth of events.

I look into her eyes for the first time since I got here—*really* look—and notice the differences I missed while I was in my own head. The slight wrinkles in the corners of her eyes and the way she parts her hair now. It's not to the side or middle, but somewhere in between. She then runs her hand through her hair, and the part is no longer visible at all. That's when I notice how her boobs have become perkier.

I have to borrow that dress sometime.

We've both changed, our age beginning to show. But she still has the same scar on the side of her face from when she had chicken pox and couldn't stop scratching. Mom told her it would scar, but like the six-year-old she was, she didn't listen.

This Lauren is still my sister, the one I used to run to when a boy I liked pushed me and stole the cookies Mom made especially for me.

I smile at her now. The new Lauren.

But the one who's still my sister.

"I'm… I'm sorry for being rude to you. I know I was hurt, but it didn't give me an excuse to treat you that way."

I let one final tear fall. "I deserved it. I'm the one—"

"I was jealous of you," she blurts.

"Of me?"

She winces like it pains her to admit such a thing. "Yes. Jealous of your carefree nature. How you just up and moved to LA and live this adventure." Then her voice changes, becoming more stern. "But that's not me. This town is my adventure."

I start to scoff but think better of it. She catches me, anyway, and glares. "You only remember the bad parts of this town. The bad memories associated with it. But if you stopped to look around at the nice people, the comfort, the good desserts at Pearl's Cupcakes, you'd realize it's not so bad." Her expression softens. "It's part of you, just like it's part of me."

"LA suits me better, though. You have to agree."

Sitting back, she smiles and shrugs. "True. It's a good look on you, but me? I'm not made for LA. Can you imagine me sitting on the beach for hours? I wouldn't last thirty minutes with wet sand stuck between my toes."

I grin, thinking about her aversion to getting messy. "But maybe more visits to see your sister wouldn't be so bad?"

"I'd like that." She grins at me as we stare at each other. Then she slowly pats her stomach. "Baby Wells would like that."

I throw my hands up and leap off the couch toward her. But this time, it's not to pull her hair or scream at her. This time, it's to hug my sister and feel genuine excitement for her and her new husband.

"Does this mean I can borrow your old clothes for the next nine months? You won't need them, right?"

She pulls back, an inch from my face. "Like I'm going to let you wear my Kate Spade in the slums of LA." She shudders in my arms.

I tremble with laughter, thinking some things won't ever change.

But the fact that I'm reconciling with my sister relieves me of so much tension that I'm ready to face what else scares me.

It's time I stop letting my fears get in the way of my own

happiness and that includes Sebastian.

With more resolve than ever, I drive to my parents' house for the night before I go back to the West Coast. As I drive, I pass through downtown, Lauren's words replaying in my head.

I start seeing the town in a different light, a positive one. It's different than LA. It's no longer my home, but Lauren's right. This place is part of me.

My breathing becomes easier as I pull into my parents' driveway, my chest not so heavy anymore. I know some things won't change between my parents and me. We may be somewhat past the wedding debacle, but they still give me shit over wanting to pursue an unconventional career path. My dad didn't even know what Instagram was, so it was fun trying to explain to him that it's a real thing.

And while I don't have their complete blessing, Lauren's right. They just want what's best for me.

Which is what I tell myself as I get out of my mom's car. It's what I repeat to myself as I open their door, ready to talk about the social media thing in more detail and to also bring up Sebastian's occupation.

They haven't mentioned it, so I assume Lauren hasn't told them like I thought she would—another thing I'm grateful for. That she is, in fact, looking out for me in her own way.

I wouldn't bother telling them now about him being a dancer for a Vegas male revue show. I wouldn't bother dealing with the backlash, but I want him back.

I'm ready to face them, feeling more optimistic than ever that Sebastian will take me back. He may have given me the space I asked for, but he still lingers in my thoughts and the way he likes all my social media posts. Like he's silently cheering me on.

That's what I want—a partner to cheer me on and believe in me.

His silent cheers have me betting I won't be too late.

And when the time comes, I want my parents to have had the time they needed to adjust.

Because when I win him over, I don't plan on ever letting him go.

CHAPTER 54

Sebastian

I knock on her door, shoving my hands in the pockets of my joggers and exhaling dramatically. We haven't spoken in a while. The only reason I know she's even still alive is from her Instagram blowing up lately.

I jerked off more times than I care to admit while looking at pictures of her at the gym, sweat dripping between her breasts. Her full breasts pushed together with a sports bra that angels themselves stitched together to make me bite my knuckles.

I knock on her door again, kicking a rock to the side and begging the universe for grace. At this point, I'd pray to a leprechaun for even one pebble of luck thrown my way.

Ty and Leo convinced me to do this, to come here and fight for her. Even if she thinks we're done, I never truly believed it. She's always on my mind—at the gym, in the shower, even when I go to the fucking grocery store.

I know Kendall was put in my life for a reason, and I'm not going to let her go easily.

Especially not after what Ty said, that she's still hung up on me, according to Emma. When I asked Ty how he knew that, he shrugged and said he attends Emma's classes when he's in town—said he likes yoga. Even though I've never seen him touch his toes or so much as try.

I didn't think too hard about it at the time because I was more concerned about Kendall and her feelings for me.

And how happy that made me.

Ty also said she was visiting her sister but got back to town this morning. So I drove straight here when I knew she'd be home.

I'm about to knock a third time when I hear a muffled voice on the other side. "What're you doing here?"

"Kendall?"

"Yes, Kendall. You're at my apartment."

I exhale in laughter, imagining her scowl. I missed that, her attitude.

I missed *her.*

There's shuffling on the other side of the door and then a pause.

It fortunately opens, but unfortunately, Kendall's in her robe with her wet hair tossed over to one side. Her face is free of makeup, and her hands are perched on her hips.

My eyes are glued to her robe, her exposed skin. Knowing she just got out of the shower drives me to the brink of insanity.

I missed her tan skin, her sassy stance, all of it. All of

her.

I'm ready to get on my knees and beg her to give us another chance. Anything I have to do to convince this goddess to be mine.

She steps closer and wipes at my mouth, her soft touch glorious on my stubbled chin. "You're drooling." She smirks.

I'm overwhelmed with her closeness. It's been so long since I last got a taste of her, since our fight on the church steps. Weeks of watching her Instagram along with the rest of the world as though I wasn't special to her. As though I don't know her on an intimate level.

Unable to stop myself, I grab the back of her head and slam my mouth to hers as I push her inside.

She stiffens at first, but she doesn't pull away.

I take it as an invitation to continue, snaking my tongue between her lips and running my hands down her arms. The silk robe "accidentally" falls off her shoulders, and the tops of her breasts make my mouth water all over again.

With a moan, she pulls back, leaving me empty but with a pleasant view of her swollen lips and perfect breasts before she pulls her robe on tight. She shakes her head. "Stop. We can't… this isn't…"

"This is everything right. This is all I've craved for almost two months." I run my hand through my short hair. "I missed you."

A throat clears behind us, the Asian woman from across the hall glaring at us with arms crossed. The woman has impeccable timing.

Kendall rolls her eyes. "Okay, Mrs. Lang. I'll be more careful about the door." She shuts it and leans against it.

After a pause, she gives me a sad smile. "You missed my body, you mean?"

I throw my hands up where she can see them. Surrendering, I plead with her, "Can we please talk? I'll behave. For now, anyway." I smile when she eyes me suspiciously, mischievously.

God, this woman will be the death of me.

She nods and smooths her hair down.

I gently grab her hand and lead her to the couch. "I don't have a grand gesture." I chuckle nervously. "But I just need you to hear me out. Please let me explain. Let me explain and then decide what you want."

"What're you even doing in LA? Shouldn't you be in Portland?"

I smile. "You know my schedule?"

"I… um…"

Her blush makes me smile wider, and my chest expands knowing she's been keeping tabs on me. It's the encouragement and hope I need to continue. "I live in LA. Most of the time, anyway."

Her eyes widen, but she doesn't say anything else.

"I live here, and I only perform part-time for Naked Heat now, mostly just in Vegas." Her eyes keep widening with every word, and I just want to take her in my arms and carry her into the bedroom. But I know we need to clear the air. I need her to know who I am now. Who I want to be. How I want my future to look.

And I want her in it. I want her to be part of it all.

Once we're settled onto the couch, I tell her everything, trying not to stare at the way her legs are spread. She sits with one foot under her other knee, and it's driving me crazy wondering if she's wearing any underwear. It's been so long since I've slept with her, with anyone, and my willpower is being put to the ultimate test.

But I refrain and tell her everything instead. About Leo signing with me for a loan to buy my dream lot. The hotel I'll build. The suite where I'll live.

With Kendall, someday. If she'll have me.

But I leave that part out, not wanting to freak her out. I'm happy she's finally talking to me, and I don't want to ruin it.

She remains silent through my whole spiel. When I'm done, she still sits quietly, watching my every move with a blank expression. I've usually been able to read her, but she's motionless now. It's confusing.

For a moment, I panic. My heart rate speeds up at the thought that I probably sound like a lunatic with my unrealistic plans to build a hotel in LA, the one place that has plenty.

I've been confident about it this whole time, confident that my plan is unique enough to stick out from the competition. But sitting next to her with this empty look on her face has me doubting my judgment. And Leo's, who's supposed to be the wise one.

"You're building a hotel? The one you've been dreaming about... you're doing it?" Her voice is level, no indication of what she thinks.

I squirm in place on her couch, pulling my arm from the back of it and onto my lap. Nodding slowly, I say, "We start building next week."

The corners of her lips slowly tilt up, and she closes her eyes before she opens them again. "That's fantastic, Sebastian."

I exhale and pull her into a hug, my large body suffocating hers. I grip her tightly, holding onto her for dear life. Because that's what she's done to me—breathed life back into my empty soul since the first night we spent together.

Even when we were apart, she was always on my mind, making me smile.

She snakes her arms around my waist, and we hold each other for several minutes, enjoying the embrace and all the comfort it brings. We comfort each other and the new directions our lives have taken.

Hopefully, our lanes will merge into one from here on out.

I pull back an inch from her lips but refuse to give her any more space than that. "Say you'll be by my side when the hotel opens." I rest my forehead on hers. "Please be with me. Take me back. I'm so fucking sorry—"

She takes my face between her hands and kisses me softly, but she pulls back.

Uneasiness mars her features.

Like she needs more convincing, but I don't know what else to say.

I thought this would be enough, so what do I do now?

CHAPTER 55

Kendall

"Why didn't you tell me about your engagement?" I fidget with my cuticles, avoiding his handsome face. I've missed it. Missed him. I didn't realize how much until I saw him at my front door.

Until I heard his deep voice.

Until he kissed me.

The two only in my dreams lately.

I got in from Alabama this morning with full intentions of driving to Vegas to see him tomorrow, after he was set to be back from Portland.

And now he's here. I'm elated he came to find me. That he wants me back and I'm not too late. I wanted to crumble to the floor in relief when I saw him at my door.

But before I can say all is forgiven, before I can really move forward, there's still so much I need to clear up, from

my end and his.

He held out on me about his previous engagement for a reason, and I need to know why. I need him to be honest with me. I can't move forward with someone who hides part of himself from me when all he's done since I met him is try to open me up.

I sit back, my shoulders tense, bracing for the impact of his next words.

To know if he's over his ex or not.

He scoots to the side to fully face me. "You were right. I wasn't over it." He holds his hand up when I'm about to protest, kick him out—kick him in the shin, even. "Not in the way you think. I'm not still in love with her or anything like that."

I relax and let him continue without thoughts of bruising his shin for being in love with another woman while he was with me.

"Truth is, it took me a long time to admit this, but she was wrong for me. Had she not done what she did, we still would've broken up in the end, but I wish it would've turned out differently, you know?"

"No. I don't understand…"

He licks his lips, his expression darkening, and scoots even farther forward so he's sitting on the edge of the couch. "You remember me telling you about my uncle? My mom's brother, the one who helped raise me?"

I nod carefully. I don't like the sudden tension in the room. The pain and discomfort written all over his face make my stomach churn.

"Joelle left me for him."

I cover my mouth with my hands.

He continues without letting me respond, not that I'd know what to say to the ultimate act of betrayal. "I saw them kissing one day in our parking lot. Outside our home." He shakes his head, angry but also seemingly at peace. Like maybe he *is* over it now. "I was so surprised that I didn't see it before. They must've thought I was such a jackass, laughing behind my back. I felt like a jackass too."

I take his large hand in mine, trying to offer as much sympathy as my tiny hand can. "You have nothing to blame yourself for. They did this. It's on them."

"They got married the weekend of your sister's wedding."

They got married?

My mouth falls open, and I cover it again, his outburst that day suddenly making sense. All the pieces falling into place, shining light on this twisted puzzle.

"I'm sorry I didn't tell you, that I took it out on you. That I projected my fears and distrust onto you."

I consider his confession, how there was more to our argument that day. He was angry at me, but also at her. "I'm not her."

"I know. And no matter what she did, how she betrayed my trust, I always disliked that she put down my job. Felt like she was always putting me down, even if that's not what she always meant to do."

I tilt my head at him in question, but he waves it off. "The point is, I know you're not Joelle. I know—"

"I didn't like you being a stripper," I blurt out.

He recoils, leaning back on the couch's armrest and putting distance between us.

"I want to be honest." Now I lean toward him, trying to close that distance. Trying to get him to understand. "It bothered me that you got naked in front of other women. But that's not even what bothered me the most."

I fidget again with my fingers, unsure of how to say it. He leans his head down to be eye level with me, forcing me to look at him. To say this to his face and hope he understands. "I didn't like what my family would have to say about it. I've disappointed them with everything I've done since I was sixteen." I throw my hands up. "Quit piano and tennis. Got in fights, mostly with Lauren. But I also punched a girl in the face. Dropped out of college." He knows most of this, but what he doesn't know is everything that happened with Adam that sent me spiraling even further.

So I take a deep breath and lay it all out there. "I chucked a rock the size of a brick at my ex-boyfriend Adam's car and busted his windshield. He'd just gotten done lecturing me—yes, *lecturing*—on how to dress. That I look like a slob, and that's why he doesn't like going out with me." I shake my head, embarrassed that I was with a guy for almost a year who said shit like that to me.

"He broke up with me after that for being 'a psychotic bitch who wasn't worth the trouble.'" I exhale, deflated, even more embarrassed that he's the one who broke up with me and not the other way around. "I took his words to heart, you know. I was in love with him—or so I thought. I loved him and believed him when he called me embarrassing and stupid." I lick my lips, swallowing my tears. "Because it wasn't the first time I'd heard these words. I've heard them all my life from people in school and Lauren and her friends. I've always felt insecure, so when I started dating Adam and he believed the same, I thought it must be true. Especially since he was so well liked by others. I thought I *must* be the problem."

Sebastian reaches for me, but I hold my hand up. If I'm going to get through this, I need to push through in one breath. "I never stopped internalizing those nasty words. They're always in the back of my head, making me feel like I'm not good enough." I take a deep breath and meet his gaze. "So I pushed you away, and I'm sorry. You made me feel the opposite, like I'm worth so much, and I didn't know how to handle it. I didn't know how to react to you."

I hold my breath, waiting for his response, the hum of the refrigerator the only sound filling the silence between us.

This is it.

Our moment of truth.

"Wow," is all he says, his gaze never leaving mine.

I still hold my breath, my face surely turning blue by now.

"That makes me like you even more."

I peek up at him through my long lashes to see if he's serious.

He laces his fingers through mine and rests our hands on his lap. "You are strong. Pure. Gorgeous. Everything about you is beautiful." His deep voice seeps with intensity, his words so honest they're almost painful.

I exhale my breath and a few fearful tears I was holding in. Relief floods my body, my shoulders releasing their tension.

"You have so much to offer. I never want to take away your light. I only ever want you to shine." He kisses my forehead, and the relief is so overwhelming, I take his face between my hands and kiss him.

Hard.

I kiss him with no thoughts of ever letting him go again.

I tell him everything—how much I care about him and missed him—with this kiss.

I yank his T-shirt toward me, pulling him on top of me on the couch, but before we can go any further, my brain turns on. "Emma…"

"I'd like to keep this between us, actually." He pulls at my bottom lip with his teeth, his eyes twinkling.

I weakly slap at him, my body ready for him. "She… she should be home any minute…" More nipping, and I become mush. "Bedroom… bed… *now*."

He pulls me up, both hands gripping my ass as he leads us to my room. Crossing the small living room, he pushes my bedroom door open and lays me on the bed. Before he crawls onto me, he does a double take toward my nightstand. "What is that?"

I scramble to throw away the calendar sitting there. "Nothing!"

"Holy shit, you have the Naked Heat calendar on your nightstand." He snatches it away from me.

"No! That's Emma's." My face is beet red, my entire body on fire from embarrassment.

He flips through it, searching every page like he hasn't seen one before. Like he's not in it several times. "Please tell me you drew hearts around my face in here."

I slap at his shoulder and then slap at the calendar in his hands so it falls to the ground. "Just for that, I'm withholding sex. You can leave."

He grabs my face and kisses me. "You are too fucking cute." *Kiss.* "And adorable." *Kiss.* "And unbelievably sexy." He stops when something falls to our bare feet, tickling us. "What's this?"

I suck in a breath, attempting to regain my composure.

When he stands back up, he turns a picture of us—the one we took when we first met—and asks, "You kept this? And printed it out?"

I nod, not wanting to embarrass myself further, but I want him to know the truth. To know how much he means to me. "I did. I missed you all this time, but I at least had the picture to keep me company when I was lonely. Which was basically every night. Emma's not much of a cuddler, so…"

He watches my lips move and sears me with his gaze. "You're so beautiful, inside and out." He wraps his strong arms around me, and I kiss him in response, thankful for his words.

For him.

"I don't need a man to tell me how to look," I tease as he kisses along my jawline.

"No," he whispers against my neck, making me tremble. His light stubble against my skin arouses me further. "But I'm going to say it every day to you, for as long as you'll have me."

I gulp. "Okay."

I melt against him just as we hear the front door open.

"Kendall?"

I move my mouth to avoid screaming in Sebastian's ear, but he's too close so I probably deafen him a little, anyway. "In here! I'm… changing."

Sebastian pulls at my robe and growls, "Let me help."

Emma says something else, but I don't catch it, only able to focus on Sebastian pushing me to lie on my back, his fingers trailing my stomach until he reaches between my legs. My robe falls completely open, and I spread my legs farther for him.

"*Fuck*," he whispers. "I knew you were naked under here. Driving me fucking crazy this whole time." He kisses me intensely before pulling back just an inch. "Next time we have a serious conversation, I'm making you put real clothes on."

I smile, liking the way he says "next time." That he wants a future for us.

Because that's what I want. I want him for the long haul.

He slides his finger inside me, making my head fall back onto the bed with a gasp.

"Love that sound," he says and places a kiss on my bare chest. "*Missed* that sound."

I look down at him, his expression one of determination. I can only whimper, especially when he slides a second finger inside and his thumb moves in circles right above my clit.

The familiar tension builds as he picks up the pace, all the while trailing kisses down my neck to my chest. My body lights on fire, and I pant his name over and over, missing the way it feels on my lips.

"That's right, baby. Come for me."

With a few more strokes, I let him take me over the edge, no longer wanting to fight it. Never again will I fight him.

He stays with me, fingers slowing as wave after wave of pleasure rolls through me.

Placing gentle kisses down my chest, Sebastian finally steps away and pulls me up.

Standing on shaky legs, I kiss him, savoring the taste of him. After months of dreaming of his touch, I finally have the real thing, and I want it all.

All of *him*.

I fumble with his jeans but stop when an idea occurs to me. I smile at his confused expression like I took away his sweet chocolate bar. "I have one last game for you." I run my finger down my chest, between my breasts, while he watches me take a seat on the edge of the bed.

He nods furiously, waiting for the rules of the game.

I turn serious, wanting him to understand that I'm serious about him. *Us*. That I'm serious when I turn his words around on him. "Strip for *me*. Let *me* see *you*."

He gulps and watches me with careful eyes.

I nod in encouragement, to let him know he can always be open with me as well. That we can find comfort in our shared defenses.

We can be each other's defense.

"No more games," I emphasize, taking back what I said about this being the last one. "No more lies. Just *us*."

He takes my hand in his and lays it over his chest, where I feel his heart beating quickly. "Just us," he repeats.

My chest swells, and I'm ready to jump in his arms. To

rip all his clothes off and leave claw marks on his shoulders.

To mark him as my own.

He places both hands on my shoulders and sets me back on the bed, my hair falling over one shoulder. I scoot up to the headboard like he did the first time he was in my apartment.

He smiles shyly, as though I make him more nervous than if this room was full of women. And that makes my chest swell even more, knowing I have this effect on him. It gives me a strength I've never known. To know I have this much power over someone when I'm simply myself.

It's intoxicating.

As Sebastian removes each article of clothing, tentatively and deliberately, his eyes are trained on mine.

The street noise is a light soundtrack to what's already been the perfect night. The perfect reunion with a man I met in Vegas and never expected to see again. A perfect man for me who's undressing now, baring his soul with each toss of his clothing.

The movements speak to me and tell a story of their own.

One of heartbreak. Of betrayal.

And when he stands in only his briefs, one of peace and no more pain.

His eyes widen as I lean over my curled knees, my hair falling over my legs. "You are breathtaking," he says, gulping again like he's scared.

That makes two of us.

Because the three words are on the tip of my tongue as he removes his briefs, revealing himself fully to me. With the moonlight casting a glow around him, he's my angel I never asked for but knew deep down I wanted.

I want to be open and say those words to him, to seal our connection with the magic of those three devastating words.

They're caught in my throat as he moves over me, nudging my legs open, his warm skin against mine. With one swift yet gentle motion, my body ready and aching for him, he's inside of me.

The gesture almost enough to pull those words out of me.

He moves the hair out of my eyes as I hold on to his shoulders for strength. "Where'd you go?" he whispers. "Stay with me."

I fight the urge to roll my eyes in the back of my head from the pleasure mixed with so many other emotions I have for this man. "I'm right here. With you. Always."

He kisses me as our bodies move together in sync, like we haven't been apart for several weeks—a lifetime with as many changes as we've made to our lives. But our bodies fall back into the rhythm, recognizing each other.

I move my hips up, meeting his every thrust, losing myself in this moment.

We both near the edge, and I fall willingly—greedily, even—with Sebastian by my side, like he's my life jacket on a sinking ship.

Because my life *was* a sinking ship before I met him.

"You're kidding," he says, laughing quietly as he faces me in bed. "You did not attack her at her wedding."

I cover my face, burying my head as far into the pillow as I can. "I wish I could say I was kidding, but I did. I pulled her hair and tackled her to the ground. Tore her wedding dress too."

He chuckles. "And the girl you punched? You have to tell me about that, mostly because I don't believe you."

"I did. I punched a girl in the face so hard I broke her nose." I shrug, trying to downplay how violent I can be when I snap.

He smiles in awe at me and my story like it's this year's Oscar winner for Best Picture.

"She called me a slut and wounded my ego, so I wounded her face. Fair, right?" Sebastian continues chuckling, the sound vibrating through my whole body, which is still tingling from his touch. "I wasn't as bad as my friend in high school, though, not Emma. This girl was more like a friend for a week. She was a cheerleader who jumped into the stands and hurled herself at another girl during a game. They'd exchanged words beforehand, and then she taunted her while we cheered. It didn't end well."

"During the game? She just went all apeshit?"

"More like Harley Quinn, but yeah."

"Well, cheerleaders are supposed to entertain."

"And she delivered." I nod at the memory, and the way some people actually cheered her on as she pulled Angela Meonich's hair. "My parents forbade me from hanging out with her after that, but of course, I did just to spite them. Which led me to egging—yes, *egging*—someone's house.

We thought they weren't home, but they were. They called the cops." I swallow. "It was fun having my dad yell at me the whole time at the station, on the way home, and for a whole year after that."

"And your friend?"

"We weren't friends after that. Not because of my parents," I point out, "but because… well, she wanted me to do meth with her. I was a rebel, but not to that degree."

He nods in understanding.

"No, I waited to do meth until after high school." This gives him pause, and I laugh. "Kidding."

"Oh? Because I was just going to say me too."

Now he gives me pause, but he follows it up with a laugh of his own. I turn toward the ceiling. "I deserved that."

We stay up most of the night, talking and laughing like we've known each other for years. And the thought of spending every night like this has me smiling from ear to ear as I fall asleep in his warm arms.

CHAPTER 56

Kendall

"Oh my God." I cover half my face with my hand. "That's her. She's here. She's fucking working out *right now*."

Sebastian looks around like he's searching for his donut on cheat day. And it warms my heart that he feels so strongly about everything I say, even when he doesn't know what or whom I'm talking about.

"Samantha Ray! She's right over there." I turn my back to where she's squatting in the corner, the sun from the open garage door beaming down on her. I point behind me so Sebastian can see.

"That's Samantha? Right there?" He gives her a once-over, her abs visible even from this far away. "I can tell why you're obsessed with her."

"Not *obsessed*. That makes me sound creepy." I slap his arm as he continues to stare. "And stop checking her out."

Instead of looking away, he grabs my hand and walks toward Samantha as she racks the barbell back in place and tightens her ponytail like I've seen her do many times in her Instagram videos.

Maybe I am creepy.

"We are *not* going over there." My panic increases with each step we take toward her.

"Sure we are."

In three more strides and two seconds away from a panic attack, I'm in the fitness queen's presence. "Hey, guys," she greets us like we've been friends for a while.

"Hey," Sebastian starts, still holding my hand while I try to hide behind his large frame. "You're Samantha Ray, right?"

Chest heaving, she nods.

"Hi," I pipe up. And inwardly roll my eyes at myself for sounding so meek and childish. Especially when I wave stiffly. "I'm Kendall, and this is Sebastian. We just wanted to say hi, and I'm a big fan, and I'm sorry we bothered you during your workout. We'll get going now. Just wanted to say hi…" I turn to leave, but Sebastian stops me.

With hands on her hips and abs on display, Samantha giggles. "Kendall?"

"Yeah, Kendall Gray." I take a deep breath, forcing myself not to ramble anymore. "I've commented on just about every one of your posts, and—oh my God, sorry. I'm not a stalker or anything."

She giggles again, shaking her legs out to keep them moving. "Well, thanks so much for your support, Kendall." She looks around before turning her attention to us. "Hey, what're you guys working out today?"

"Legs," we say in unison.

"My favorite!" She claps and heads back toward the squat rack. "Want to jump in here with me? We could switch off spotting. I'm working out alone today, so I could use the extra hands."

"We thought you'd never ask!" Sebastian says as he all but shoves me toward her. "We'd love to. Jeez, one hundred and ninety-five pounds? Wow." He rubs his hands together and then shakes out each leg before turning to me. "We have some work to do."

"Keep up!" she says before she unracks the weight and walks it back before getting into her squat position.

And just like that, I'm working out with Samantha Ray—my role model. The one woman other than Emma who got me into fitness. The one who made me believe I could make a living out of being an Instagram athlete. And although I've had trouble growing a following, I haven't given up. I'll get there, one squat at a time.

Throughout the workout, I beat my personal record in just about every exercise, impressing even Sebastian. I can tell by the way he looks at me with awe. With him by my side and Samantha's encouraging words, I was able to push myself.

Sweat dripping down my whole body and legs growing more and more sore with every rep, I smile, happy to be at the Mecca—Gold's Gym.

Only person missing is Emma. I asked her to come with us before we left, but she was busy. Although she was just sitting on the couch with a protein bar and didn't seem to have anywhere to be.

At the end of the workout, Sebastian pulls his hat off to wipe at the sweat on his forehead, then puts it on backward. He challenges Samantha to a backflip contest, believing he can do more in a row than her. I laugh because that's the first thing Sebastian said when I talked about Samantha. He said he'd challenge her to a backflip contest if we ever ran into her.

And of course, he follows through.

She doesn't hesitate for a second. While they get into position in the open area to the side of the gym covered in turf, I sit back with my camera ready to record the whole thing.

Sebastian flies backward effortlessly, flipping the length of the open area. When he gets to the end, he doesn't miss a beat before he does a few front flips and ends up in front of me. He holds his hands out for high-fives, face blood red and smirk in place.

Samantha nods, clapping sarcastically at him. "Okay, that was good. But don't get too cocky just yet." With a deep breath, she goes into a handstand and walks a few feet on her hands before she goes into a backbend and stands. Without a pause, she turns around and does so many backflips, it looks like she's in a hamster wheel. After the last one, she goes into the splits and shoots Sebastian and me her own cocky grin. I can't help but laugh, especially as onlookers give her a round of applause.

"This is rigged!" Sebastian yells, throwing his towel to the ground sarcastically.

On our way out, I take a selfie with Samantha, both of

our hair sticking to our necks and foreheads. Nothing cute about it, but I already have it ready to post to my social media before we even make it to our car.

"It was so nice meeting you, Kendall." She gives me a one-arm hug before she high-fives Sebastian. "And your gym bae."

"And you're sure you don't want to tell us about your secret gym bae?" I try one last time to get any details out of her.

She seals her lips and waves, laughing as she walks backward.

I smile the whole way to my apartment while Sebastian holds my hand over the console. "Perfect morning."

At a stoplight, he looks at me with a content expression. "Really was." When he turns his attention back to the road, he says, "And it's not over yet. We still need our mid-morning snack. Starbucks?"

"Or that place around the corner up here. What's it called? The one we went to last time with Ty and Emma?"

"Oh yeah. I think it's called Orgasm in a Bowl."

"Is not!"

"That's what it should be called."

I roll my eyes but can't help the giggles escaping me, my heart ready to explode at the whirlwind of the morning. The last few weeks, really.

My whole life has changed for the better.

When we get back to my apartment with tacos in hand, I'm still riding the high of this morning, my heart racing. Once inside, I check my phone and just about faint. And not from the intense workout, either.

"What?" Sebastian asks, dropping the keys in the bowl on the entryway table. "What're you looking at?"

"My Instagram." My eyes widen at the number of hearts on my notifications and number of new followers. "What the fu…?"

He peers over my shoulder. "Holy shit, Kendall."

With a trembling thumb, I scroll through my notifications and see that a few people reposted my video of their backflip contest.

"Holy fuck, Samantha Ray shared your post!" Sebastian yells. "Her one million followers saw your post!"

I drop my phone to the ground. Shocked, I turn to him while the door to Emma's room cracks open. "Hey, I didn't think you guys would be back already," she says, tugging at her shirt and closing the door quickly behind her. "What's going on?"

It's noon, and she's still makeup-less? At any other time, I'd ask her if she's feeling okay, but I'm too shocked.

Plus, she looks fine. Her hair's a little tousled, but otherwise, she even seems happy.

Sebastian picks my phone up, and Emma peers between us at the screen. Samantha's profile is pulled up, our faces on her most recent post with the caption *So fun meeting Kendall and her #gymbae Sebastian this morning for a good old-fashioned backflip contest. Who do you think won? Comment below! Then go follow this beautiful soul @ kendallgray. #strongissexy #chickswholift #backflips*

"Oh my God, Kendall!" Emma screeches in my ear before covering her mouth. "You got over a thousand new followers just this morning?"

Sebastian scoops me up while I bury my face in his chest. Emma joins in on our group hug, and I burst into tears, feeling like this is the beginning of an exciting adventure.

For the first time in a long time, I'm hopeful for what the future brings. With Sebastian, my family, and finally my career.

With the people I love most around me for support, this is the beginning of the rest of my life.

And it's looking pretty damn bright.

CHAPTER 57

Sebastian

A squeal from the living room has me shooting up in bed. Movement beside me makes me jump back and hit my head on the wall. "Shit, motherfucker." I rub my head while Kendall holds my other hand and kisses my cheek.

It's been over two weeks since I knocked on her door, and although I've slept here the last three nights in a row, I haven't gotten used to the change of scenery just yet. We stay at my place most of the time for more privacy.

Because when I have my way with Kendall, I want no interruptions or restrictions. I want her free on top of me, bare and vulnerable. Every night.

I'll dance my last show in the fall in Vegas. I'm slowly backing off since I live in LA now, but I still dance every weekend for the extra cash while the hotel gets going.

Lauren and Rhett plan to come to the show too, and

I'm thrilled to see Kendall getting along so well with them. Lauren can still be a snob, but deep down, she has a kind heart. Rhett won't actually be going to see the show; he already made it clear that "watching dudes get naked" isn't his thing.

After Kendall hung up the phone that night, after making plans for them to come out, she and I agreed we'd visit her hometown again, with a better ending to the weekend this time. I squeezed her hand over the popcorn bowl, and she laid her head back against the couch as we continued watching *The Breakfast Club* since she'd never seen it. Apparently, all she likes are scary movies.

But I'm slowly converting her as we settle into our new lives, *together*.

She tugs at my briefs now, needy for morning sex. Ever since I told her that's my favorite, this is how we wake up now, with her eager to have me inside her.

And I always oblige—no need to ask me twice.

I'll never get enough of this woman.

Especially not with her trailing hot kisses down my stomach, toward my throbbing dick.

Loud shuffling from the living room makes us stop, my head still hurting from hitting it on the wall and from the massive hangover. We went out last night with my friends, including Ty, who had to crash on the couch after too many shots and losing his phone.

I groan, her mouth two inches from my dick. "This is the biggest tease," I complain as she crawls to the end of the bed. I let my head fall against the headboard with a thud and give her the biggest pout I can muster.

But she's looking elsewhere. Farther south.

"You like what you see, hmm?" Taking this as an opportunity to tease her as well, I grip my length and slide my hand up and down.

Her mouth visibly waters, the sight turning me on, especially as she stands there naked, her body on display like the most expensive work of art at the Met. I could stare at it all day.

She's perfect.

And she's mine.

She snaps her attention back to my face as something crashes in the kitchen. "What if we're getting robbed, and we're in here fucking while they steal my Keurig?"

I don't stop what I'm doing, and when she saunters over to me, her hips swaying, I think I've won.

But instead, she slaps me and pulls me off the edge of the bed. "You're going to let me get *taken* by the robbers?" She scowls as she puts her robe on.

"They'll last two minutes with you and that menacing scowl."

She narrows her gaze at me before rolling her eyes and turning toward the door. Just as she opens it, I move as quickly as a cheetah and quietly as a cat toward her. Pushing my length against her back, loving the way her silk robe feels against me, I whisper, "Hurry back."

She leans into me but opens the door before I can lead her back to bed. Cabinets are banging, so I grab my gym shorts from the floor and step out as well.

We open the door just in time to see Emma slap Ty across the face and stalk off toward her room, toward us.

She jumps back when she sees us, but her body doesn't stop trembling. She's fuming. Ty chuckles in his spot in the kitchen, shirtless with his jeans hanging low. He looks like he enjoyed the slap, gently caressing his cheek like there are lip prints on it instead of a hand outline.

"Why the fuck is he here?" Emma's angry, but she also sounds breathless. I've never seen her so emotional. She's usually so composed, probably from all that yoga and charity work. She's like a saint, but apparently, Ty is where she draws the line of niceties. She turns back to him and spits, "This isn't a hostel. The shelter around the block takes in strays, you know."

Kendall and I exchange glances, wondering what we've missed.

Ty sticks his hand down the tub of oats and shovels a handful in his mouth, small specks littering the floor. "Rage is a good look on you, with your hair all wild and untamed. I bet you're a firecracker in bed." He grins, more oats falling to the ground.

She starts toward him, fist in the air, but Kendall grabs her before she can get very far. "Like you'll ever find out. Only in your dreams, buddy boy."

"Buddy boy? Good one."

Emma struggles in Kendall's grasp, her thin tank top strap falling off her shoulder to one side. I make a move to help but catch Ty's gaze instead. It's on Emma's bare shoulder, and an idea hits me.

Emma and Ty?
Hmm...

"Like you have anything better, asshole." She stops

struggling in Kendall's arms and runs into her room.

Before I can reel Ty in, Emma emerges again from her bedroom. "And stop eating my fucking food. This is not a bed-and-breakfast!"

We all jump when she slams her door.

I turn toward Ty, who's now guzzling orange juice straight from the jug out of the fridge. "Dude."

He wipes his mouth and offers us the jug, unfazed by the earthquake Emma just caused. "Oh, you guys want some?"

I roll my eyes, unable to control the maniac.

I need to warn Emma against him if what I saw in his eyes was lust.

She would not be able to handle him, and it would not end well.

But instead of getting involved, I do myself a favor and haul Kendall back into the bedroom to finish what we started.

CHAPTER 58

Kendall

I try to check on Emma, but she's already in the shower.

Rolling my eyes in Ty's direction in the kitchen, I open the door to my room and crawl back into bed with Sebastian. He nuzzles my neck, ready to pick up where we left off before Emma and Ty's scuffle. But I have other thoughts on my mind, ready to burst if I don't talk to him. And in the name of being open with each other, I have to ask him. "So, when am I going to meet your mom? You've met my whole family. I'd like to meet yours."

He told me about their strained relationship, how they haven't spoken in two months. Not since she tried making him attend his whore of an ex's wedding to his uncle. But me reconciling with my family has me feeling like I could do more to help him with his situation.

I don't expect him to forgive and forget with his uncle

anytime soon, if ever, but his mom is all he has now. I wouldn't be a good girlfriend if I didn't meddle.

Which is what I tell him, making him back up and chuckle.

"I know you want to help, and I appreciate your big heart." He turns me to face him and holds both my hands up to his chin. "But that's not going to happen for a long, *long* time. If ever. She's not very nice, so I'm doing you a favor."

"But she's your mom. She's part of what makes you *you*." I pout, but he only takes my bottom lip between his thumb and forefinger, nostrils flaring.

His voice is low and barely audible when he says, "Not falling for it." He looks up from my lips. "We'll probably be married way before you meet her."

I laugh. "We haven't even said 'I love you' yet, but sure, let's talk marriage."

He grows serious, but he beams toward me. "I haven't said that to you yet? I feel like I did."

I match his smile and shake my head from side to side. "No."

"Must've just been in my subconscious since I met you, and you refused to dance with me."

I shrug. "Have to have something to tell the grandchildren."

"So we'll have kids someday?" His smile falters, not because he doesn't look excited but because he wants a serious answer from me.

And the truth is, two months ago, talk of marriage and kids would've freaked me out. Like sent me running to

Hollywood Hills and hiding behind the giant H.

But things have been going well with Sebastian—really well. My Instagram has picked up since meeting Samantha. I've even run into her once again a few days ago and had another great workout together.

I've even made good use of my collection of pictures on my phone, mixed in with the not-so-glamorous ones of my cheeks puffed out while doing squats. People seem to enjoy both kinds of posts, and my following is growing every day.

I've had positive responses, and the negative ones haven't bothered me as badly as I thought they would've.

Maybe it's because I have Emma and Sebastian to lean on. Lauren too. She called yesterday to gripe about one of the negative comments, and I appreciated her "wanting to slash their tires" for calling me unoriginal.

My friends and family loving me for who I am makes those nasty comments bearable. They help me focus more on the positive ones, the ones that reflect the good I'm doing by being transparent with other people who are insecure about themselves.

Some of my old classmates have even reached out to thank me for sharing my journey, that it's helped them make their health a priority too.

Sebastian broke ground on the hotel. I was in awe when we visited the site last week. It's going to be a nice boutique hotel in an amazing location. From what he told me, he had to fight to outbid the others interested in the lot, but with Leo's help, they made it happen.

I couldn't be prouder.

Smiling, I snuggle closer to him. With Lauren married

and having a baby, I've warmed up to the idea of marriage. She always talks about the glories of both, and I think it's because Rhett is the right person for her to be enjoying the journey with.

Sebastian feels like mine.

With his goofy grin and smoldering eyes, I could get used to all of him.

But I can't tell him that. Not first, anyway. I need him to take the plunge first.

Or...

An idea hits me.

"Yes, but first things first." I pause with my hands in his like we're at the altar already, the pillow acting as the minister. "We say it at the same time."

He nods in understanding, another reason we're good together. Not just anyone can read me as he can, and vice versa. "On three." He counts down, mouthing the numbers to me, barely able to contain the excitement rolling off him and swirling around us in a cocoon of happiness.

On three, we both say, "I love you," and smile at each other like we spent the last hour getting high and now have the munchies.

We're hungry for one thing, at least.

Sebastian slowly peels my clothes off me, his fingertips grazing my bare skin. We hold each other's gaze, unable to look away as we strip the barriers between us.

Facing each other, free of our clothes, we simply exist. Exist in our love and attraction for each other.

He tentatively grazes my cheek with his rough hands, and I close my eyes, letting myself feel everything he gives me. I part my lips, needing him like I've never needed anything else. Needing this moment, where the world stops just for us.

Before long, he has me pinned beneath him on the bed. Cupping my breasts in each of his hands, he slides inside me with slow, sensual movements. He lights me on fire as he kisses me and whispers he loves me with every thrust.

"I love you, Kendall Gray."

Thrust.

"You are my everything."

Thrust.

The words and feeling of him all warm me. I'm content and bursting with joy as we move in sync. He's everywhere, clouding my senses, and I wouldn't have it any other way.

Not with this man I love. A man who fought for me because he saw beauty in me—something not many people stick around long enough to uncover. Even though I pushed him away, made it as difficult as possible to let him close to me, he stayed. He fought. He loved me, anyway.

And when we fall off the cliff together, we watch each other, admiring the unfiltered love between us as our light shines as one.

EPILOGUE

Seven months later…

Sebastian

I run my hands down my crisp button-up shirt. Ty said it was the right choice for tonight. White shirt with gray slacks and matching jacket—classy but not too aging.

He forgot to mention *hot as fuck*.

This thing traps heat and kills me slowly. Or maybe it's because it's LA, and even during the winter, it's not really winter.

Even so, it also has to do with the fact that I'm about to change our lives forever tonight.

Hopefully.

I gulp, using the paper with my speech on it to fan myself. Then Ty shows up, slapping me on the back. I shouldn't be startled—it's his signature move—but my nerves are unpredictable at the moment.

"Ready, man?"

I don't move. I don't say anything. All I can hear is my breathing. All I can smell is the faint salty scent of the ocean close by. That and Ty's cologne. That snaps me out of it. "Dude, did you swim in a pool of cologne? What is that?" I cover my face with my hand, the other still fanning us.

He shrugs, pulling at his collar. "Waitress and I got a little handsy in the liquor closet. Had to use my backup cologne to cover up her pussy on me. You know my backup is shit."

I blink several times, mostly angry that my staff is already wandering on such an important night. And the fact that I thought Ty and Emma would be together by now. Their constant flirting hasn't gone unnoticed, but they deny any attraction to the other anytime it's mentioned.

Ty's the only one who knows what I have planned for the hotel's grand opening. That in itself has me near tears, but I'm more nervous about Kendall.

Ty sniffs his red button-up, pulling it through his dark gray vest, then smooths it back down. "You ready?" His hands move to his hips, and he looks toward the door. "Party's in there."

I gaze back out at the ocean in front of me, much like I had the night in San Francisco after I left Kendall. After I almost ruined my chances with her.

How she pushed me away for weeks after I tried to make it right with her.

I clutch my chest, though not out of anguish, not this time. It's only been full—happy—since I showed up at Kendall's apartment to win her back.

Her Instagram took off after she finally met that Serena girl—I mean *Samantha*. *Oops.* Glad she can't hear my fumble. Kicking a small rock, I chuckle at the scowl she would've made had she heard me.

Since then, she's gotten some momentum going, growing her influence. She's an affiliate for a couple of apparel companies, marketing their gym clothes to her followers. And she's entered a contest by a major supplement company for a sponsorship. We're still waiting for her big break, the industry not easy to get into, but we hope to hear good news from the contest soon.

Maybe then she can finally quit the shoe store, much to George's dismay. He needs her southern sass like he needs his nightly cocktail. But quitting is something she's looking forward to more than her birthday next week, and she *loves* celebrating her birthday.

"What're you doing?" Ty asks.

I inhale deeply. "I'm ready." I smooth my shirt down one last time, thinking we're both in a good place, personally and professionally. This is the right time for us. "Let's do this."

He hesitates, not convinced of my readiness. "We can stand out here some more. Nice view that's perfect for a powwow, if you want. A touching heart-to-heart before you make the biggest mistake ever." He grins widely, jokingly.

He's been with me through the hardest times, and now I have no doubt he'll be there for me through the good. Making jokes the whole way because he doesn't know anything else.

"Happy for you, Seb." He shakes my hand and pulls me

in for a bro-hug, the gesture making me tear up.

When we pull apart, I laugh lightly on an exhale. "Never thought I'd be doing this again."

His expression loses all humor. "You deserve to be happy. If I didn't think Kendall would be the right one for you, I wouldn't let you do this. Not this time."

I tilt my head in confusion, but he only shrugs and looks away. Guilt consumes his features, his lips forming a tight line.

"Hey." I pull on his arm. "What're you talking about? Nothing was your fault."

"I should've stopped you. We all should've been there to stop you. We knew Joelle was wrong for you, not that we could've predicted her and your uncle Sid's relationship. But we knew she was wrong. You didn't have that energy about you like you used to. Until you met Kendall, anyway."

I'm surprised by his comment, and touched.

"Look, I don't mean to bring you down, man." He grabs my shoulder. "I just want you to know that me and the guys? All we've ever wanted was for you to be happy. And you're doing it, Seb. Your hotel. Your girl. You're making a life for yourself, no matter the shit you went through. What your mom still puts you through."

I flinch at the mention of my mother. She and I have fallen back into a somewhat normal routine—whatever that means for us. But she still "couldn't squeeze in" my life's dream turning into a reality. Just for one night, she couldn't make the necessary plans to be here, even though I told her months ago.

"She's proud of you, you know. Even if she doesn't know

how to show it."

I'm taken aback again at his comment, rarely getting this serious side of him. "You turned out all right, you know," I say with tears in my eyes, so many unsaid admissions passing between us. So much tying us together as brothers. I gulp. "I know this time of year gets to you, and—"

"You don't have to do that. I'm trying not to bring you down, remember?"

"Yeah, and I appreciate it. Thank you for so many things. For one, I'm glad you're here, even though I know this month as a whole is tough on you." He nods, squinting at the ocean, so many memories flashing before his eyes. Ty's pain, heartache, helplessness—I can't even imagine what he went through and still goes through. "Your sister would be proud of you."

He nods and pulls me in for a bear hug, foregoing the handshake. "Thanks." He pulls back and stuffs his hands in his pockets. Smiling, he adds, "If only I could settle down, right? Then again, if my sister were still alive, she'd lose it if she knew there was actually a woman out there who could handle me." Although it's sad, he chuckles and kicks at the ground.

I open my mouth to ask if he's found someone, to suggest Emma for the hundredth time, but he pats me on the back, still smiling. "Go get your girl."

With him leading the way, we enter the hotel, the one I've dreamed about for years. I'm finally standing inside of it.

She's small but fierce, much like my Kendall.

The light gray interior goes well with the white and red

furniture in the small banquet room that's more of a bar and lobby put together. Movie posters line the walls, and a red carpet is rolled out front. I went with a vintage Hollywood theme, each room different—mafia, boxing, even romance. Posters of *Casino* and *Gangs of New York* line the walls of this room, much to Kendall's dismay. She wanted to add Freddie and Chuckie to the mix, but I had to kindly distract her with my lips to get her off that idea. I can't go scaring guests with posters of Freddie's bloody claws and wild eyes.

She let up when we added a movie room with a projector and reclining seats. Kendall thinks it'll be fun to have a weekly movie night for guests.

We're still growing and are eventually going to add that spa Kendall suggested. But those are plans for down the road, among many others.

Once inside, I take it all in. The many hours poured into this place the last several months. It's finally happening, with my friends gathered around—my family.

Our investors and their guests are sprinkled among them as well, so I stand a little taller, but I don't focus on them.

Not once my eyes land on her.

My angel with blond hair and an ass that kills.

I lick my lips at her choice of attire for tonight. She's wearing a romper that hangs off her shoulders with sleeves that reach her elbows. The light blush of it gives her a feminine look, but the way it exposes her shoulders and a hint of cleavage is sexy, especially paired with her tall wedges.

As I walk up behind her, each step is one toward my

future.

Moving her low ponytail to the side, I kiss her shoulder, startling her, but she tilts her head to give me better access. Once I turn her around, Leo's voice sounds throughout the room from the front. "If everyone can please turn their attention to the center of the room, we have a very important announcement from the man of the hour himself."

I can't hear what else he's saying with the blood rushing to my head from everyone's eyes on me. I've been on stage countless times—naked, nonetheless—but this feels more vulnerable, more terrifying. My hand trembles as it reaches into my pocket and fingers the velvet box that's been nestled there all night.

Kendall steps away from me with her glass of champagne in one hand and her clutch in the other. She smiles at me, thinking I'm about to make a speech that doesn't include her. Before she gets too far, I pull her toward me and give her champagne to Emma for safekeeping.

She looks confused at first, scanning the crowd for answers. But I'm the one who needs an answer. Hopefully, one with three letters instead of two.

"Kendall," I start, taking her hand tentatively, "when I first met you, I was fascinated. You're way funnier and prettier than anyone I'd ever met, and you definitely have the most attitude."

I chuckle as a tear falls down her cheek. I wipe it off and revel in her small smile. "You have the biggest heart and an infectious drive to show up every day and be better. You helped me take the leap and open The Martini Inn, my dream hotel." I pause to take a deep breath. *Here it comes.* "I hope you'll help me realize another dream too."

She gasps as I get down on one knee and hold out the ring for her. She covers her mouth with both hands and squeezes her eyes closed. More tears fall, but she's smiling when she pulls her hands down.

"Will you marry me?"

Leaping at me, her arms wrapped around me, she whispers, "Fuck yeah."

Cheering surrounds us, but all I can hear are those two words. Those two words allow me to exhale, relieved that she wants to spend the rest of her life with me.

I kiss my fiancée in front of our friends and family, pulling back in time for her parents to walk up. Her mother is crying into a napkin, but she's smiling too. Her father trails behind her, unable to keep up.

I'd invited them weeks ago, right after I asked them for permission. I knew she'd want me to ask her parents for her hand, but what I didn't know was how thrilled they'd be.

They might not have wanted her with a stripper, and I might not have made a good first impression, but Kendall and I have both tugged at them from all angles for acceptance.

Lauren and Rhett likely put in a good word, as well.

Kendall shrieks, "Mom? Dad?"

"Sweetie!" her mother cries, her dad still behind her with his phone raised. "Congratulations, honey." She smooths Kendall's ponytail down and paws at her smudged lipstick, thanks to me.

Kendall swats at her hands like she's still ten and her mother's getting her ready for her school pictures.

Some things never change.

I cover my smile with my hand, but Kendall still catches me and glowers.

I hear more shrieking, but it sounds muffled. I look around. Emma and the guys are all huddled over here too but keeping their distance so Kendall can have her family time.

Kendall grabs her dad's phone after he gives her a hug. More like traps her in his large arms—the guy's seven feet tall, if I had to guess. Crying into the phone, she holds her hand up with the sparkling diamond on her finger. Emma joins her, wrapping her arms around her waist and talking into the phone. "Our girl's engaged!"

She and Kendall laugh more at whoever's on the phone, and the guys all congratulate me. Leo pulls me in for a hug. "Congrats, man. You deserve this. All of it." He pulls back. "Proud of you, sailor."

I nod, at a loss for words, the moment too overwhelming with Leo, my friend and mentor, looking at me like he means it. He may only be four years older than me, but he's wise beyond his years. I never had a mentor, not like him—one I could trust. His words reach deep inside me and warm my chest.

Kendall bumps into me. "Check out my sexy fiancé!" She holds up the phone, Lauren's face filling it.

She screams at both of us in excitement, and I can't get a word in. "Holy shit, Sebastian, the size of that rock! Oh my God, strippers *do* make good money. You sure you don't want to do that part-time? You could—"

Rhett appears then, taking the phone from her. Cringing

at her screams, he nods at me. "Congratulations, you two. I think it's bedtime for this new mama." He winks at Lauren and ends the call.

Kendall pulls me toward her friends and parents. With her bouncing about, I'm scared she'll twist an ankle in those shoes, so I wrap an arm around her waist.

Her dad shakes my hand, and her mom hugs me.

This is better than I could've hoped for. I have the girl of my dreams, but her family welcomes me too. I gained a fiancée and a warm family.

For the rest of the night, Kendall and I drink, dance, and laugh. We laugh *a lot*. Our friends stay until the very end, after yet another of my speeches thanking the investors for coming and for, well, making this all possible.

At the end, I thank my fiancée for supporting me and believing in my dreams.

For believing in me.

My fiancée.

I never thought I'd have another one. It just took the right girl to strip for me to make it happen.

The End

ENJOY THIS BOOK?
LEAVE A REVIEW!

Did you enjoy Sebastian and Kendall's story? Please consider leaving a review!

Reviews have such a big impact on a book's success, especially for a first-time author, so please take a moment to review *Strip for Me*. You can leave one on any site you like: Goodreads, Amazon, BookBub, Apple Books, etc. The best part? You don't have to write a long, tedious review! It can even be one line, if you want. Anything to show how you feel about this book would be super helpful! And I'd forever be grateful. Thanks so much!

ACKNOWLEDGEMENTS

Thank you, reader.

Thank you for taking a chance on a first-time author and picking up this book. It's one that I hold close to my heart. One that I poured myself into for almost two years. One that I'm proud of. I loved writing and sharing it with you, and I hope you enjoyed reading it!

This has been such a rush.

Publishing a book has always been a dream of mine. Up until last year, I thought it would be one of those things that was just out of my reach. Something that I wanted but wasn't sure I was good or smart enough to make happen. But with a lot of hard work and persistence, it's finally happened—I've published a book!

I wouldn't have realized this dream if it weren't for all the people who helped along the way. Thanks to the ladies at

Hot Tree Editing. You rocked it with the content and copy editing! A big thank you to Kari for working your cover design magic. Thanks so much for entertaining each of my crazy, nitpicky ideas and working with me to produce a final, amazing cover! Thanks to Marla for your proofreading expertise. I knew we were meant to be when we found out we share a wedding anniversary! Jill—you're a rock star with all your formatting skills and the fantastic teaser designs. They brought my story and characters to life in a way I only dreamed of. Courtney, you're a blurb-writing genius. Thanks so much for all your great feedback in writing a kickass blurb. It was my first time going through the whole process of writing a book, editing it, and putting it together for a finished product, and all you ladies made it so smooth and awesome.

A big, huge, gargantuan thank you to this amazing book community who is so generous with your time and wisdom to help a newbie out. I appreciate all the authors I've met along my journey who helped get me started and offered their support as I navigated this publishing thing. I met so many amazing people at Inkers Con this year who gave me that final push through the publishing finish line. You guys have answered all my questions and offered words of comfort that I'm not alone in this crazy writing thing. There are so many of you whom I want to thank but would be too many to list! You have all been invaluable. You've been mentors to me throughout this whole process, even when you didn't know it. Special thanks to Rachel who gave me my first big taste of the writing and publishing process. It has been a joy helping you with your work, and in turn,

I've learned so much about my own projects and process.

Thank you to bloggers, bookstagrammers, and readers who've helped spread the word about this book. A special thanks to Dani and Wildfire Marketing Solutions for all your promotional wisdom. Marketing this book has been a fear of mine since day one, but Dani—you gave some great advice and helped make this book a success. Couldn't have gotten the word out without you!

There are several—and I do mean, *several*—people who stuck by me from the beginning stages all the way to the end. You listened to me rant on the phone about writing but also the headache that is the Internet. When Facebook hated me, you all were there to laugh with me and push me. When I doubted my writing ability, you were there all the same. Thank you for reading all the terrible first drafts, the snippets of dialogue, the scenes I was unsure of. Thank you Jody, Meli, Prisda, Shelby, Heather, and Haley for all your constructive feedback and words of encouragement along the way. A special thanks to my Book Bitches—Crystal, Jessica, and Chelsi—for your support. Thank you all for not blacklisting me and changing your phone numbers. I'm so grateful for you all.

These next two people will be difficult to thank. These words are not enough, but hopefully they will due for now. They're in print, after all—that has to mean something! LOL. First, my mom. Where to begin. You were the one I first uttered the words to. When I was in the eighth grade, I followed you around as you filled the salad bar at the family restaurant, as I always did after school. But this was not an ordinary day. It was the first time I told anyone that I wanted to be an author one day. Right next to the baked chicken and green beans, my words were, "I want to go into authoring one day." We laughed about it then, but it was the start of all this. And you've been with me ever since, encouraging me and helping me in any way possible, even if it was to walk around campus with me while I checked out a graduate school. You're proud, and I can feel it in my bones every time you say it. That means the world to me.

Next, my husband. My person. My forever. We like to joke a lot, but when it comes to this dream, I've never doubted how much you believe in me. How much you love me for going after this thing. When I first told you I wanted to quit my salary-paying job to pursue writing, you didn't hesitate to push me to go for it. You smiled like it was your own dream. And you've been the same ever since. I love you for that and for so many other things. It hasn't always been easy. I've often stopped listening to you in order to listen to the characters in my head, but you've been supportive and patient with me, nonetheless. You're my best friend. My rock. My own happily ever after, and I'm so thankful for you. I love you forever and always.

ABOUT THE AUTHOR

Georgia Coffman is a romance author with a Master's in Professional Writing and loves all the warm and fuzzy feels she gets after reading a love story. She's obsessed with rompers and the TV show *Friends*. When she's not reading or writing, she and her husband enjoy working out and playing with their two pups. Georgia loves to connect on social media or through email, so feel free to reach out with any questions, your fave book recommendations, or even a funny joke!

Website
www.georgiacoffman.com

Facebook
www.facebook.com/ghcoffman

Instagram
www.instagram.com/ghcoffman

BookBub
www.bookbub.com/profile/georgia-coffman

Facebook Reader Group
www.facebook.com/groups/2274938956095355

Subscribe to Georgia's newsletter for all her new release details, exclusive giveaways, behind-the-scene snippets, and more!
www.georgiacoffman.com/newsletter